kissing
games

kissing
games

STEFANIE
LONDON

Entangled Publishing, LLC
10940 S Parker Rd
Suite 327
Parker, CO 80134
rights@entangledpublishing.com

Amara is an imprint of Entangled Publishing, LLC.

Edited by Lydia Sharp
Cover illustration and design by Elizabeth Turner Stokes

Manufactured in the United States of America

ISBN 978-1-64937-353-3

First Edition March 2022

At Entangled, we want our readers to be well-informed. If you would like to know if this book contains any elements that might be of concern for you, please check the book's webpage for details.

https://entangledpublishing.com/books/kissing-games

To anyone who ever felt like they don't fit in, the right people will love you just as you are.

CHAPTER ONE

Ryan Bower had a lot of reasons to wake up in the middle of the night. Being a superstar major league pitcher with a busted knee and a contract about to expire was one reason. Being thirty-five and watching his games get taken over by a twenty-year-old prodigy was another. He'd even had the occasional nightmare about walking onto the diamond in front of thousands, with his pants around his ankles.

All normal reasons to be blinking into the darkness.

Squeaking bedsprings, however, were not a reason to be waking up in the middle of the night. Especially when those bedsprings belonged to his parents.

Ryan cringed as he swung his legs over the edge of his bed and planted his bare soles against the worn, wooden floorboards of his childhood home. Outside, insects chirruped and tree branches scratched against his window, disturbed by the breeze.

Squeak, squeak, squeak.

Lord help him.

He took a step forward, his movement slightly stiffer than usual thanks to a torn ACL, which was in the latter stages of recovery and the very reason he was even in his parents' house right now, having to listen to this torture. Raking a hand through his hair, Ryan pulled on a T-shirt and a pair of sweats, and walked out of his bedroom and into the hallway, where a thin beam of light shone from under his parents' doorway.

Squeak, squeak, squeak.

"Oh, come off it," he muttered, wrinkling his nose.

Okay, sure, he was glad his parents were still in love, because he'd definitely prefer it over the alternative. But he really, *really* didn't want to listen to the intricacies of them being in love. And since brain bleach wasn't a thing, there was a high chance that this would scar him for life.

"Yes, Alfie!" his mother cried out. "Like in chapter twenty-one!"

Chapter twenty-one? What kind of books were they reading?

Ryan contemplated pounding on their door and telling them to keep it down, but frankly, the thought of hearing even a second more of whatever the hell they were doing was way too much to handle.

He headed into the living room and went out the back door, almost tripping over himself in his hurry to get outside. What had happened in the time he'd been away? His sweet, mild-mannered parents had turned into horny college kids. Ryan scrubbed a hand over his face.

The worst thing was that this was the *third* night in a row. And Ryan had only been back in Kissing

Creek for three days. That was a 100 percent hit rate...no pun intended. The first night, he'd popped one of the sleeping pills he kept for long-haul travel, and then the next morning, he'd acted like nothing had happened. Last night, he'd stuffed a pillow over his head and made sure he was out of the house early so he didn't have to watch his mother humming up a storm as she made breakfast.

Maybe it was time to book himself a room at the local bed and breakfast. The only reason he *hadn't* done that in the first place was because he wanted to keep a low profile. Also, if he came back to Kissing Creek and didn't stay at home, his mother would disown him.

However, his low profile had been blown on day one when some kid studying at the local college had spotted him at a café, because Ryan wasn't human until he'd had his daily double shot. He'd been *sure* the low-slung Boston Celtics cap and sunglasses would have kept his identity hidden. Apparently not.

Now he'd been badgered into giving the college baseball team a special visit and pep talk. Normally, he'd be all over something like that—he loved encouraging young players and inspiring them to work hard for their dreams. But right now, nursing a bad knee and a bruised ego, he wanted to bury his head in the sand and pretend the baseball world wasn't rotating without him.

Too bad the rest of the season was gone. His *best* season...at least it should have been.

Inside the house, there was a loud thump. Ryan

tipped his face up toward the sky and wondered why he'd even bothered coming home. His penthouse apartment in Toronto was perfectly comfortable, and he had a great view of Lake Ontario.

"You know why," he said to himself.

Ryan would *never, ever* admit it out loud, but when he was licking his wounds, all he wanted was family around him. He'd been that way since he was a kid.

Yet that wasn't the only reason he'd bolted out of Toronto at the first opportunity.

He could see the stadium where his team, the Blizzards, played from his living room. It was also the place where they would be hosting their games after making the playoffs for the first time since a massive rebuild. He'd put up with the growing pains of the rebuild, like sloppy defense work while they rotated through position players, trying to find the right combination. He'd put up with stale bats and poor morale and a losing streak that had almost broken a franchise record. He'd put up with all of it for the hope of what would come.

And this season they'd sparkled like gold. Their young designated hitter was smashing balls out of every park, their third baseman was in line for MVP, and Ryan had his sights set on a Cy Young award.

All it had taken was one wrong move. Assisting a rundown between second and first, which would have been an important out for the game but nothing wildly out of the ordinary. Certainly nothing he'd thought would end his season.

But he'd twisted to avoid a collision with the runner and felt something give as he laid the tag down—a flare of pain so sharp it'd made his eyes water and a cry catch in the back of his throat. Despair had flooded him as he'd pounded his fist into the earth, knowing in his heart it was more than a sprain.

He *should* be there right now, taking the mound, securing the win, bringing his team to victory. Not hiding away at home.

Ryan pushed up onto his feet. It was no good sitting alone with his thoughts right now—*that* was the reason he'd come home. Distraction. He'd needed to be surrounded by people that wouldn't walk on eggshells around him, who wouldn't dwell on what he'd lost. Who wouldn't remind him of how easily everything he'd worked toward could disappear.

How long had he been outside? Surely, long enough that his parents had run out of puff, so to speak. Tentatively, he made his way to the door and creaked it open, ears straining. *Silence.* For a second, Ryan thought that "chapter twenty-one" might be over.

"Not like that," his mother's voice sounded through the bedroom wall, which backed onto the living room. "Bend over a bit more. That's it."

Squeak, squeak, squeak.

He was officially done.

Thank God he'd been cleared to drive. He needed to get out of here, and driving around the sleepy, nighttime streets of Kissing Creek was the best option he had. As he walked through the house on the way to the front door, he spotted a book sitting on the coffee table.

Stormy Pleasures was mostly black and white, but the spine and back were bright red, and this version had library stickers. A Post-it Note stuck to the front said *book club with Sloane Rickman*. Wow. Looked like the library book club had gone a little risqué.

The squeaking intensified.

Okay, a *lot* risqué.

Shaking his head, Ryan headed to the front door and snatched his keys from the hook on the wall. Today, he was going to find a new place to stay and *then* he was going to jam *Stormy Pleasures* through the garbage disposal.

• • •

Sloane Rickman was living the dream.

Granted, her *personal* dream looked a little different from the kind Hollywood tried to sell her. There was no tripping through city streets in an expensive pair of stilettos. No fancy apartment with a glittering view of a famous skyline. No hero waiting to scoop her up if she fell.

Sloane was quite happy scooping herself back up at the moment. Not that she would reject the right Prince Charming if he and his white horse happened to trot on by. But her dream was more of the variety that included a small home with a veggie patch, friendly neighbors, and a coffee shop where someone asked her if she wanted "the usual."

Belonging. Now *that* was the dream.

"Hello!" A woman named Audrey, aka the best barista in town, waved as Sloane walked into the Kisspresso Café. "I saw you heading down the street, so I took the liberty of making your vanilla latte, extra shot, like always."

"You're the best." Sloane grinned and all but bounded up to the pastry counter.

Kisspresso Café might be her favorite place in all of Kissing Creek. Well, aside from the library, where she worked. The café looked like the Barbie Dream House version of a Starbucks, where all the staff wore pink aprons, and they even made specialty pink white-chocolate mochas that were totally Instagram ready. No filter required.

"Did you want your almond croissant, as well?" Audrey asked, her hands already reaching for the tongs inside the pastry cabinet.

"Yes, please." Sloane dug her wallet out of the crossbody bag she had slung over her outfit. "How's school going?"

"Good, busy. Amazing." Audrey grinned. "I know I must be the only student who thinks every second of college is the best thing ever because of what happens *inside* the classroom. But I'm happy to be a weirdo."

"You're talking to the woman who dresses almost exclusively in things with dinosaurs on them." Sloane swept her hands down to show off her fifties-style black dress patterned with rainbow silhouettes of brontosauri. "We can be weirdos together."

"That is one seriously cute dress," Audrey said, popping Sloane's croissant into a paper bag. "Did you know the name Brontosaurus means thunder lizard in Greek?"

"I did, actually," Sloane replied. "Did *you* know Mick Jagger has three different extinct creatures named after him? *Aegrotocatellus jaggeri*, *Jaggermeryx naida*, and *Anomphalus jaggerius*."

Audrey's face lit up. She was a sponge for interesting facts. "That's so cool!"

Sloane laughed and pulled her credit card out of her wallet to pay, but Audrey waved it off.

"It's on the house." Audrey slid the takeout coffee cup and the paper bag containing her croissant across the counter. "My sister is going to flip when I share this new fact with her. She watched a documentary on the Rolling Stones while she was staying with our aunt and now she's obsessed. I guess it's better than her watching TikTok videos."

"Are you sure I can't pay?"

"Please." Audrey held up her hands as the bell tinkling behind Sloane signaled that more customers had entered the café. "It's my treat."

Sloane's chest warmed at the kind gesture. "Well, let me buy some of your muffins for the library staff, then. I'll get four of the blueberry bran, please."

Shaking her head and laughing, Audrey piled the muffins into a bag, and this time she allowed Sloane to pay. "I hope everyone enjoys the muffins."

"Oh, they will!"

Sloane stuffed a five-dollar bill into the tip jar before popping the bag of muffins into her tote and grabbing her breakfast. She nibbled on her croissant right out of the bag as she headed outside into the sunshine. October was Sloane's favorite month, because of the pretty fall foliage, and this weather was the cherry on top of an already perfect morning. The trees were ablaze in shades of gold and rust and a rich red, and it was finally cool enough to wear a sweater over her dress.

She took the long way around to the library, walking past the off-leash dog park so she could admire all the adorable furry creatures racing around in the morning sunshine. By the time she arrived at work, ready to relieve the librarian on the opening shift, she'd finished her croissant. Dusting the flakey crumbs from her dress, she touched up her lipstick before heading inside.

The library had geared up for Halloween. Cutouts of Jack-o'-lanterns, wailing ghosts, and black cats decorated the high wall in the children's area, and the "what's hot" display out front had a great selection of spooky and atmospheric novels perfect for Sloane's favorite time of year. She sipped her coffee and took a moment to straighten a book that had been moved out of place on the shelf, trying to decide what she was going to borrow next.

Maybe it was time for a re-read of *Interview with the Vampire*.

"Sloane, I've been dying." One of the other librarians, a woman in her sixties named Pat, rushed over. She had dark, close-cropped hair flecked with silver, deep brown skin, and was known for her funky, bold accessories. Today, it was a thick stack of bangles and a hand-knit shawl in ruby red. "I slept in and didn't get my coffee on the way over."

"You should have told me. I would've picked one up for you." Sloane frowned.

"Yes, yes. And then you wouldn't let me pay you back and I would have to feel bad because I know you've sunk everything into that little house of yours." She waved a hand in the air, and the stack of bangles clattered as they slipped down her arm.

"Well, I bought blueberry muffins," she replied. "So no need to buy snacks, at least. I got enough for the team."

"You're a sweet soul. I'm taking my break now."

"Go, go." Sloane shooed her colleague away. "I can't have a dead librarian on my hands. My sleuthing skills aren't good enough to get me through a murder investigation."

"You've been reading too many of those cozy mysteries." Pat shook her head, laughing, and grabbed her purse from the shelf behind the main counter. "I'll be back in a bit."

The library was quiet now, but it would be busier later. Most days they had one to two programs on the schedule to keep patrons rolling in. Sloane particularly enjoyed the toddler story-time sessions and after-school arts and crafts. But her favorite thing of all was running the Believe in Your Shelf Book Club. They met the third Tuesday of every month and had been doing so for almost ten years. Taking over such an established club was a huge honor, and Sloane wanted to bring her A-game.

In the past, they'd stuck to typical book club–style books, like critically acclaimed fiction, memoirs, and wannabe commercial blockbusters that the publishers pushed in the hopes it would create the next Nicholas Sparks or Dan Brown.

Sloane wanted to shake things up a bit by putting her own stamp on the club and broadening the fictional horizons of its participants. She'd always read widely and encouraged others to do the same. This year alone they'd tried a bunch of new styles—from a horror graphic novel that was a surprise hit and an eight hundred–page epic fantasy that had challenged everyone's idea of how much they could read in a month.

And then there was *this* month's book.

Holy moly. Sloane felt her cheeks grow warm thinking about it. *Stormy Pleasures* had been a bold choice, and she hadn't been sure how well it would go over. They'd done romance novels before, but erotic romance was a whole different ballgame from the warm and fuzzy happily-ever-afters they'd read in the past.

She was a bit behind on the reading schedule herself, with work being busy and the upgrades she'd decided to tackle in her house. Oh, and the extra community activities she'd volunteered for. But at five chapters in, Sloane was already starting to understand why the book had been so talked about on release.

Sloane stashed her bag behind the main counter, catching a glimpse of the book in question peeking out between the handles. The red spine stood out, calling attention to itself. Not that she had any concerns about reading a spicy book in public. Her job was to fly the flag for *all* books, and she enjoyed any chance to spark up a conversation with a curious potential reader.

Sloane pottered around the library, stopping to say hello to the young mother and her toddler sitting in the kid lit area, and pushing the book cart around so she could return the returned books to their rightful homes.

As she was going about her work, an electronic chime signaled that the front doors had opened. Sloane didn't need to greet everyone who came in, but when the library was quiet, she tried to at least wave or smile to make people feel welcome. She poked her head around the end of the aisle and blinked.

The man who walked through the front doors of the library didn't look familiar. Kissing Creek might be a small town, but it was also a college town, and she didn't know everyone who lived here. Something told her even if she'd only passed this man on the street, however, she would have remembered him.

He was tall—easily six foot two or three, maybe more—and broad. He wore a fitted T-shirt with long sleeves that perfectly showed off the sculpted muscles in his shoulders, arms, and chest. Dark hair poked out from under a baseball cap, and even at this distance, she could see his eyes were an arresting, electric blue.

He walked into the library with an air of confidence Sloane had always hoped to embody but could never quite get right. Maybe being taller than everyone else naturally lent itself to having a presence. Maybe the air was better quality up there.

Or maybe he was born like that.

He wandered over to the nonfiction section and began to peruse the shelves. Hmm, he was a reader?

You know better than to judge a book by its cover.

Even if the cover was in *pristine* condition. Talk about cranking the hot meter up to eleven. What was better than a big, muscly guy who loved books? She should probably go over there and see if he needed help selecting one. That was her job, after all.

Yeah. Going to talk to him is all about work, right.

"Shut up, brain," she muttered as she finished shelving the last book on her cart. Then she took a moment to smooth out the fabric of her dress, fluff up her ponytail, and check her teeth in the reflective material of the cart to make sure there were no rogue pastry flakes. But before she'd even made it past the front desk, the glass doors to the library slid open.

And a llama walked inside.

CHAPTER TWO

A blood-curdling bleating sound startled Ryan so suddenly he would swear it carved a decade off his life. "What the hell was that?"

There was an older woman browsing in the same aisle as he was, and her head lifted as wide eyes swung in the direction of the front of the library.

"It's the llama." She pressed her lips into a line, and Ryan peered around the edge of the bookshelves.

"Oh shit. It *is* a llama. What the hell is a llama doing in here?" He looked back at the woman. "Did you know they made that kind of a sound? It's terrifying."

The poor woman looked pale. "She makes that sound when she's mad."

She? Okay, so the llama must be known around town. Her coat was mainly white with patches of a warm brown on her face, neck, and hindquarters, and she looked like she'd run through some bushes thanks to the leaves and other bits of natural debris trapped in her fur.

"Dammit, Lily!" someone scolded the llama, but the beast seemed unperturbed. Lily stamped her foot. Or was it a hoof? Did llamas have hooves? They were related to camels, right?

This is no time to lament how you should have paid more attention in school.

The creature made that awful bleating sound again, taking an aggressive step toward a shorter woman who shrieked at the sudden movement.

"That llama is a menace." The older woman shook her head. "You should help the poor librarian."

Do I look like the kind of guy who knows how to herd farm animals?

Uh, no. Ryan had about as much experience with four-legged creatures as he did with any kind of farm animals…which was to say none. But in Kissing Creek, you helped your neighbors. End of story. Didn't matter if it was a flat tire or a cat stuck up a tree or clearing the road after a storm had blown through…*or* shooing a giant monstrosity of a llama.

"Can someone call Devon?" the woman, whom Ryan assumed was the librarian, called out. "I don't want to make any sudden movements to get my phone. Tell him Lily's loose again."

"I'll call." The older woman grabbed her phone and tapped at the screen.

But the llama was clearly after something. That's when Ryan spied a bag sitting on the checkout counter. He recognized the Kisspresso Café logo. Was it after the food? That had to be one hell of a nose.

He walked out from the aisle and crept toward the front of the library, the llama seeming to grow bigger with each step he took. She was, as his pitching coach would say, "an absolute unit." He'd put her at three hundred pounds and a hair under six feet tall, making her bigger than any of the hard-hitting sluggers he'd faced at the plate. Heck, he was pretty sure he'd seen smart cars that were more compact.

"Are you okay?" he asked the librarian.

"That remains to be seen." She turned to him, attempting to smile but looking more than a little frightened of the creature.

Her hair was the shade of espresso, and she wore a novelty dinosaur-printed dress. She had full lips and eyelashes that were thick and dark, making her eyes seem big and luminous. Starry eyes. The kind that shifted in the light, changing from silver to gray to blue and refusing to be put entirely in one category.

"I think she's after the muffins," she added. "I've heard stories about how she's always terrorizing the poor staff in the café, but I thought it was an urban legend."

The llama bleated again.

"Can we sacrifice the muffins?" he asked.

"If we must," she replied with a sigh. "But I bought them for the team."

"If we get out of this alive, I'll take you out for some replacement muffins." The words shot out of him before he had time to think about whether it was wise to flirt with a woman while he was in his hometown. Or while they were being stared down by a giant llama.

If muffins are considered flirting, man, you're way off your game. Maybe you should ask her if she knows about chapter twenty-one.

"Did you proposition me in a life-or-death moment?" The librarian shot him an amused look. "Talk about taking advantage of the situation."

"*If* we get out alive." He glanced at the llama, who was growing impatient. "Which is definitely not guaranteed."

Lily ambled forward, toward the checkout counter, but there was a railing in front, which usually directed traffic and was decidedly *not* sized for a beefy llama. The blood-curdling bleating sound happened again.

Ryan shuddered. "Right now, I'm putting our odds at fifty-fifty."

"Devon said he'd be here in five," the older woman said from her safe vantage point in the aisle. "He also said to get her outside if we can."

"And how exactly are we supposed to do that?" The librarian frowned. "Maybe if we throw the muffin outside, she'll follow. I don't suppose you have a good arm?"

Was she being sarcastic? Or did she have no idea who he was?

"I'm sure I can toss a muffin." He crept closer to the swinging door that led to the circular area behind the checkout counters. "Can you make sure the doors stay open? I don't want her running through glass and hurting herself."

"Cute, loves books *and* animals. Wow."

Did she just call him cute?

"There's a button by the door. I'll go over there slowly. Keep her distracted." She looked at him. "Ready?"

"We got this." He let out a breath.

There were a few other people in the library, and they were all hiding in the aisle, watching from a safe distance.

"Hey, Lily." Ryan made some kissy noises. Did llamas respond to that? He was *so* out of his depth. "Don't pay any attention to the nice librarian lady, okay? Keep your eyes on me."

He pushed through the swinging door to get behind the checkout counters and reached for the bag of muffins. The llama's eyes locked onto him with laser-like focus. She had long white lashes and crooked teeth that jutted out. He would swear she narrowed her gaze at him as if to say, *Who the hell do you think you are, telling me what to do?*

"Since when does this town have a menacing llama?" he muttered.

Ryan reached for the paper bag, and the rustling sound was like fireworks in the quiet library. He extracted a muffin from the bag, and the llama's nostrils twitched.

"Smells good, doesn't it?" He held the muffin up. "If you leave these nice people alone, then you're going to get this tasty treat."

The llama stamped its foot again. Ryan had to admit, the muffin *did* smell good. The llama was getting impatient. She was moving her head back and forth, a slight snorting sound coming from her. Uh oh. The librarian got to the front doors just as the llama charged at the railing.

"Oh shit! You'd better hurry. She's getting mad."

The librarian hit the button for the doors to open, and the second there was a sizable gap, he threw the muffin as fast and hard as he could. He could only hope that the beast realized he didn't have it in his hand anymore. The muffin sailed through the air, and in that moment, Ryan learned two things. One, muffins made surprisingly decent fastballs, and two, there was nothing like having a large animal scream at you to make your life flash before your eyes.

But to Ryan's relief, Lily was laser-locked on the muffin sailing right through the doors. It bounced onto the sidewalk, breaking into several crumbly pieces. She immediately trotted outside and started sucking them up like she had a vacuum attachment for a mouth.

"Close the door!"

The librarian jabbed at the button, but the doors weren't closing. The llama lifted its head and looked as though it was about to come back inside, when thankfully someone outside got her attention. A guy in a buffalo-plaid shirt whistled, and Lily went from being a demonic, muffin-hungry nightmare to a docile, fluffy farm animal.

The man raised his hand in thanks and led the llama away as if this was a totally normal occurrence.

Ryan left the checkout area and went to the

librarian, who looked mildly traumatized. "Are you okay?"

"I'm fine," she said. "That was a hell of a throw."

"No sweat," he said with a laugh that sounded *way* more high-pitched than he wanted it to.

"I'm Sloane, by the way." She stuck her hand out.

"*You're* Sloane Rickman?"

"Yep, that's me," she said.

This cute, *young*, innocent-looking woman wearing a dinosaur-print dress was the one who'd introduced his parents to chapter twenty-one? What the heck?

• • •

The way he'd said her name sounded like caramel sauce, sweet and decadent. But for some reason, it also made her feel like she was sitting outside the principal's office. Maybe because a pair of bright blue eyes were staring her down like twin laser beams in a sixties superhero movie.

"I was picturing someone…older," he said.

Sloane raised an eyebrow. "Librarians come in all shapes, sizes, *and* ages, you know."

"I guess I do now." Standing next to her, he seemed even taller than when she'd noticed him walking into the library. Sloane was five-four, if she made an effort with her posture. Apparently, that was average for an adult woman, though right now, standing next to one giant hunk of a man, she felt like a resident of the Shire.

Minus the hairy feet.

He folded his arms across his chest, and Sloane tried not to stare too obviously at the way it made his biceps bulge. Lordy! Maybe it was the pages of *Stormy Pleasures* she'd read last night, but she was having a hard time doing the polite thing now and not ogling the man's body.

People don't come here to be judged for their appearances, even if they warrant an A+.

"You didn't mention your name." She walked back to the front desk and motioned for him to follow. He walked slowly, with a slight stiffness to his gait, almost like he was nursing sore muscles or an injury. The raised platform behind the front counter was a much-needed addition to the conversation. It might only be a few inches, but she didn't want to get a crick in her neck.

"Ryan Bower," he replied.

"Nice to meet you, Ryan Bower. Thank you for helping with the llama situation."

The counter and the raised platform did nothing. Ryan still towered over her, and his eyes were still boring into hers. They were almost hypnotic, so blue she wondered if the color was from contact lenses. But they suited him too well to be fake. They were the perfect balance to his other sharp features—a nose that looked as though it had gotten into a fistfight or two, and a jaw that was so sharply angled it would make an architect weep with joy.

"You're welcome."

"So, how do you know my name?" she asked. "I don't think I've seen you around town before."

He cleared his throat. "I'm aware of your book club."

"Adults' or children's?" she asked.

"Adults'." His lips tightened. "Seems you're reading a very…engaging book this month. Stormy something."

"*Stormy Pleasures*?" Oh boy. Now Sloane was going to have the perfect fantasy man to pop right into that story next time she got back to it. Ryan Bower was everything the hero of a book should be—at least on the outside and Sloane knew better than to make assumptions about what people were like on the inside. "If you're looking to borrow a copy, I'm afraid we're all out. The book club gets first dibs, and it turns out this month has been quite popular."

"I don't want to borrow it." He held up a hand and shook his head. "Look, this is a family-friendly town."

"Excuse me?" She blinked.

"I mean this place is…" He moved his hand, as if trying to conjure up the right words. Then he finally settled on, "Wholesome."

Sloane blinked. Did he…did he imply she was a bad influence? Her surprise morphed into irritation as heat crawled up into her cheeks. She took her role in the community seriously. Kissing Creek was the place where she'd finally set down roots, and while roots were something most people took for granted, she absolutely did not.

Choosing Kissing Creek as her home wasn't a decision she'd made lightly.

"I know. That's why I moved here," she said, folding her arms across her chest. "And what's wrong with romance novels? Happily-ever-afters are totally wholesome."

"Not that kind of romance novel." He wrinkled his nose as if he smelled something rotten. "That's all about the *other* kind of happy ending."

Ryan Bower's shine was wearing off faster than the enamel on a piece of costume jewelry. He was attractive. Hell, even if muscular giants with jaws strong enough to crack a nut weren't your thing, you couldn't deny it.

But no one criticized her book club picks and got away with it.

Besides, all the members were adults, and she'd given them fair warning that this book was steamier than what the book club was used to. Nobody was forcing them to read it. And that had only made them *more* curious to join the fun. So who did Ryan Bower think he was, coming into her library and trying to make her feel like some skeevy book pimp? Not cool.

"Look, I'm sorry if your parents haven't had the birds and the bees chat with you, but here's the condensed version: lots of people have sex. If that's something you're not comfortable with, I suggest you don't read this book."

Ryan blinked—clearly, he hadn't expected her to

fire back. Maybe along with his misconception that all librarians were old, he'd also expected her to be a mild-mannered little mouse.

Sorry to disappoint, bud.

Sloane prided herself on being generous and welcoming and kind…but that didn't mean she wouldn't bite when necessary. An ex had once compared her to chili chocolate—sweet with an unexpected kick.

"Who says I'm not comfortable with sex?"

"You basically said it yourself," she replied, flipping her ponytail over one shoulder.

"I simply questioned your view that *all* romance novels are inherently wholesome and somehow that means I'm uncomfortable with sex?"

"Sorry, let me clarify. You're uncomfortable with anything beyond boring, vanilla, lights-off, race-to-the-finish-line, missionary sex," she said with a saccharine smile. "Is that better?"

CHAPTER THREE

This five-foot-nothing, dinosaur-wearing, ponytail-flipping librarian was giving him shit about his sex life? Uh, no, that was *not* going to happen.

"If you think missionary is boring, then you haven't had the right man on top of you," Ryan said, returning fire—as quietly as he could. But even in a lowered tone, his voice seemed to boom around the library. "As for racing to the finish line, I don't mind a quickie every now and then. It's good for the warm-up round."

Sloane tipped her face up to him, pale eyes peering at him from behind the lenses of a pair of oversize tortoiseshell glasses. "I bet that's what all quick-finishers say."

She was feisty, he'd give her that. And not at *all* what he'd expected. Ryan had definitely fallen into the trap of stereotyping.

"Got a lot of experience with quick finishers?" He met her gaze head-on, and her jaw tightened, as if she was clenching her back teeth. "I bet I could change your mind about quickies."

Yeah, you talk a big game, Bower, but when *exactly was the last time you brought someone home?*

Irrelevant. His argument stood and he wasn't

about to bring his two-year-long self-imposed drought into the conversation.

"That's a bold statement for someone who has a problem with a book." Sloane folded her arms across her chest and looked up at him with a self-assured smirk. "I would think a man so confident in his sexual prowess wouldn't have an issue with some steamy fiction."

"I don't have a problem with the book itself," he said. "Just who you're getting to read it."

He watched as the puzzle pieces clicked into place.

"I'm going to put my best Nancy Drew skills to work," she said, tapping a fingertip to her cheek. "There's a Gaye Bower in the book club—a sweet-as-pie woman in her fifties who talks about her three sons, two of whom live out of town. Both athletes, if I remember correctly, which seems to fit."

"Seems to fit, how?"

"Tall, muscular, larger-than-life ego." She waved a hand in his direction. "Throws a muffin like a champ. I'm going to say…baseball."

"That would be correct."

"And you didn't deny the larger-than-life ego, interesting."

Why would he? As a professional athlete, if you didn't expect to win, then you were running a race with a ball and chain around your foot. Ryan went into every game with the same mentality—*I will win*. Did that happen every single game? Hell no, but it wasn't an excuse to think otherwise. Mental toughness was as important as the speed of his fastball. It was as important as the diligence he put into reading the scatter reports. It was as important as his consistency in the gym.

"Confidence intimidates some people." He shrugged. "Call it what you want."

"Right. Now let me guess," she said. "You're one of Gaye Bower's boys and you've come home to visit your family only to find your mom reading a spicy romance novel in the family living room. Or maybe she was even reading it—gasp—at the coffee shop. How scandalous."

He ground his back teeth together. "Wrong, Dino Woman."

"I take that name as a compliment."

"You would."

"So let me guess, if it's not the reading that's bothering you, then…" She gasped and clamped a hand over her mouth, eyes crinkling with stifled laughter. "You're complaining for another reason."

Before he could respond, Ryan heard the front doors swish open a few feet behind him. Tension crackled in the air as he remained focused on the librarian. He hadn't even planned to mention it! He'd only come in to borrow some books, since he knew he would grow tired of binging shows on Netflix while he rested up, and he'd accidentally left his ereader back in Toronto. If it wasn't for the llama incident, he wouldn't have said anything to her at all.

"Sloane?" A woman's voice behind him made

Ryan turn around. "Ryan Bower, my goodness! I heard you were home."

"Ms. Irving, it's good to see you." He turned on the charm as easily as turning on his shower, smiling in the older woman's direction. "It's been a while."

"We've been following your progress with the Blizzards." She came over and squeezed him in a hug, her jewelry jangling with the motion. "You won't take me away from my beloved Red Sox, but we're rooting for you in our house."

Sloane raised a brow as she watched on, her expression curious.

"I was so sorry to hear about your injury." She shook her head. "A nasty, unfortunate incident."

Like he needed the reminder.

"Pat, it's good you came back," Sloane said to the older woman, a wicked smile brewing on her lips. "Ryan has some feedback about our latest book club pick."

What was she up to? Mischief seemed to dance around her like fireflies. Her eyes sparkled from behind her glasses. She was enjoying this.

"Oh yes?" Ms. Irving asked.

"Apparently, Gaye is enjoying it so much, it sounds like he's *heard* all about it," she said, barely containing a laugh.

Damn her.

Thankfully, Pat Irving seemed to miss the innuendo in her tone. "Wonderful. I love to hear about our patrons enjoying their books. It's why we do what we do. Now excuse me, I need to finish off my break. Say hi to your mom, Ryan."

"I will," he replied smoothly, watching as she disappeared into a back room.

Sloane never took her eyes off him, however. He could feel the intensity of her gaze like warmth on his skin. She stood smugly behind her checkout desk, leaning forward on her forearms and grinning like the freaking Cheshire Cat. "Yeah, say hi to your mom, Ryan. I look forward to telling her that I finally got to meet one of her lovely sons."

Ryan shook his head and turned on his heel. The easiest way to deal with this problem was to find somewhere else to stay. If his parents were going to continue to hump like rabbits, fine. He was happy their marriage was as strong and lively as ever.

But he didn't have to torture himself by listening to it.

He'd find himself a place to rent for the rest of the month, long enough to wait out the post-season. Then he'd return home to Toronto, focused on making sure the next season was his best yet, and he'd forget all about this interesting—no, *annoying* encounter with this adorable—dammit—*troublemaking* librarian.

CHAPTER FOUR

Not only were his parents driving him batty, but now he'd struck up some weird antagonistic relationship with the local hottie librarian.

The local hottie librarian who was convinced he was boring in the sack.

What the hell was going on in his life right now? It was almost as if things had been going *too* smoothly prior to this year and fate had decided to punch him in the nuts to keep him humble. Maybe he should pack his bags and go somewhere he didn't know anyone, where nobody could mess with his head.

Why did he even care what some dinosaur-wearing, pocket-rocket of a woman thought of him anyway? Ryan wasn't a people-pleaser by nature. He was too focused for that, too driven. He had his eye on the prize from the second he woke up in the morning until his eyes finally shut at night. His whole life was dedicated to one goal.

But what happened when that goal was suddenly on ice, at least for the moment? He had no idea how to live.

He wasn't even his usual self. Instead, he'd turned into a gloomy, prickly, picking-silly-fights version of himself. He *wasn't* that guy.

On the drive back to his parents' house, he resolved to keep his head down and stay out of Sloane's path. Something about her pulled him like a magnet. She demanded his attention, and a woman like that was not in his plans, no matter how intrigued he felt.

Maybe in another life.

Only Ryan didn't want another life, he wanted his old life. His *normal* life. His baseball-and-nothing-else life.

He pulled his car up alongside the curb in front of his parents' house. The rehab appointment had gone well and he'd grabbed a coffee on the way home, which meant it was time to have a serious chat with his folks about him finding somewhere else to stay.

Ryan let himself into the house, surprised to see the living room empty. Both cars were parked out front, so his parents should be home. Maybe they'd gone for a walk. But then a cry came from the back of the house.

"Again?" Ryan scrubbed a hand over his face. However, it became quickly apparent that the cry was not one of pleasure, but one of pain. Ryan jogged through the house, worry coiling like a snake in his gut. "Dad? Mom?"

"We're in here," his mother replied. He found them in their bedroom.

His father was on the bed, lying at an awkward angle with his face twisted in a grimace, his tanned forehead covered in a sheen of perspiration. He was wearing a ratty old white T-shirt and shorts, a sure sign he'd been working in the garden.

"What happened?" Ryan frowned.

"Your father tweaked his back," his mom replied with a heavy sigh. Her blue eyes—the ones shared by Ryan and both his brothers—brimmed with concern. "He bent down to deal with some of the weeds that have been bothering our peonies, and a muscle spasmed."

His dad tried to move and grunted. "It's not the damn peonies."

Gaye shot her husband a look that had "shut the hell up" written all over it. She folded her arms across her chest, obscuring the faded logo of an old tourist T-shirt from a family trip they'd taken to Hawaii almost two decades ago. She must've been in the garden, too.

Ryan raised an eyebrow.

"It's that book," his dad said, squeezing his eyes shut and stifling a groan. "Chapter twenty-one. It's not even humanly possible."

"Alfred," his mother snapped. "Stop it."

She all but dragged Ryan out of the room and closed the bedroom door. He didn't even want to think about *what* they'd been doing that might have aggravated his dad's old back injury, sustained from a nasty trip down some icy steps years ago. This freaking book was going to haunt him the entire time he stayed in Kissing Creek.

"Come out to the kitchen and help me with some heat packs for your father," his mom said, walking briskly down the hall. "I've given him a few painkillers, and the physiotherapist said he'd pop around on his lunch break for a house visit."

"That's kind of him." Ryan followed his mother into the kitchen. "So, the peonies, huh?"

She narrowed her eyes at him. "I know you don't want to hear the ins and outs."

Ryan cringed at her choice of wording. "I really don't."

"Then I won't talk about it. Your father will be fine." His mom grew up the daughter of an ER nurse and had been raised on the "unless there's arterial spray, you'll live" kind of mentality. "His back plays up every now and then because he doesn't keep up with the stretches the specialist gave him."

"So, it's all his fault?" Ryan arched a brow.

"I didn't say that." She dug a handmade fabric bag filled with oats and lavender and shoved it in Ryan's direction. "Put that in the microwave. Two minutes."

Ryan did as he was told, while his mother started pulling out some bread to make sandwiches. She knew her husband well—the better fed he was, the less he complained.

"I know you're supposed to be resting at the moment," she said as she laid the slices of bread and sandwich ingredients out in the same methodical way she'd made lunches for the entirety of Ryan's life. "But your father is going to be out of action for a week or two, at least. Same thing happens every time he pulls that muscle."

"So long as it doesn't put any strain on my knee, I'm here to help. Whatever you need." He jabbed at the buttons on the microwave and watched the grain bag slowly turn. "I can drive him to appointments and stuff."

"It might be a bit more than that, I'm afraid. He agreed to sit on the town festival committee, and they're gearing up for some big Halloween event. I think there's plans for a parade in the afternoon, before trick-or-treating kicks off." She shook her head. "He was supposed to be in semi-retirement this year, and then he filled all that spare time with even *more* work."

Ryan couldn't help but smile. That was his dad in a nutshell—he had to be busy all the time. If he wasn't tinkering with something around the house, he was helping a neighbor rake leaves or fix a broken fence. "I'm not sure what expertise I can lend to a parade committee, but if it will help…"

"It will. You know how your father hates to let people down. He's got a big thing about pride and the family name." His mom shook her head. "You'd think he was running for mayor with how seriously he takes this stuff."

Ryan snorted. "Mayor Bower. Now *that* I'd like to see."

"Don't you dare put any ideas in his head." His mother looked up from the cutting board to make sure Ryan knew she was serious.

Chuckling, he held up both hands. "I won't breathe a word."

"Good." She nodded. "I don't think I could handle that."

Ryan wasn't so sure. His mom was built of tough stuff—she'd had to be to raise three rambunctious boys who'd been pure hyperactivity the second they exited the womb. She was also the pillar of the family, ready with a swift shove in the right direction if one of her sons needed it. She wasn't the kind of mother who coddled her kids or worried about every bump and scrape, but he'd never doubted that she was there for him, despite the jokes about the youngest, Ace, being the favorite. Gaye had somehow managed to be at every single one of Ryan's little league games, every swim meet for Ace, and every one of Mark's weightlifting competitions until they all left for college.

At one point, Ryan wondered if his mother was secretly a set of triplets masquerading as one person. Either that, or she'd been able to be in three places at once. Four if you counted her always being there for her husband, too.

"It's really good to have you home, Ry," she said. "We miss you."

"It's part of the job, Ma. You know that." He drew her into a firm hug. "I'm doing what I love."

"I always knew you'd make it. The first time I saw you hold a bat, while all the other little kids looked like they were trying to pick up Thor's hammer, you took to it like a duck to water."

He smiled. "Took a while to get my swing down."

"You were a natural. All my boys are talented to the core." She squeezed him and then stepped back. Ryan was surprised to see her looking a little misty eyed.

"Hey, what's this about?" He narrowed his eyes. "What's going on?"

"Some days I miss having you all under one roof is all." She gave herself a little shake, and then she was back to her brisk, practical self. "Now, take that heat pack to your father and make sure he puts it on the right spot. I'll bring lunch in a minute."

"Can do." Ryan thought about how to broach the subject of him staying somewhere else. He really didn't want to hurt his mom's feelings, but… "So uh, about me staying here—"

"It'll be a big help with your father laid up," she said, cutting the sandwiches into neat triangles and not looking at him. "You know I need someone tall to reach things on the top shelf."

"That's the weakest excuse I've ever heard," he muttered, pulling the heat pack out of the microwave.

She glanced at him over one shoulder. "With your father laid up, I might have to sleep in the spare room anyway so he can stretch out."

Message received. There'd be no more X-rated action in his parents' bedroom while his father had an injured back, which meant Ryan might get a peaceful night's sleep after all. He'd give them one more chance, but the second *anyone* uttered the words "chapter twenty-one," he was out of there.

• • •

Three days after the "major league jerk" incident, Sloane was feeling herself again. She suspected that was due to a few causes. For starters, she'd finally gotten in touch with her mother, who was apparently somewhere in central Europe. Location undisclosed, as usual, but she was alive, and Sloane knew not to ask for more than that.

They'd chatted for five minutes, without video. Her mother claimed the internet was bad and video caused too much lag, but Sloane knew that was code for her mom being on a job she couldn't talk about. She'd always said, "The less you know, the better."

Growing up, her mother's work had taken her—and Sloane and her dad—across the world. A year here, two years there. Whenever people asked what Sloane's mother did for work, the answer was always the same: consulting. Consulting for what, exactly, Sloane was never quite sure. Security of some kind. Tech security, maybe? Or maybe it was more private security. All Sloane knew was that she got paid enough that they always stayed in the fanciest of places.

Oh, and that her mother's job had ruined Sloane's parents' marriage.

Her father had never liked playing primary caregiver, even though he was a great dad. But he'd given up a lucrative engineering career to follow his wife around the world. And what was the point of a master's degree when all you ended up doing was cooking breakfast and washing dishes?

Her parents lasted until Sloane went to college. Barely. She got the "we're getting a divorce" call twelve days into her first semester. Within two years, her father had remarried and started working on the kind of family he'd always wanted, one with a wife who leaned on him and was willing to pop out a football team of children. Not like in his first marriage, where Sloane's mother didn't need anything from anybody. Which was precisely why Sloane had two rules when it came to relationships:

1. Never follow someone around the world.

2. Don't play second fiddle to someone's career.

It wasn't that she expected to end up with a man who had no ambitions in life—not at all. But there was a big difference between being ambitious and having that kind of hard-wired, single-mindedness her mother had that eclipsed everything and everyone around her.

What she'd learned from watching her parents' marriage crumble was that it took more than love between two good people to make a relationship work. It took common goals, too.

Shaking off the memories, Sloane walked into Kissing Creek's most beloved pastry shop, Glazed and Confused. They specialized in donuts—a bold strategy coming from the state that founded Dunkin' Donuts—and, like most businesses in town, capitalized on kiss-themed puns.

"Mornin' sugar." The woman behind the counter smiled in greeting. She had a black apron over a floral dress and hair that was the exact shade of a new copper penny. "What can I get you today?"

"A dozen, please." Sloane crouched a little to look at the vibrant display. "Three of each— Frenching Vanilla, Chocolate Smooch, Caramel Canoodling, and...what's the special this week?"

The woman behind the counter gestured to a tray of specialty flavors. "This week we've got Pashing Pumpkin and XoXo, which is an almond praline with a hint of salted caramel."

"Oh pumpkin, yes. Three of those as well, please." Sloane clapped her hands together. "I don't know how you keep coming up with all these adorable names."

"We have a brainstorming board out back." The woman reached for a piece of tissue and began carefully placing the donuts into a white box. "Anyone who has an idea pops it on the board, and then each month we pick one or two to experiment with."

"That's so fun! I've always thought it would be cool to have a job naming things. Like that person who gets to name all the lipstick shades at a cosmetics company," Sloane said.

The woman behind the counter filled the box and then brought it over to the cash register.

"Are these a gift?" she asked as Sloane tapped her card to the machine. "I can put a pretty ribbon on the box, if you like."

"Nah, no need for that. They're team-building

donuts." Sloane reached for the box and bid the woman a goodbye.

Today was a big day. For two of the three years she'd lived in Kissing Creek, Sloane had been part of a local volunteer group who helped organize community initiatives for the town. Sometimes it was about cultural enrichment—like their Shakespeare in the Park event, which had theater majors from the local college putting on their version of *Taming of the Shrew*. Other times, the events aimed to raise funds for various charities, like the fun run for ALS they did last year.

But this time around, it was a Halloween parade, with no other goal than making the local kids have the best Halloween possible. And Sloane was in charge. It was perfect for two reasons—one, because she was very good at organizing things, and two, because Halloween was by far the best day of the year.

People went gaga for Christmas with all its glittering snowflakes and peppermint-flavored everything. Even Thanksgiving seemed to get higher billing. But to Sloane, Halloween was everything you could possibly want.

Excuse to wear a crazy costume? Check.

No one judging you for how much candy you were eating? Check.

Black and purple, aka the best color combination in existence? Check.

Every Halloween, Sloane took her costume game to the next level. Always dinosaur-themed, of course. She'd done Ellie Sattler and John Hammond from *Jurassic Park*. Another time, she'd gone as the Dilophosaurus complete with the frill and some green water for "spitting venom," even though it was noted by a famous geologist that the Dilophosaurus was unlikely to have had the frill and been able to spit venom like the movie portrayed.

But Sloane figured Halloween was more about the drama than paleontological accuracy.

She walked down Main Street, carefully carrying the box of donuts. It was a good thing the council offices, where the committee was granted use of a meeting room once per month, was only a few blocks away. She didn't want to look too wilted while running her first meeting.

This might not have seemed like a big deal to a lot of people, but to Sloane, it was a sign people trusted her. The committee president, a retired high school principal, had tapped her on the shoulder for this job. He said she showed great leadership skills and had the kind of upbeat, positive attitude he liked to foster in the group.

That was a high compliment and proof she was an accepted member of their community, something she'd wanted for the longest time. She belonged. She made an impact. People noticed and remembered her.

And she wouldn't waste this opportunity.

Sloane headed into the council buildings, walking straight to the front desk to sign in. The meeting room was already open; some of the members liked to gather early and catch up. They weren't due to start for another ten minutes, and Sloane's stomach was filled with nervous butterflies.

Most of the prep work had already been done— the date picked, permits acquired, and a safety plan had been signed off by government officials. It was Sloane's job to bring the parade to life and motivate her team to get everything done on time.

She walked into the meeting room with a big smile on her face, ready to do the best job possible. But the smile slowly died on her lips as she caught the intense, electric-blue stare of the absolute last man she wanted to see today.

Ryan Bower.

CHAPTER FIVE

Ryan blinked. Okay, the universe was *definitely* screwing with him.

That was the only explanation for why, when he was trying to do a good deed and keep his parents happy, he was thrown into Sloane's path once more. The only thing that made him feel slightly better was the fact that she looked about as happy to see him as he was to see her.

She swanned into the room, wearing an attention-grabbing novelty dress. It was purple with a fitted top, a full skirt, and little frilly sleeves that made her look like something that belonged on top of cake. The fabric itself was covered in jack-o-lanterns, witch hats, dinosaur skulls, and white ghosts.

"Wait, which event is this parade for again?" he joked. "Your outfit isn't sending a clear enough message."

Sloane's perky smile turned brittle as she placed the donuts on the table in the middle of the room. "Ryan, what a surprise."

The members already in the room gravitated to the sweet treats, but Ryan stood his ground, waiting to see what Sloane would do next. As everyone dug in, she came to stand next to him.

"Are you lost?" she asked, keeping her voice low enough that the other committee members wouldn't hear. "I assume you're here to complain about something, but complaints are usually lodged with the customer service desk on level two."

Shots fired.

"I'm very much in the right place." He threw her a saccharine smile that instinct told him would get under her skin.

"Well, you're not part of my team," she replied. "So, no, you're *not* in the right place."

Behind her chunky black glasses, her eyelids were painted with something sparkly that made her irises look more silver than gray. Every time she blinked, he got flashes of pink and purple and gold, like tiny fireworks exploding.

It seemed fitting.

"Yeah, I am. My dad threw his back out..." He contemplated telling her how, but he figured she'd turn that into yet another opportunity to cast aspersions about his sex life. "In the garden."

"And you put your hand up to take his place? That's noble," she said. "But all volunteers need to be vetted by the committee president."

"Mr. Shaw? Don't worry about that. He used to coach me in little league." Ryan's grin grew wider as Sloane's jaw grew tighter.

"We still have to follow the process."

At that moment, the man in question walked into the room. Douglas Shaw was a towering tree-trunk of a man and possibly the only person in Kissing Creek who made Ryan feel average in height. But despite his imposing size, he was a man driven by his personal values—love for his family, his community, and his sports.

"I heard a rumor that the pride and joy of Kissing Creek was back in town." Douglas walked over and clapped Ryan on the back so hard it very well could have shifted an organ. They didn't call him Big Doug out on the field for nothing. "Welcome home, son."

"Sir." Ryan nodded. "Dad's had an issue with his back, so he asked me to step into his spot. You know I relish any chance to help out."

He couldn't help but throw a cocky glance in Sloane's direction. She looked like she was trying to set his head on fire with her eyes, but the second that Douglas turned to her, the look evaporated like a puff of smoke.

"I understand we need to vet—" she started, but her words were cut off by the raise of Big Doug's hand.

"Consider Ryan vetted. We're blessed to have such a fine young man back on home turf. Although I don't want you doing anything to impact the recovery of your knee, of course. Gotta have you back on the mound next season, doing us proud."

"Don't worry, I'll make sure I keep it out of harm's way," he replied.

As Douglas moved on to greet some of the other committee members, Sloane turned to Ryan. "Quite happy with yourself, aren't you?"

He didn't even try to hide his smugness. "Very."

"Why do you want to be here? You seem a little too uptight to be spreading joy and happiness."

"I think I'm going to need some medical attention for that third-degree burn," he quipped.

She snorted. "Okay, so you have a sense of humor. Noted."

"I'm not an asshole, much as that might surprise you." Although he was aware in having to make such a statement, that probably weakened his position rather than strengthening it.

"A prude with a heart of gold, then?" She shot him an unrepentant smile.

"Just because I don't want to hear my parents banging doesn't mean I'm a prude," he said, keeping his voice low. He shouldn't bite back, because that was clearly what she wanted. But he couldn't help himself.

"Well, you did originally come to the library for some reading materials, right?" She tilted her head, appraising him through the lenses of her glasses. Her long brown hair was styled differently today, half up and half down. The loose strands were lightly curled, and they bounced around her shoulders. "Why not read *Stormy Pleasures*?"

Was this sassy little librarian seriously calling his bluff?

Ryan knew the adult thing to do would be to say, *No, I'm not interested in reading the same smutty book my mother is reading.* But there was a deeply rooted sense of pride being dented here. Part of him had some caveman-like urge to prove he wasn't a boring, stick-up-his-ass, pearl clutcher.

Was it childish? Probably. Pointless? Abso-freaking-lutely.

Was he going to do the mature thing? Uh, nope. Hard pass on that.

"Sure," he replied with a nonchalant lift of one shoulder. "I'll read it when you have it back in the library."

Sloane looked at him like she was trying to figure out whether he was full of shit or not. "I finished it last night. You can have my copy."

Okay, so she was *definitely* calling his bluff.

He stopped short of puffing his chest out like an actual primate, but he didn't dare break eye contact with her. Little Miss Button Presser was about to get a lesson in stubbornness from a pro. One didn't make it all the way to the Major Leagues without knowing how to hold his ground. Ryan was a gold medalist in digging his heels in. Call it a Bower family trait.

"Hand it over," he said coolly.

Sloane reached into her bag and pulled the book out. The flashy red spine wasn't the least bit inconspicuous, and she seemed to take great pleasure in handing it over as slowly as possible, so everyone could see. "Don't you dare doggy-ear the pages."

"I'm not a monster." He turned the book over in his hands, aware that some of the other people in the room were watching. But he wasn't going to back down, no siree. "And I'll make sure I return it on time. I know how you librarians hate books being returned late."

Sloane's full lips quirked up into something halfway between a smirk and…well, something teasing. "Study up, Ryan. There's going to be a pop quiz."

"Don't worry," he said, taking a step closer and scoring himself a point when her nostrils flared and her pupils widened behind the lenses of her glasses. "I'm an excellent student."

"We'll see if that's true."

If Sloane Rickman wanted a challenge, then a challenge he was going to bring her. Ryan didn't back down for anybody. And maybe, despite the rocky start to his trip home, this was exactly what he needed right now. Something to keep his mind off his knee and his career and all the fears about how fast the future was rushing toward him.

• • •

Later that afternoon, Sloane *should* have been feeling on top of the world. Her first meeting had gone well. The volunteers seemed enthusiastic and had lots of good ideas—well, except for Ryan, who sat in the back, watching her with his unnerving blue eyes in a way that made her all tingly.

But, that aside, she could chalk it up as a win. Douglas had sat in on the meeting to make sure it ran smoothly, and he'd pulled her aside afterward to tell her what a great job she was doing. She had "massive leadership potential" apparently. That really meant a lot to her, because he could have picked someone with much more local knowledge and experience. Someone who'd been on the volunteer committee for years.

She wouldn't let him down.

And this was a big checkbox in her "Operation Perfect Home" plans. When she'd driven her beat-up red sedan into Kissing Creek three years ago, tears in her eyes after yet another place turned out to be wrong for her, she hadn't expected much. But within a week, Sloane knew this place was different—people here were kind and open, willing to chat to strangers while waiting in line for a coffee.

She'd found herself a house to rent for the first year and then extended for one more. Then she'd bought one of her own. It was wild to have a little piece of land with her name on it, a place where she could plant what she wanted, paint the walls bright colors, and make any change she liked. Coming home every day from work still made her giddy with excitement.

And yet...

Sloane stood in the middle of her living room, limbs twitching with restless energy. Yesterday she'd rearranged the furniture again, trying to get everything in the perfect spot. The new couch was supposed to complete the room, but now that she looked at it again, something was bugging her.

No matter how hard she worked, or how

many things she tweaked, there was part of her that wondered if she'd ever feel like the house was "done." Three years was the longest she'd ever lived in one place—because even in her college days she'd transferred halfway through her studies, telling herself the move was about finding the right school environment.

But there was a niggling part of her brain whispering that it was a big fat lie. That she moved because moving was all she knew. It was muscle memory to her. Packing her bags and starting over was comfortable in some ways, familiar.

And living in the same town for three years wasn't.

This was *supposed* to feel like the dream. She finally had a home that was hers, a town she'd handpicked because it suited her needs perfectly, and a job she loved. So why did she feel restless?

"You've never lived alone before," she reasoned with herself. "Maybe that's it."

The house *did* seem empty—not because it lacked furniture and things to fill the space, but empty in a different way. Empty of life. Empty of sound. Empty of love. But how was she supposed to fix that? It wasn't like she could conjure up the perfect life partner to fill that void. Maybe it was time to get herself a pet. A dog seemed like a lot of work, so perhaps a cat was better. Or a goldfish.

Sloane chewed on her bottom lip. Even a goldfish seemed kind of scary. What if she forgot to feed it? Or what if she sprinkled *too much* fishy food and the little guy overate and Sloane came home from work one day to find him floating on his side, dead.

She shook her head. Maybe a house plant was a safer place to start. Even if she killed a house plant... well, that wasn't *so* bad, right? They didn't have pain receptors. Lots of people killed plants and nobody seemed to judge them for it.

She'd mull on the idea of a house plant, but right now she felt like getting out of the house was necessary...even though she'd only just returned home. Ugh. Why did she have this weird energy today? She couldn't sit still for five minutes.

Maybe she'd pop into the library and see how Pat was doing.

Resolved to go and visit her friend, Sloane turned around and walked back out of her house, feeling a sense of relief as she locked the door behind her.

Fifteen minutes later, she pulled her car up in front of the Kissing Creek library, with two coffees nestled safely in her cupholders. She grabbed the drinks and got out, bumping the car door closed behind her with one hip. Pat was inside, checking out a student with a large stack of books. Sloane waited patiently for the boy to finish up and head on his merry way.

"What on earth are you doing in here on your day off?" Pat frowned, though her expression softened a touch when she saw the coffee in Sloane's hands.

"Caffeine delivery," she replied with a perky smile, pulling the cup out of the snug holder and then placing it on the library checkout counter.

"You're too sweet for this world, child." But she took the coffee anyway, inhaling before taking a big sip that left a perfect imprint of rich burgundy lipstick on the lid. Today Pat was in a floaty dress and wore a strand of chunky beads around her neck in shades of fuchsia, sunset orange, and a vibrant sunflower yellow.

"It's no trouble." Sloane took a sip of her own coffee. "I appreciated you switching shifts with me so I could run the meeting for the Halloween parade."

"How'd it go?"

"Good." Sloane bobbed her head, her mind immediately going not to the content of the meeting but to one irritatingly handsome volunteer. Well, volunteer-under-duress, she suspected. "We've got some big ideas. It'll be a lot of work, but I think we can do it."

"I would expect nothing less." Pat laughed. "With all these activities you're throwing yourself into, when do you have time to do normal young-person things?"

Sloane cocked her head. "What do you mean 'normal young-person things'?"

"Like going out for dinner with your friends or seeing a movie." Pat gestured with her hand, and a large silver disc on her ring finger flashed in the light. "Or going on a date."

"I do all those things," Sloane protested, but even as she said the words, she knew they were a lie.

The last time she'd gone to the movies was more than a year ago, *and* she'd gone alone. As for

going out for dinners and drinks with friends, well…
Sloane was almost ashamed to say that even though
she had a ton of acquaintances and was friendly with
everyone she met—major league pain in the asses
aside—she was a little short in the "real friends"
department.

She'd spent her whole life longing for a group of
friends that she could call when she felt blue, or who
would lean on her when they needed support. The
kind of people who'd pile onto her couch and share
a pizza from the same box and laugh over silly inside
jokes. Friends like she saw in all the TV shows she
watched growing up.

Unfortunately for Sloane, no matter how friendly
she was and how hard she tried, she only seemed to be
good at getting to the "wave hello in the street" phase
and not the "sharing pizza from the same box" phase.

"We could always go to dinner tonight," Sloane
suggested hopefully.

"As much as I appreciate the offer, *I* have a date."
Pat shimmied.

"Really, with who?" Sloane leaned on the
counter. "Tell me everything."

Pat glanced around to make sure there were no
customers within earshot. The library was quiet at
this time, and barring a few people milling about the
shelves, there wasn't anyone waiting for assistance.
"Hilary Maxwell's grandfather."

"Hot grandpa?" Sloane gasped. "Go, you!"

Hot Grandpa was the nickname given—secretly, of

course—to Steve Maxwell, a local mechanic who was built better than men half his age and had a total silver fox thing going on. Plus, he was a sweetheart to boot.

"Don't you dare tell anyone." Pat waggled a finger in her direction. "Since the divorce, I haven't really done the dating thing, so I'm nervous."

"Don't be. I'm sure you'll have a great time." Sloane grinned. "Well, forget I said anything about dinner. I would *not* want you to miss out on a hot date."

"Don't you want to hang out with people your own age, anyway? I'm old enough to be your mother and then some."

Sloane rolled her eyes. "Age is just a number. Besides, everyone my age is getting married and having babies and they don't always have time for a new friend."

She'd meant to brush it off with a cavalier attitude, but clearly, she'd sounded a little sadder than she'd wanted to, because Pat came out from behind the checkout counter and wrapped Sloane into a big hug.

"Oh, honey," she said. "Don't worry. It's hard making friends as an adult, especially in a new town."

"It's not a new town. I've been here three years," Sloane said, her words muffled because Pat was cradling her head against her perfumed bosom. As much as she didn't want to admit it, it was nice being hugged.

It'd been a long time.

In fact, she remembered the last time her mother had almost hugged her…it had been the day she'd moved into her dorm room right before her first semester of college. Her roommate also had her parents there. All three of them had been giggly, tearful, and excited, love radiating like a fluffy pink cloud around them.

In contrast, Sloane's parents were barely speaking and her mother had patted her awkwardly on the back when it was time for them to leave. Instead of goodbyes and I-love-yous, her mother had told her to make sure she registered with the local doctor's office should she need to have any tests done.

That was her mother's parting wisdom—try not to get an STD.

"You have to keep putting yourself out there." Pat pulled back. "Everybody loves you. You have such a big, sparkling personality, and anybody in this town would be lucky to call you a friend."

That was easier said than done.

Sloane put her hand up for everything—she ran the book clubs, volunteered on the town event committee, manned bake sales, and handed out posters for missing cats. Anything she could do to ingratiate herself in the eyes of the Kissing Creek residents, she did it. And Pat was right, people *did* like her.

But liking someone didn't make them a real friend. Sadly, Sloane didn't have too much experience in taking that next step. She had a lifetime of experience to make her an expert at the "getting to know you" conversations. And her quirky outfits made people remember her—but she never quite seemed to figure out how to take the relationship to the next level.

And it hurt a bit, seeing all these kind folks out having dinner with one another and never having an invite herself. Not that anyone tried to exclude her on purpose, of course, but they never seemed to think of her, either. Was it completely pathetic to be twenty-seven and not have any true friends to speak of? Probably.

You know what was worse? The fact that she'd googled "how to make friends" more than once. Ugh. If that wasn't the saddest internet search in history, then she didn't know *what* was!

Seriously, some people might be ashamed of the weird, kinky things they looked up on their incognito browser, but Sloane would go to her grave hoping nobody found out she'd tried to get Google to help her make friends.

Still, she'd screen-capped one of the articles and saved it on her phone.

1. Start small with people you know and ask someone to hang out.

2. Get to know the other person by asking questions.

3. Be open—you have to let people in if you want to make friends.

4. Be there for them when they need you.

5. Make an effort to keep in touch.

At that moment, her phone buzzed in her pocket, and when she saw who'd messaged, a smile automatically curved her lips. Ryan. They'd exchanged numbers after the meeting earlier that day, just in case she needed to contact him with changes to meeting times or other official business.

But it seemed Mr. Grumpy Guts was determined to prove a point.

RYAN: *Settling in for a reading session. Kitty does not look impressed.*

A photo followed of a cat with a very sour expression on its face, sitting next to the book. For some reason, the message made something warm and fuzzy stick in her chest.

Clearly, Ryan was thinking about her. Enough that he took the time to text, anyway…although that could be a simple act of revenge for her calling his bluff today. Whatever the reason, it made her feel a little less alone.

SLOANE: *Tell me when you get to chapter three, that's when it starts to get juicy.*

RYAN: *Literally juicy? I'm not sure I like the sound of that :/*

Sloane snorted, and Pat shot her an amused look. "Maybe you should invite out to dinner whoever is making you blush like a schoolgirl."

"Nah. He's not a friend." She shook her head.

"More like an antagonistic acquaintance."

"You don't look very antagonized. Besides, what harm could it do? The more you put yourself out there, the easier gets. It's like working a muscle."

Sloane looked at her phone screen and considered Pat's advice. Maybe there was some truth to it—like a practice run, perhaps? She needed to figure out how to take the next step—because it was becoming clear that while Sloane was respected and part of the community here, there was a big difference between being welcome and actually belonging.

And she really wanted to be more than a familiar face on the street.

Maybe Ryan Bower was the perfect person to practice on. He wouldn't be sticking around, since he had big shiny career dreams waiting for him on the other side of his injury rehab. He was low risk. He was leaving anyway, so if she made a fool of herself, then what was the big deal? Besides, if she could get Ryan Bower to like her, then she could convince just about anyone.

1. Start small with people you know and ask someone to hang out.

He was someone she knew…kind of.

"You know what," Sloane said. "I think I'll do that."

Maybe not dinner, since that seemed a little intimate. But lunch, perhaps. No, a working session! Ryan couldn't say no to that after he made a big song and dance about not needing to be vetted today.

Waving goodbye to Pat and wishing her luck for her hot date, Sloane headed out of the library with her coffee in one hand and phone in the other.

SLOANE: *No spoilers here. You'll just have to read it and find out yourself…then you can meet me after work tomorrow.*

RYAN: *You want a verbal update?*

SLOANE: *Maybe. A photo of the book doesn't mean you're actually reading it.*

RYAN: *Don't tell me Dirty Rainbow Bright has trust issues.*

Dirty Rainbow Bright? She snorted. Now *that* was a nickname.

SLOANE: *Actually, I need your help picking up some supplies for the parade. Two birds, one stone. Meet me at The Craft Shed at 6?*

Three little dots blinked on her phone screen before Ryan typed his confirmation. Sure, this wasn't quite the "dinner with friends" activity she was missing in her life, but it was a start.

And Ryan Bower was going to be her guinea pig whether he liked it or not.

CHAPTER SIX

As much as Ryan would never admit it out loud, he was enjoying *Stormy Pleasures*. He'd always been a nonfiction reader—performance psychology, memoirs, books on resilience and success mindsets and achieving greatness.

Fiction had always struck him as something people used to escape, and he wasn't the kind of guy who wanted to escape his life…usually. But last night when he'd settled into the comfy chair in his old bedroom, *fully* prepared to hate every word on the page, Ryan found himself swept up in the story. The characters were compelling, the plot was intriguing. As for the sex? Well, let's just say he'd taken a cold shower before bed.

Worse than that, he'd woken up in the middle of the night, hand gravitating under his bedsheets and images of Sloane on his mind. Cue cold shower number two. The last thing he wanted was picturing the perky, bespectacled brunette wearing only a pair of hot pink panties and doing some of the things he'd read about. And Sloane was right—chapter three *was* juicy.

Now he had to face her in the light of day. He was going to try *really* hard not show that the book had affected him at all. The plan was simple—read the damn book, act like it was nothing, walk away feeling like he'd protected his manhood.

Ryan walked up the street toward The Craft Shed. Sloane was waiting out front for him at six on the dot, looking surprisingly normal. Jeans that hugged her curvy hips and slim legs, a white T-shirt with a graphic of the Flintstones on the front, and a bouncy ponytail. The only nod to her usual retina-searing style was a pair of hot pink sneakers.

"Jeans and T-shirt." He gasped in mock shock as he got closer. "What happened? Did the rest of your closet catch on fire?"

"Hardy har." She rolled her eyes.

"Although I see you still got some dinosaurs in there. Flintstones, classic."

"I always thought the pet dinosaur was underrated in that franchise," she said.

"I'm more of a Bamm Bamm guy myself."

"The character who could only yell and bash things with a club? Why am I not surprised?" She shook her head. "Come on, the shop closes in an hour, and we've got work to do."

Sloane strode toward the entrance, and Ryan took a moment to admire her from the back before he followed. Who knew Sloane was hiding such a great ass under all those flouncy dresses?

Stop it. This whole "all work no play" thing is clearly messing with your head. You do not *find her attractive.*

If only it were that easy to ignore the fizzing,

zinging sensation in his veins. It seemed to get stronger every time he saw her, as if fueled by the challenge in her pretty gray-blue eyes and the tight purse of her lips.

"So, what do we need in here?" he asked. Maybe the quicker he got this over with, the better chance he'd make it through without sticking his foot in his mouth.

"All the parade floats have been assigned to the local groups who want to take part. *That* was a hell of a spreadsheet exercise," she said. "The good news is, however, that the committee itself is only responsible for two floats *and* we already have trailer bases that we can use. Therefore, all we have to worry about is decoration. I've assigned one float to Jenny, Marty, and Tricia. Then I thought you and I could tackle the other one."

Ryan raised an eyebrow. "You voluntarily *chose* to partner with me?"

Sloane headed down the first aisle of the craft store, which was brimming with pom-poms and fringe and a whole lotta shit Ryan didn't know the names for. "Why not?" she said. "You're on the committee, aren't you?"

"Yeah. But I figured you'd probably want someone on your team who knew what they were doing." He shrugged. "The one and only time I tried to decorate anything, I got dumped."

Sloane's eyebrows shot up. "That's a story I need to hear. Right now."

"I was dating this girl in college." Christa. It'd been more than a decade and he still remembered the humiliation like it was yesterday. "Her twenty-first birthday was coming up, and I had the grand idea to surprise her by decorating her dorm room and baking her a cake."

"Aww." Sloane pressed her hand to her chest.

"Don't *aww* yet," he replied, shaking his head. "Anyway, she loved stars and moons. Even had a little tattoo of a star on her ankle. So I ordered some cardboard stars online to hang from the ceiling along with some fairy lights. I thought the stars looked nice, and they had these circles around them."

Sloane's eyes grew wide. "Oh no."

"Yeah, so turns out they weren't stars. They were pentagrams." He raked a hand through his hair and let out a self-deprecating laugh. "So, yeah, I accidentally covered my girlfriend's dorm room in devil worship symbols."

Sloane snorted but at least tried to look sympathetic. "That's not *so* bad, is it?"

"It wouldn't have been that bad if her parents hadn't dropped her back to school after a long weekend. Including her father…who's a minister." Ryan cringed, and Sloane gasped and slapped a hand over her mouth.

"No!"

"Yeah." He sighed. "It also gave the writing on her birthday cake—happy birthday, my little devil—a whole other meaning."

"That's priceless!" Sloane cackled. "What did they do?"

"Her father wasn't impressed. She basically shoved me out of her room, and then she called me the next day to break things off."

"Poor Ryan." Sloane ran her hand along some sparkling tinsel-like garlands. "I would have thought you were Mr. Slick in college."

"Because I was a jock?" He lifted one shoulder in a shrug. "I mean, I wasn't short on attention."

"Found yourself another girlfriend, did you?"

"Sure did." He laughed. "And I learned my lesson. No more decorating."

"Well, I'm sorry to end your 'no decorating' streak, but you've got to dust off your crafting skills and try again. Good thing is, this is a Halloween parade, so if you want to get all satanic, that's totally fine." She grinned.

"I'll pass on that. Thanks."

"I was thinking we could do something a little more…prehistoric." Sloane waggled her eyebrows, and Ryan couldn't help but laugh. There was something strangely appealing about a woman with a goofy sense of humor.

"You want to go dinosaur-themed. I'm shocked," he deadpanned. "I hope you know what you're doing, then, because I'm far out of my element."

"That's fine. I like being in charge." She looked at him over one shoulder before yanking off some bright-green fringe from the shelf and slinging it over one shoulder.

Was it his imagination or was she being a little saucy with him?

"I figured if you're reading a book like *Stormy Pleasures* you probably liked it the other way around," he said under his breath.

"I heard that."

"You were meant to."

Sloane pulled a few pieces of foam sheeting from another shelf and shoved them into his arms. On top of that went a set of vibrantly colored paints and some more fringing.

"Now I know why you brought me," he quipped. "I'm nothing but a pack mule to you."

"Yeah, but you're such a pretty pack mule," she shot back with a saccharine smile.

He followed her around the store, carrying an increasingly teetering pile of craft supplies. "Pretty, huh?"

There was silence on the other side of the pile of craft items. Ryan lowered them enough that he could peek over the top. Sloane appeared to be studying some type of heavy-duty glue gun thing, but he could see that her cheeks were starting to turn a shade of pink that matched her sneakers.

"I was being sarcastic," she said.

"That blush doesn't lie. Don't tell me you brought me here because you have a crush on me." He said it loud enough that a woman further down the aisle turned and looked on with interest. "Oh, hi, Mrs.

Waterman."

The older woman waved and smiled in their direction, which only seemed to make Sloane more agitated. "I don't have a crush on you," she said. "Not even a little bit."

"I don't believe that for a second."

"Not every woman in the world is attracted to you, you know." She huffed.

"I know that, because not all women are attracted to men. But the ones who are tend to like me." He stifled a laugh behind the craft goods in his arms. It was way too much fun winding her up.

"You're not my type."

"And what exactly *is* your type?"

Maybe it was a bad idea to bait the woman who'd already proven she was more than okay with challenging him, but Ryan felt like Sloane had one up on him. So far, he hadn't been able to fluster her, and this was the closest he'd come.

One little taste…and he wanted a big ol' bite of satisfaction.

"You really want to know?" she asked.

"I could guess based on what I've read so far in the book," he said. "But I'd prefer to hear it in your own words."

She pulled a foam block out of his arms, which cleared his line of sight to watch her more closely. The aisle was empty now, and Sloane's cheeks were pinker than before. She also had a few specks of glitter on her cheek that'd likely transferred from something. It was adorable…in an angry pixie kind of way.

"My type is equal parts smooth and rough," she said, tipping her nose up at him. "Strong enough to handle me when I'm being bossy, but I like him to have a gentle mode if I'm feeling romantic. I don't care about packaging too much, only the way he makes me feel."

"You don't care about packaging, huh?" He raised a brow.

"Nope. I'm not superficial."

"Well, he sounds like quite the guy," Ryan replied.

"Want to know the best bit?" she asked, leaning forward as though she was going to share some great big secret. "I can switch him off and throw him in my underwear drawer when I'm done."

Ryan felt his body temperature shoot up a couple hundred degrees. Turned out he had a new fantasy to add to the one of Sloane in her bright pink underwear…one of her touching herself with the help of a battery-operated friend.

"Now who's blushing?"

"I don't blush," he said. "Trust me, after what I read in chapter three last night, a little chat about your vibrator is nothing."

"Verdict?"

"I never judge a book based on a first impression."

"And people?" she asked, her gray-blue eyes looking molten hot behind the thick lenses of her glasses.

"I'm always prepared for people to surprise me."

Sloane's lip curved up into a sly smile. "Good. I like surprising people."

• • •

Sloane headed to the front counter of The Craft Shed to pay for all the items needed to make the float design. She was doing her best not to let Ryan see how much he was affecting her, but something told Sloane her initial impression of him might have been inaccurate.

He was *not* a prude.

In fact, the heat that flared in his eyes when she'd thrown the little barb at him about her favorite sex toy had been near enough to melt the clothes right off her body. It had been a long while since a man had looked at her like that. Like maybe the kind of friendship she was looking for wasn't exactly the kind he was interested in dishing out.

She'd never met a guy who'd done such a sharp one-eighty like Ryan Bower.

Eye on the prize. You're supposed to be looking for a practice friend, not a boink buddy.

They headed outside with all their spoils, and Ryan helped her pack everything into the trunk of her car. "Thanks for your help," she said.

"My pleasure."

Ryan leaned against her car, looking devilishly handsome—no pun intended. He was dressed in faded jeans, tan lace-up boots, and a black hoodie that stretched across his broad chest and shoulders like a dream. His hair was wavy, and the wind ruffled it a little, carrying the scent of crisp air, crunchy leaves, and a hint of cologne right to her.

This is the part where you say, "Hey, want to grab a drink?" and see what he says.

But the words lodged in her throat. She'd tried this tactic before—finding someone she liked enough to ask to hang out. Something low-key like coffee or a drink at the local wine bar. Maybe even a few appetizers at the Italian restaurant, Mille Baci.

Every single time the response had started with "I wish I could but…insert excuse here"—picking up the kids, studying, family duties. Or they already had plans with their actual friends. Sloane never got the impression that people meant to hurt her feelings, but it did all the same. The rejections had piled up like a mound of rose thorns, until Sloane wasn't so sure she could put herself out there again.

But she had to try. Because what would her perfect dream home and dream town be if she didn't have friends? And making friends was a skill like anything else. All she needed was a little practice.

"We should drink," she blurted out. "Together."

Smooth. Like the back of a Stegosaurus.

Ryan quirked a brow. "I know you find my company questionable, but if you really need alcohol to put up with me…"

She knocked his arm, trying to cover her embarrassment with action. "I didn't mean it like that. I just meant, maybe if you didn't have plans, we could…"

God, why was her heart beating so fast? This shouldn't be *so* nerve-wracking.

"I heard the wine bar has free peanuts during happy hour." Nope, that wasn't much better. Gee, no wonder she struck out swinging so often.

"Sure," he said.

Sloane blinked. "Sorry?"

"I said sure." Ryan looked at her like she was being strange. "Let's grab a drink. In fact, we could always get something to-go then work on the float, if you want."

Happiness bubbled up in Sloane's chest, but she tried to act cool. "Great idea. That sounds…efficient."

"Yeah, efficient is what I was going for." Ryan snorted. "Come on, I'm sure we can do better than free peanuts."

CHAPTER SEVEN

Forty minutes later, Ryan and Sloane were sitting on a pair of stepladders in his dad's garage—which was more of a workspace than a place to park a car. He'd called home to ask if they could use it for float preparation and his dad had readily agreed. After all, the physio had ordered him to keep from doing any manual labor, so he didn't have use for it right now.

Ryan had suggested they get lobster rolls. Now, they were happily munching away while they tried to figure out how to tackle the float design. But he couldn't seem to keep his eyes off Sloane—or stop his imagination from running wild while he watched her tuck into the buttery, rich meal with gusto.

"This is *so* good." She made a moaning sound that sent a jolt of heat straight through Ryan's body. "I've been missing out."

"How come you never tried them before?"

"I don't know. Lobster seems like a rich person thing." She wrinkled her nose. "Now, if I knew it tasted this good, I might have tried it earlier."

"I thought you were supposed to be Little Miss Adventurous." He raised a brow. "Or does that only extend to your…fiction?"

She paused from eating and looked up at him,

mischief dancing in her eyes. Her glasses had slid down her nose a little, and the wind had whipped her ponytail around so that a few extra strands had fallen out and floated around her face.

It socked Ryan in the gut. God, she was beautiful.

Sure, he knew Sloane was attractive. He'd been able to tell that the day he walked into the library, but this was the first time he'd seen her relaxed and open. Without her guard up. People always said the way to a man's heart was through his stomach, but perhaps that was more universal than people gave it credit for.

"Why are you so curious about my reading habits?" She took another bite, a dot of the creamy sauce clinging to the edge of her lip. She swiped her tongue out and caught it, and Ryan found himself having a hard time swallowing. "I thought I was just a smut peddler to you."

"Maybe we got off on the wrong foot."

"Ya think?" She snorted. "How would you feel if I came into your workplace and started picking on the way you did your job?"

"Oh, you mean like every single sports reporter and person on the internet? Sorry if that statement doesn't resonate with me. I'm used to people picking apart my every move."

Lord knew the headlines after his injury had been like a billion grains of salt in a very open wound.

BOWER STARING AT THE END OF HIS CAREER? VETERAN PITCHER'S BODY CAN'T KEEP PACE.

PREDICTION: BOWER WILL MAKE IT BACK TO THE MOUND,
BUT HE WON'T BE THE SAME.

MLB'S YOUNGEST AND BRIGHTEST TO REPLACE BOWER.
HAVE FANS ALREADY FORGOTTEN WHO SET UP THEIR
PLAYOFF RUN?

"Is it really that bad?" she asked, cocking her head.

"Some days, yeah. I get it, people are trying to do their jobs and criticism always gets more clicks than praise." He shrugged like it didn't hurt, even though he'd almost sent himself into a deep, dark hole in the early days after his surgery. "But it can get into your head."

Sloane looked confused. "But you're at the pinnacle of your career."

"Yeah, and what's on the other side of a pinnacle?" A sheer drop to the bottom. "It's all downhill from here."

"Oof." Sloane put a hand to her chest. "That got me right in the feels."

"Not to use a well-worn cliché, but the higher you climb, the harder you fall, right?" He shrugged. "It's inevitable. Professional athletes have a shorter career span than most people."

"You talk like you're done."

"I'm *not* done." He shook his head emphatically. "But the media likes to spin it that way. Thirty-five and basically one foot in the grave. It's bullshit. I've got years ahead of me."

But even as he said the words, there was a

niggling little voice inside him that asked: *But do you?*

How did he know this ACL injury wouldn't be the end? How did he know he wouldn't be relegated to the bullpen, stuffed into a group trade like the forgotten footnote on the game's history? How did he know that he wouldn't be permanently replaced?

Fact was, he knew nothing.

"So, you'll be going back to Canada next season?" she asked.

"Sooner." He smoothed his palms down the front of his jeans. He hadn't expected to answer any questions about himself today—especially not those surrounding his career plans and his insecurities. Hell, that was one of the reasons he left Toronto.

"Can't hide out forever, huh?"

"I'm not hiding," he said coolly. "I'm taking the opportunity to visit my family while I'm off work."

"Hmm," she said with a nod, her expression indicating that she wasn't quite buying it.

He bristled. "There's nothing *hmm* about it."

"If you say so."

"I do say so."

Silence settled over them for a minute while Ryan held Sloane's inquisitive gaze, not giving her an inch. Something crackled in the air, like a current passing between them. To be honest, it was refreshing to have someone challenge him. In his younger days, he had enjoyed the attention he got as an elite sportsman, all too happy to bask in the adoration. But if he was being totally honest with himself, these days he found it...dull.

It felt like his life went from one extreme to another—online, everyone was a critic, and in person, everyone was a sycophant.

Sloane, however, was delightfully in-between.

"You know, all the articles I read painted you as this unflappable, laid-back kinda guy. You're way more argumentative in person."

"All the articles you read, huh?" He couldn't help the smug grin that spread across his lips at the moment Sloane's eyes widened, realizing she gave herself away. "What prompted the Googling?"

"I wanted to know who you are." She looked down at her food, pink tinting her cheeks. "It's not every day I get a six-foot-three slice of man wall walk in my library, claiming I'm corrupting the innocent people of my town."

A slice of man wall...was that a compliment?

"Six four," he corrected with a cocky grin.

"Fixated on inches, interesting."

Ryan stuffed the last bit of his lobster roll into his mouth and wadded up the paper wrappings in his fist. "Seems like you are, too, if your reading taste is anything to go by."

"You made it to chapter five already. I'm impressed." She laughed. "Now, either you're trying to rush through it as quickly as possible to prove a point, or..."

"Or..."

Her eyes sparkled, and she neatly folded the

butcher paper around the discarded end of her roll. "You're *really* enjoying it."

"Which of those two things do you think it is?"

"If I take you with a surface-level view, then I'd say you're rushing through to prove a point. But something tells me you're the kind of guy who's more than meets the eye." She studied him, her gaze roaming over him and leaving a soft, warm burn in its wake. It was like she was trying to figure him out, like he was a puzzle that needed solving. "I'm going to say you're enjoying it."

"Then you'd be wrong," he lied. He wasn't even sure *why* he felt the need to tell a little white one— which his mother always said were as bad as the real deal, unless you were telling Grandma that her pecan pie didn't have the texture of cement.

"I'm not wrong often," Sloane replied. "And I don't think I'm wrong now. It's okay, Ryan. I won't judge you for liking an erotic novel. Quite a few of our male book club members are really into it."

"Gee, I wonder why."

"Great character development, an interesting plot with twists and turns, atmospheric writing…" She ticked the items off the list.

"Nothing to do with the sex scenes?"

"If people only want that, they can watch porn. This story is about the *whole* experience."

Truthfully, he agreed. But he didn't like being proven wrong…and he still hadn't forgiven Sloane for being the reason he had to listen to his parents screwing like bunnies.

"Hey, who knows?" she said, lifting one shoulder in a shrug. "It might even provide some good life guidance."

"Yeah, the next time I happen to end up at a high-end sex club by accident, drinking cosmos with my BFF after getting snubbed at the Oscars, I'll know exactly what to do." He snorted.

"I was talking more in the bedroom," she replied sweetly.

"I don't need any help there."

"Well, I can't comment on that because I wouldn't know. I can only go by the information that's presented to me." She looked far too smug for her own good. Damn, this woman enjoyed baiting him.

"Which is?"

"That you might be a bit of a prude."

"Maybe I'm just a grumpy asshole."

She shook her head. "But you're not, are you? Everybody *loves* Ryan Bower, the town golden boy. I swear, I can't mention your name without someone pouring on the praise like maple syrup on pancakes."

"You're talking to people about me as well as Googling me? Awkward."

"You weren't supposed to notice that bit," she said, pursing her lips.

A cool breeze blew in from outside, sending a few crunchy brown leaves skittering along the garage's concrete floor. Sloane shivered and rubbed her palms vigorously up and down her arms. The action brought

Ryan's attention to her bust line, where her white T-shirt was pulled tight and showing further evidence she was chilly.

He could even see the subtle scalloped edge of her lace bra underneath the thin white cotton. He coughed, turning away and trying to get the image out of his head.

"Not dressed for the weather, huh?"

"The temperature is up and down like a yo-yo at the moment. It was hot this afternoon." She jumped up and down in place.

Ryan tugged at the hem of his hoodie and pulled it up over his head. "Here you go."

"Now you'll be cold."

"Nah. You'd be surprised to know I grew up playing as much hockey as I did baseball, so the cold is my friend." He thought about adding how it wasn't even really that cold, but he didn't want her to reject the offer of a warm sweater out of stubbornness. "We're used to it here. I'm guessing you lived somewhere warmer before coming here."

"A little town in South Carolina. They don't get winter like we do here." She accepted the hoodie from him and slipped it over her head. The hem fell all the way to mid-thigh, and she had to roll the sleeves back a few times, but she immediately stopped shivering.

"I don't get a Southern Belle vibe from you."

"Because I'm not a proper lady?" She did a mock curtsey and laughed. "No, I was born in California, actually. Sacramento. But we'd already moved from there by the time I was four. I spent my first year of school at an international school in Madrid. Then a year and a half in Luxembourg, another year back in Madrid, then off to Singapore, and a year in Vienna."

"Wow. You moved around a lot."

"There's moving around a lot, and then there's what we did." She smiled, but it didn't quite make the edges of her eyes crinkle the way they did when she teased him. "I swear, I thought my name was 'new kid' until I was about twelve."

Ryan found himself curious about the intricacies of her, but before he could ask any of the questions bumping around like balloons in his brain, Sloane clapped her hands together.

"Right," she said. "Now that we're refueled, we should probably start working on the float."

Sloane went to her purse and fished out a piece of paper. It was crinkled as though she'd folded and unfolded it many times, a coffee stain dribbling off one edge. Bright purple ink was scrawled across the page, a crude design bracketed by notes and question marks and squiggly arrows. Clearly, she'd given this a lot of thought.

"So, the theme is…" She held up her hands and paused for dramatic effect. "Dinosaur Olympics."

"I'm sorry, what?" Ryan blinked.

"Let me paint you a word picture." She grinned, and Ryan motioned for her to go on, laughing at the absurdity of it. "You know how you can get those inflatable T-Rex suits."

He wrinkled his nose trying to picture it. "Uhh…"

"Oh yeah, I forget you don't know how to have fun—"

"Hey!"

"There are these blow-up T-Rex suits and they're hilarious. They remind me of those sumo suits. I got to thinking, well, dinosaurs battled back in the day, right? Survival of the fittest…and then I thought, what if we took *fittest* literally?"

"Dinosaur athletes…dinosaur Olympics, got it." Ryan snorted. "That's pretty out there."

"You can come as a baseball-playing dinosaur."

"Hang on a minute," he said, holding up his hands in protect. "I agreed to step into Dad's place to help out with the committee, but I did *not* agree to dress up."

"How can you ride on the float if you're not dressed up?"

"I also did not agree to ride on the damn float."

Sloane frowned and folded her arms across her chest, which bunched up the fabric swimming around her small frame. "But why wouldn't you want to?"

"Parades aren't my thing." He shrugged. "I guess I'm more of a behind-the-scenes kinda guy."

She snorted. "Forgive me if I can only see that as a steaming pile of cow dung."

"Why?"

She waved her arms in his direction as if the answer was obvious.

"I'm hot, so I should automatically want to stand

up in front of a crowd?" he asked, feigning innocence because he knew it would get under her skin.

"Your ego knows no bounds, huh?" She rolled her eyes. "I meant given your very public career choice, you spend all your time in the spotlight."

"Exactly. So why would I want to do that in my spare time?"

"Don't act like you don't love it," she said, throwing him a disbelieving look. "I've seen you in interviews. You lap up the attention."

"Interviews, plural?" He sucked on the inside of his cheek to try and stop from laughing, but he couldn't quite help himself. "How many did you watch?"

Sloane tipped her nose up at him, clearly trying to cover the fact that she'd been sprung. Again. "Enough to know you would have no problem riding on a float."

"Fell into an internet rabbit hole, did you?" He swaggered toward her, noting the way her eyes grew even bigger behind the lenses of her glasses and the way her tongue darted out to moisten her lips. "Lay in bed with your laptop, falling asleep to the sound of my voice."

"I didn't have much choice. Your voice has a very sedative effect." She smiled sarcastically at him.

"Nice try, Sloane. But you wouldn't have cheeks the color of cotton candy right now if you'd been bored."

"This hoodie is too warm."

He raised an eyebrow as a chilly breeze whipped

into the open garage. Outside, dark clouds were starting to gather in the sky. October was always unpredictable like that—hot one minute, stormy the next.

"Take it off, then. If you're so overheated."

Sloane glanced outside and practically shivered at the turn of the weather. Seemed they were getting into a habit of calling each other's bluff.

"Nah. I'm good."

"Smart. It's always better to admit you're lying than to go cold." He chuckled, and she shot him a sharp look. "So, let me reiterate," he said. "I'll help you build this thing, but I am *not* wearing a dinosaur costume, and I'm not riding on a float."

"We'll see," she said airily. "I can be persuasive when I want to be."

Something told him that Sloane being persuasive was *not* a bluff. In fact, he was quite sure it was a warning. She was the kind of woman who went after the things she wanted with the ferocity of the very pre-historic creatures she loved so much.

"I'll bet you can," he replied. "Now let's, as my dad would say, quit jibber-jabbing."

"Jibber-jabbing?" Sloane's face crinkled up in laughter.

"Yeah, like flapping your gums…I think. It's British. Dad likes to watch TV shows from all around the world and incorporate the phrases he learns."

"That's cute."

Ryan shrugged. Truth be told, he never really understood what the word "cute" meant because women seemed to apply it to everything. Fancy latte art? Cute. A new pair of shoes? Cute. Babies? Cute. His father adopting idioms from other countries? Also supposedly cute.

"I had an idea for the float setup," Sloane said. "I was thinking a sign at the back with the Olympic rings on a green background. We can use the chicken wire attached to some wooden posts and do that thing where you stuff the holes with tissue paper and glue so it creates a textured appearance."

Ryan nodded as if he had any freaking clue what she was talking about. He might be a small-town guy, but his childhood had been filled with early starts and driving to tournaments and having to skip events like parades in order to play ball.

Truthfully, he wasn't sure he'd ever been to a parade...unless he'd been too young to remember it.

"Then on the back, we've got a few sporting-related businesses to advertise, so they can have their own signs hanging there. Oh! And we need a dinosaur head at the front, preferably with a mouth that opens and closes."

Ryan rubbed a hand over his face. He was going to need reinforcements. One, he wasn't supposed to lift anything heavy so he wouldn't put unnecessary pressure on his knee. Secondly...he could handle basic handyman things, but his skill didn't extend to making a dinosaur head whose mouth opened and closed.

"You know how to do any of this?" he asked, already knowing what her answer would be.

"That's why you're here," she said sweetly. "You're going to help me figure it out…unless you're not too good with your hands."

She was taunting him again, the sassy little minx.

"You know this is not a two-person job, right? Especially not with me needing to protect my knee."

She sucked on the inside of her cheek. "Uh, well, all the other volunteers have been assigned."

"It's a good thing I know a few handy folks around here," he said. "We're going to need all hands on deck."

"Great. You can make the calls." She grinned. "Do you mind if we leave the stuff here? I don't have any workspace in my garage."

Ryan laughed and shook his head. "Do you always get your way?"

"Like I said before, I'm persuasive."

It would be easy to look at Sloane and write her off as some colorful sprite of a woman, to label her as being more style than substance. But that would be a mistake.

She was a force. A tiny rainbow hurricane who'd mow down everything in her path if that's what it took to achieve her goals.

And he respected that.

But there was no way he was wearing a blow-up dinosaur suit and riding on some float. End of story. Because as persuasive as she might be, Ryan was equally stubborn. And he certainly wasn't about to get blown over by Hurricane Sloane.

CHAPTER EIGHT

RYAN: *Chapter nine is done! Barely breaking a sweat.*

SLOANE: *You're only supposed to sweat if you're re-enacting the book, not reading it. Unless your brain is working overtime reading something other than scatter reports?*

RYAN: *Harsh.*

SLOANE: *I kid, I kid.*

RYAN: *You know, I think chapter eight might be my favorite so far.*

SLOANE: *The scene where he takes her to dinner? Why?*

RYAN: *The buildup. Tension, ya know. It made me keep reading.*

SLOANE: *The anticipation of what's about to come next.*

RYAN: *Exactly.*

SLOANE: *I like that bit, too.*

RYAN: *Sleep tight, Sloane. If you want to fall asleep to the sound of my voice, then check out this interview.*

Sloane would rather poke her eyes out with blunt pencils than admit that she *had* clicked on the link Ryan had texted her and watched the whole interview all the way through. Twice.

It'd been filmed well over a decade ago, when Ryan had been called up to the majors. He was fresh-faced, wide-eyed, and someone her former teenage self would absolutely have swooned over. Sharp jaw, intense blue eyes, and a mop of dark hair. But if she was being honest with herself, it was nothing compared to the man Ryan was now.

He was older, broader. Hotter. He'd lost that smooth, early-twenties, baby-faced appearance and now had a delightful crinkle at the edge of his eyes and the hard stare of someone who'd figured life out a bit more. And *damn* if she didn't find that appealing.

The ironic thing was, he made her feel like a giddy teenager—lying in bed, texting back and forth in the darkness, a giggle bubbling up in the back of her throat. They'd done the same thing for the last three nights. And every one of those nights she'd fallen asleep with visions of him dancing in her head—of the way he'd looked at her while daring her to remove the hoodie she'd borrowed from him.

And then she'd dreamed of him removing it... and more.

Sloane rubbed her fists into her eyes as she walked from the kitchen into her living room, waiting for the coffee machine to do its thing. The house was so quiet she could hear the slight suction noise her bare feet made on the titles as she shifted impatiently from foot to foot. Quiet, she had discovered, was *not* a good thing when she had a man on her mind.

The quiet made room for thinking. For imagining.

Before she'd had too much of an opportunity to let her mind wander to things that bothered her, a melodic chime rang through her house. The sound was coming from her laptop. Sloane grabbed her cup of coffee and headed into the living room, to where her laptop was perched on the coffee table, and clicked on the button to answer the Skype call.

"Slo!" Her five-year-old half-sister, Molly, clapped her hands together. Slo was Sloane's nickname, because Molly had never quite been able to remember the "n" sound at the end. "You're here."

"I'm here, Molly-Dolly." She grinned. "Did you steal Daddy's laptop again?"

"Nuh-uh, he *gave* it to me."

Sloane raised an amused eyebrow. There was about a two percent chance that was true, since Molly was jokingly called "Little Miss Hulk" for her strength and habit of breaking things. But Sloane wasn't about to give her dad any sympathy. If he didn't listen to her advice about password protecting his laptop, then that was his problem.

She knew why he didn't, of course. He'd lived

in a relationship with secrets before, and he did everything in his power to avoid them now. His new wife was as open and honest as they came, and Sloane was certain that was a huge part of the reason he'd married her.

"I'm very happy you called," Sloane replied. "Do you have some good news to tell me?"

"I've been at school more than four weeks." Molly extended her hand toward the computer screen, her chubby little fingers splayed out into a five. Sloane laughed and didn't bother to correct her. "I'm going to be an adult soon."

The little girl nattered happily for the next few minutes, and Sloane settled back against the couch, balancing her laptop on her knees while she sipped her coffee. She supposed that some people might resent the "new family" of a parent who'd basically decided to start their life over sans kid number one, but Sloane had adored Molly from the second she was born. She even liked her father's second wife, Amy, and could understand why he wanted to be with someone who was the antithesis of Sloane's mother.

Sometimes she wondered what her life might have been like if Amy had been *her* mother instead. If she'd grown up in a normal house, hadn't moved every six to twelve months, and had parents who loved each other and told each other the truth about things. If she hadn't grown up playing second fiddle to her mother's taxing, secretive, and ever-moving career.

"I made a new friend. Well, five new friends,

but one of them is extra special." Molly practically glowed. The little girl had strawberry-blond hair, like her mother, and the big gray-blue eyes of her father. They were the same as Sloane's, right down to the almost imperceptible crescent-shaped line of silver running through them.

"Tell me everything."

"Her name is Melody, which is kind of like my name because we both have *M*s. We both like *My Little Pony: Friendship Is Magic*, and our favorite color is green." Molly shook her head as if to say, *We're basically the same person*.

"And you have the same favorite color? Huh."

"I know." Molly nodded. "Now we're best friends."

Was that all it took when you were a kid? A TV show in common and liking the same color? If only it was that easy now. These days, it felt like unless you'd known someone most of your life, then you would always be on the outside.

You didn't feel on the outside with Ryan.

That was true. They'd laughed and joked, teasing each other as they worked. Despite their rocky beginning, she felt like she could be herself around Ryan. Maybe it came from the fact that during their first encounter, she hadn't tried to impress him the way she did with most people. Sloane was always trying to put on a good face, to be funny and likeable and perky and…everything.

She hadn't done that with him. She'd just been herself and not cared what he thought of her.

"Is that...Molly!" A deep, fatherly voice boomed out of the laptop's speakers, and Sloane couldn't help but laugh at Molly's deer-in-headlights expression. "What have I told you about taking my laptop?"

"I was calling Slo." She turned around, almost dropping the laptop, and the view tilted sharply skyward. Sloane caught a glimpse of her father's stern but amused expression.

"You can't be calling Sloane whenever you feel like it, Mol. She's busy."

If only. Truth be told, if it wasn't for work and her putting her hand up for every volunteer gig around town, then she wouldn't have anything to do at all on her days off.

Her father righted the laptop and patted his daughter's head lovingly. "Why don't you check on your brother and sister? I need to talk to Sloane, anyway."

"Okay. Bye, Slo!"

Molly was off in a flash, and the view lifted, revealing the large bookcases of her father's office as the laptop was settled back into its rightful place. A second later, his face filled the screen. He looked a little bedraggled, whiskers coating his jaw and his dark hair sticking out in all directions.

"Rough night?" she asked, sipping her coffee.

"Beyond rough." He reached behind the screen and pulled out a mug, wrapping both hands around the exact way Sloane was holding hers. The similarity made her smile. "Beau was up half the night, screeching like a banshee."

"Is he okay?"

"Yeah, he's going through a phase." He raked a hand through his hair. "I can't believe I was convinced to do this a third time."

The number stuck in the back of Sloane's throat. "Well, fourth…technically."

"Shit, Sloane, you know what I mean. And besides, you were an angel child. Slept through the night almost the second you came out of the womb. In fact, you slept so well, I constantly had to come in and check you were still alive."

She looked down into her cup. The glossy dark brown liquid reflected her eyes, making them look almost cartoonish behind her glasses. Sometimes she got the impression her dad said things like that more out of how he'd *wanted* things to be rather than how they actually were. He tried to be a good father to her. But she saw the difference in him with Molly and the two younger ones. That warmth and confidence and indulgent happiness he had with them…she couldn't conjure that from a single memory of her own.

"What did you want to talk to me about?" she asked.

"Thanksgiving." He placed his mug down with a soft *thunk*. "It turns out Amy's sister has finally finished renovating her house in Cape Elizabeth. She's invited us all up for the weekend."

"Oh nice, Cape Elizabeth is lovely. *And* that's going to cut my drive down by half." She grinned, but her father's faltering expression made the little bubble of happiness burst like it had been stuck with a cactus prickle. "Oh…I'm not invited."

Clearly "us" didn't include her.

"It's not that you're not invited, sweetheart." Her father cringed. "But the house isn't as big as the place we normally go."

"Right, you don't have room for me. Much better." She couldn't keep the bitterness out of her voice. No matter how much of an effort she made with Amy and her family, she'd never be considered part of the "real" family.

"Don't be like that." To his credit, he did look genuinely sorry about it. "With Beau now and Vic's twins, the extra rooms are all taken up with baby stuff. I can't imagine why you'd want to come anyway. Three kids under a year, another four in single digits—it's going to be chaos."

"Sounds horrible," she lied, her voice barely strong enough for her father to properly hear it through the computer speakers.

Truth was, Thanksgiving was the excuse she'd leaned on to visit her family. Her father had always said she was welcome, but that never seemed to translate into an actual invite. There was always something going on—vacations of their own, busy times with her father's work, Amy's parents coming to stay. Sloane herself never seemed to rank on the list.

"Are you upset?" he asked.

Part of her wanted to tell her father the truth—

that it hurt to be excluded. That it made her feel like shit when he chose his new family over her. That she wanted to come with them and be welcome.

But why bother? There was no point trying to guilt an invite out of him, because that wasn't a proper invite at all.

"No, I'm not," she said, crossing her fingers below the view of her laptop screen. "I understand."

"You should do one of those…what are they called?" Her father snapped his fingers a few times in quick succession. "Friendsgiving things? Yeah, that's it. People have all their friends over and do a whole turkey and all the sides. I'll get Amy to email you that yam recipe you really like."

Sloane hated yams.

"I have to get going. I've got a busy day planned." She tried to hide how much he'd hurt her feelings by pasting on a smile, figuring that one little fib to save some awkwardness wasn't the worst thing in the world.

"Sure, of course. Sorry about Thanksgiving, I know you love coming up to see the kids."

"And you," she said, feeling a sudden rush of prickling at the back of her eyes. She blinked. No way in hell was she going to cry over this like some sad little girl!

"We'll do a family catch up another time, okay? You can come up, and I'll put the girls together so you can sleep in Molly's room." He smiled, and there was a hint of relief in it.

"Another time." She nodded.

"Maybe after the holidays. It's going to be crazy here for a while."

Of course it was. "Sure thing, Dad."

She bid her father goodbye and ended the call, slumping back against the couch, her heart aching. Sloane sipped her coffee. It was tepid. Part of her had really believed moving to Kissing Creek and finding her own place would make everything feel…well, not perfect. But close to it. She was sure that if she found the right place to call home, then everything would magically fall into place.

She was trying, that was for damn sure.

But three years in and she still stood at the fringes, peering in, hoping someone would make space for her. Hoping she would find her people. Hoping she'd be able to make up for all that lost time where friendships moved through the revolving door of time quicker than she wanted. And the older she got, the more her father grew his new family and the less time and energy he had for her.

"You are *not* going to wallow over this," she said to herself, gulping down the remainder of her lukewarm coffee and plunking the mug on the coffee table. "Wallowing doesn't achieve anything."

Snapping her laptop closed, she picked up her mug and wandered into the kitchen. A whole day off—no responsibilities, no volunteer meetings, nothing to keep her occupied. It *should* be a dream. A glorious, relaxing dream. But Sloane felt tighter than a screw that had been cranked a few too many times, and restlessness rippled through her veins. The call with her father…ugh.

There was no point being angry at him; the guy was just living his life. Three young kids, a doting wife, thriving social life, the job he'd always wanted—she got it. She also wanted a life filled with those things.

Maybe it was time to do a little more practice friendship-making.

She reached for her phone and swiped her thumb across the screen. Ryan's texts came up because that's what she'd been looking at last. Was it too early to ask to hang out again? Did that make her look desperate?

1. Start small with people you know and ask someone to hang out.

She'd done that once with him, and it had worked out well, so maybe trying again might give her a boost of confidence. What did she have to lose? If he said no, then she would be no worse off than she was now. Without giving herself a chance to think about it too much, she quickly typed her message and hit send.

SLOANE: *Hey, what are you up to this morning? I was wondering if we might be able to work on the float?*

It was silly, but Sloane's heart hammered in her chest as the three little dots blinked in response.

RYAN: *Sorry, duty calls. I'm taking my dad to a physio appointment this morning…you know, to work out the kinks from his sex injury.*

Sloane snorted. He was never going to let her live this one down.

SLOANE: *You should be grateful. An active sex life increases life expectancy.*

RYAN: *Unless they die in a freak chandelier accident first...or tie themselves up so well that one of them ends up in the emergency room.*

SLOANE: *You're at chapter thirteen already? I'm impressed.*

RYAN: *I aim to please. Then I'm heading to the college baseball team's practice this afternoon to give them a pep talk.*

SLOANE: *That sounds fun.*

RYAN: *Yeah, so they can all ask how my team is doing without me. Super fun.*

Sloane's heart panged for a moment. On the surface it might look like a case of FOMO, but in some ways, Ryan watching his team play on without him was kind of like Sloane watching her dad move on with his life and all the little ways it was obvious she didn't fit there anymore. Or maybe that was her trying to connect...but she understood how he felt, anyway.

SLOANE: *Sounds like you're going to need some cheering up.*

RYAN: *Got any suggestions?*

SLOANE: *Movie night at home. That always works for me.*

Should she suggest that she come over and keep him company? Number five on the friendship-making list: *Be there for them when they need you.* That was skipping ahead a few steps, though.

Before Sloane had the opportunity to mentally chew over her options, Ryan replied.

RYAN: *What time are you coming over?*

Sloane sucked in a breath, happiness filtering through her system and smoothing over the dents and bruises on her heart. It would've been easy for him to brush her off if he didn't want to see her, but that was twice now he'd agreed. She felt as giddy as Molly had when describing her new best friend, and while Sloane wasn't under any illusions that she and Ryan would be *real* friends, this was certainly the confidence boost she needed.

SLOANE: *8pm? I'll bring snacks.*

RYAN: *See you then.*

• • •

Ryan was pretty sure this was the *only* time in his life

that heading toward a baseball diamond filled him with dread. He knew some guys struggled with the pressure of the game, getting rattled if they loaded the bases or if they got pulled out of a game earlier than planned. It was a slippery slope. Baseball was a mental game, and if you didn't walk up to the mound believing you were going to win, then you could easily get swallowed whole.

Ryan wasn't the kind of person who doubted himself.

Self-belief was something his parents had fostered in him since he was a kid. The words "you can do it" were spoken often, always with a gentle shove in the right direction. Getting drafted in the first round with a signing bonus big enough to make most people's eyes bug out of their heads had certainly helped. Not to mention finding his place as one of the youngest starters in the game. He'd been a hot ticket since day one, confidence fueled with the evidence of his talent to back it up.

Unfortunately, that hadn't prepared him for the realities of the job—namely, that one day it would come to an end and that he would never be ready, no matter how clearly he saw it coming.

"Ryan Bower, what a pleasure! Janice Walker." The marketing associate for Harrison Beech College rushed forward, her brown heeled boots crunching over some fallen leaves, and she walked toward him, hand extended. "Now, I can't say I'm happy about the outcome of the Jays and Red Sox game the other night, but I guess I can't blame you for that."

She smiled, and Ryan could tell the comment was meant to be lighthearted, a joke, but it stuck in his chest. Rather than taking his own crap out on some poor woman doing her job, he covered the feeling with a practiced, media-ready smile.

"I'll pass it on to the team," he said breezily, clasping her hand. "I'm sure they'll be happy to hear it."

They'd won 3-2. The starter would have pitched a complete game, if not for the Sox hitting a two-run homer in the bottom of the ninth that sent them into extra innings. Not that he'd been watching, of course, because the whole point of hiding out in his hometown was to avoid the damn thing...but he'd seen it on Instagram. That's what he got for scrolling on social media. Maybe he should have stuck to *Stormy Pleasures*. At least then the most confronting thing would have been a new sex position.

"The team are excited to have you here," Janice said. "I don't know how much you've kept up to date with the Flames, but we've got a young star-in-the-making named Pace Arterton. He's..."

Ryan tried to focus while Janice prattled on about the young pitcher who was supposedly the "next" Ryan Bower. God, he hated that sentiment. He *was* Ryan Bower, and there didn't need to be a new version. It was like they were trying to replace him before he'd hung up his glove.

Irritation prickled across his skin, but he tried to shake it off. These were his issues to deal with. The last thing he wanted was to come across like some jaded asshole in front of a bunch of people passionate about his favorite sport.

Why did I agree to do this?

A deeply ingrained sense of responsibility, perhaps. The "you have to set an example" attitude that his mother had drummed into him from the second his middle brother had been born. A message only fortified when Bower baby number three had come along.

"In fact," Janice continued, "he's got a unique windup that really does remind us of you. The coach has high hopes for the season."

"It takes more than a windup to make it to the majors," Ryan said, the words spilling out before he could think to stop them.

Janice blinked. "Oh, of course."

"I mean…" Ryan shook his head. "I work a lot with the young kids about the importance of staying strong mentally. That fortitude is a critical element of playing in the big leagues that often gets overlooked when everyone is focused on physical performance."

Jeez. *That* made him sound approximately a hundred years old.

"It's important that they have mentors," Janice said. "I think they all come to this with stars in their eyes, but I can imagine the reality is grittier."

Ryan bobbed his head. "Yeah, it is."

They came to the edge of the diamond, where a practice match was in progress. Ryan leaned against the railing, aware of the shift in energy once the players noticed him. Awareness rippled through the air, spreading from player to player. They stood taller, chests puffed out like they wanted to impress. The pitcher Janice had told him about was on the mound. He was a reed of a kid—already towering at over six feet, with long, skinny limbs and a laser-like focus.

The batter shifted at home plate, swinging his bat around in preparation and then bringing it back over his shoulder. Pace lifted his hands over his head to begin his set at the mound, his knee came up high, and then he slowly released out of the position, but right before his foot touched the mound, he paused. The batter twitched, his focus momentarily broken by the change of momentum, and when Pace released the ball, it sailed right past the batter, who swung at the air.

Ryan bobbed his head. "Impressive."

"Right?" Janice smiled and clapped her hands together. "The Flames have had a few rough seasons, but with Pace on the team, we've got high hopes."

It would be a matter of time to see whether those hopes propelled or crushed the young pitcher. The windup was good, Ryan could admit that, and his control also seemed good—two important things. But all the talent in the world didn't matter if you choked in the big moments.

The batter knocked the end of his bat against the ground, kicking up some dirt. He reset at the plate, but he was no match for Pace. Two more pitches and the batter went down swinging. Pace jogged off the mound for the sides to switch, graceful despite his gangly appearance.

The rest of the practice game played out quickly. Turns out not only did Pace have an impressive fastball, but he was also working on refining a changeup that had a *lot* of potential. Everyone loved to focus on the speed of a fastball—always seeking out that mph milestone—but having consistent and strong command over an off-speed pitch was important. Nobody wanted to be a one-trick pony. Because once a good batter clocked your style, if you had nothing else to offer, then you'd be done.

As the players milled about on the field, chatting and swapping notes, the coach came over and stuck out a big, meaty bear paw of a hand.

"So good to meet you, Bower. Name's Casey Gluck." He pumped Ryan's hand and smiled openly. He had that friendly Midwestern thing going on, but Ryan would bet that easy-going, laidback charm would disappear in a flash during a tense game. "We're sure glad to have you here."

"Of course." Ryan nodded. "Looks like you've got a great team."

Casey made a clicking sound with his tongue. "They're gettin' there. Pace is obviously our superstar, but we've got a catcher that throws a ball like it's a bullet. And our first baseman is a slugger if I've ever seen one. There's real potential here."

The unsaid truth hung in the air—*but not everyone will make it.*

Most wouldn't, in fact. Ryan knew that firsthand. He had friends from college who'd gotten stuck in triple-A, never developing to the point required to get the call up. A couple *had* gotten the call, only to be sent back down when they couldn't perform under the pressure. He'd seen some with promising careers halted by persistent injuries. Others who ended up playing in the overseas leagues like Japan, Korea, or Italy in order to keep the dream alive.

Playing was always better than not playing.

But the big shiny goal of walking into Fenway Park and facing down the Green Monster…that was only for a select few. And even if you made it, there was always a chance it would be taken away. It took big shoulders to carry that kind of weight, and Ryan had been building his strengths for years. Staying in the majors was as hard as making it there in the first place.

Don't be pouring all your personal crap onto these kids.

Ryan put on a big smile as he felt himself slip into "public" mode. He couldn't let anybody see the fear he had about his career, because being vulnerable would *not* give you an edge in sports. It would make him seem weak, reinforce the rumors about him being on the way out. And Ryan would only leave baseball when someone dragged him out.

"Why don't you introduce me around?" he said smoothly, tucking every worry and doubt into the deepest, darkest corner of his mind.

Right where they belonged.

CHAPTER NINE

Sloane walked up the driveway of the Bower house, her arms clutching a box of movie-night essentials, including her popcorn maker, in case the Bowers didn't have one of their own. In her mind, the fresh stuff—drizzled with her secret honey chili sauce—was *far* superior to anything you might find in a bag at the supermarket.

She'd also packed some corn chips and salsa and made a batch of her bake-sale staples—salty bacon and chocolate-chip cookies. For a moment, she wondered if she'd put forth too much effort. Was there such a thing as trying too hard?

Too late now. She didn't even get a chance to ring the doorbell, because Ryan happened to walk through the front of the house and spotted her through the window. A second later, the door opened up.

Sloane's breath caught in the back of her throat. Ryan's hair was a little damp, as if he'd just showered and dried it off with a towel. It was longish around his ears, and stubble coated his jaw. All that dark hair made his eyes look even more intensely blue. Otherworldly blue. A white T-shirt stretched across his broad chest, tight around his pecs and biceps, making the most of his athletic physique. On the

bottom he wore a pair of light gray sweats that well…
they hid nothing.

Sloane snatched her eyes back up to Ryan's face
in time to catch the tail end of a fleeting and very
amused smirk.

"You judging my outfit?" he asked, holding the
door for her. "I didn't think I needed to dress up for
movie night."

"It's fine," she squeaked, and then she cleared
her throat. *Get a frigging grip, girl.* "I didn't dress up,
either."

It wasn't a lie, exactly. She was wearing a pair of
purple Converse sneakers and her favorite galaxy
printed leggings in shades of bright pink, purple,
black, and blue. On top was an oversize T-shirt that
had the word *unstoppable* above a picture of a T-Rex
holding a grabber claw in each hand. Casual, right?
But the skin-tight leggings made the most of her legs
and butt, and the T-shirt had a habit of slipping off
one shoulder.

Had she purposefully chosen this outfit to look
cute? Yes. Was she judging herself for it? A little. At
least five times she'd already reminded herself that
this was a friendship experiment, not a date. But it
was like her brain hadn't quite gotten the memo yet.

"I like your space tights," Ryan commented as she
entered his house. To her surprise, it was totally quiet.

"Thanks." She tipped the box toward him. "I
brought snacks."

"I can see that," he said, peering inside. "Enough

to feed an army."

"What's the point of movie night without stuffing your face, right?" She grinned. "Besides, I didn't know if your parents might want to join us, and then I had to make sure I had enough."

"They won't be joining us. They've gone out."

"Oh?" Sloane would be lying if she said that little fact didn't make it feel like there was a fairy in her chest sprinkling happy, glittery dust everywhere. Sloane toed off her sneakers and left them by the front door. "Where have they gone?"

"Friends of theirs got a new grill. Mom said Dad could go if he didn't mix beer with his pain meds and if he promised to take his back-support cushion." Ryan snorted. "She has him on a tight leash."

"Most people would be lucky to have someone care about them the way your mom cares about your dad." The words slipped out of Sloane's mouth before she could think about how telling they were, but Ryan didn't seem to notice the slipup. He simply nodded in agreement. "I've gotten to know them quite well through some of my volunteer work and through the library."

"I know. Mom can't say enough good things about you." He shook his head.

"At least someone in your family doesn't think I'm a bad influence on this sweet little town." She winked and nudged him with her elbow.

Ryan rolled his eyes and headed toward the family room. "How long did *that* last, huh? You've been here for three-point-two seconds and already you're taking jabs."

"Oh, come on, you can take a little jab here and there." She followed him, taking a moment to observe the home.

It was a nice, cozy place, but it wasn't exactly what she'd expect for the parents of a baseball player who was worth millions. Not to say it was shabby, but it felt so…normal. Well, expect for the giant TV in the family room. She would bet that was a present from Ryan.

But it had lots of other normal things—like a comfy, lived-in couch, some outdated artwork on the walls, and tons of family photos. Sloane paused to look at a picture that appeared to have been taken at one of those cheesy mall photography stores. A smile lit up her face, and Ryan caught her looking.

"Okay, I need to know the story behind this photo," she said. "Where was it taken? How old were you? Is this an annual thing, and can I see the rest of the photos? You were so lanky!"

"That was my awkward phase." Ryan scrubbed a hand over his face. "I was thirteen. I grew three inches that summer."

She gawked. These kinds of family photos fascinated her. Truthfully, she'd always wanted one of her own. But her mother had a thing about having her photo taken—apparently it wasn't good for her work—and it seemed weird to go with her dad by themselves.

"You and your brothers look so alike," Sloane

replied, studying the photo. They were like the dictionary definition of a family—parents who loved one another, siblings who shared facial features and personal passions, a vibe of wholesome goodness around them. "Especially the middle one."

"That's Mark, and the youngest is Ace."

"He's adorable."

"He's the favorite," he joked, leaning against the wall. "Even Mom says so."

"She does not."

"But she *thinks* it."

"Don't tell me you're jealous. Aren't you basically living every teenage boy's fantasy life right now—a pro athlete, travelling all the time, having any woman you want?"

"Who says I can have any woman I want?" Ryan came closer. His arms were crossed over his chest, enhancing his biceps in a way that looked primally good. He was strong. Confident. And, despite his question, totally aware of his appeal.

Sloane made a scoffing sound. "Please. You're trying to tell me that skirts don't lift whenever you walk past?"

"Yours doesn't."

She gulped. "I'm not wearing a skirt."

"Lucky. That would be quite embarrassing if it suddenly flew up of its own accord." His lip quirked.

"I'm not talking about me, specifically. I mean… women in general. Doesn't baseball have groupies like other sports? I bet you don't get turned down that often." Crap. She was really digging a hole for herself with this conversation. "Or maybe you don't even have to ask."

"Yeah, I head to the mound and women start throwing their panties onto the field," he said sarcastically. "Believe it or not, that is not my life."

There was a serious intensity to Ryan that Sloane had noticed the first day she'd met him. Sure, he could joke around and have a laugh, but underneath it all was a sense of…burning sincerity, which sounded like an oxymoron, but it wasn't. Everything about Ryan Bower was an arrow pointing toward the future. Pointing toward his goals. She sensed that maybe he was a bit insulted that she thought his interest lay in using his career fame to score off the field.

"Maybe that's a bad stereotype," she admitted.

He shrugged. "It's stereotype for a reason. I know plenty of guys who enjoy that part of the lifestyle as much as they like playing ball. But I also know a bunch of guys who are settled down with a wife and kids, and a couple who want nothing but to improve their game."

"Let me guess which category you fall into," she teased softly.

"What's the point in working hard for something your whole life and not taking every opportunity to be the best you can be?" He hesitated, as if unsure whether he should continue. Sloane held her breath, not wanting to do anything that might spook him into clamming up. "Sorry. I guess when you have one too many interviewers grilling you on the perks of the lifestyle, it can make you sensitive about it. I've made a lot of sacrifices for my career."

"Like leaving your family?"

"Yeah." He motioned for her to follow him into the kitchen.

"Do they find it hard with you living away?" she probed, her curiosity growing as they walked.

"Of course. I'm not home as much as they would like, and I miss birthdays and special events."

They entered the kitchen and she set down the box of snacks on the countertop, while Ryan fetched some drinking glasses.

"I know your mom is so proud of you and your brother for chasing your dreams. She talks about you both all the time."

He laughed, but it felt a little forced. "Mom and Dad *are* proud. But they also want to see me settle down and have kids. Honestly, it's hard for the families of professional athletes. Sure, the money is great, but…"

"They're the second priority."

"In a lot of cases, yeah." He nodded as he reached into the fridge and pulled out two soda cans. "One guy on my team got divorced recently because his wife couldn't take the constant moving. He was traded to three teams in less than two years, and it was affecting her career."

Sloane's heart went out to the woman. "That sucks."

"The first game he pitched after that was a disaster. If he doesn't find a way to perform now, he might be out of the majors for good. It's a lot of pressure, and frankly, I don't need extra distractions."

Sloane nodded. "That totally makes sense."

It was like Ryan had voiced every issue with her parents' marriage.

"I bet that was a bit more truth than you bargained for, huh?" He smiled, and it was the most delightful, crooked, self-conscious smile that she'd ever seen. It crinkled the edges of his eyes in the sexiest way, and he swept back a lock of dark hair with one strong hand. Holy moly. Attraction bolted through her body like a squirrel scampering up a tree.

But the vulnerable look was gone in a flash. Unfortunately. She felt like she'd glimpsed the Ryan behind his public persona, the softness behind the intensity. The goodness behind the grump. And beyond every sensible thought in her head, she wanted more.

"I appreciate the candid response," she replied, and Ryan looked a little relieved.

"So, I saw a popcorn machine in your bag of tricks," he said as he poured the sodas.

Sloane wasn't sure whether she wanted to steer the conversation back or not, because Ryan was a puzzle she wanted to solve. He seemed to have everything he could want, and yet there was this restlessness to him. This dissatisfaction because he knew he could have more.

Sloane wasn't like that. She had her list of

goals—her sketch of her perfect life—and once she got all the bricks in place, then she wouldn't want for anything else. She could just be satisfied and happy and…still.

"I like to make it fresh. I even have my own special sauce to drizzle on top." She pulled the popcorn maker out and handed it to Ryan. Then she fished out the bag of kernels and the little tub of sauce she'd already mixed up.

"You've thought of everything," he said with a hint of genuine surprise. "It's been so long since I had a movie night."

"I figured maybe you'd want something fun and mindless after today."

His eyes flicked over her. "Why do you say that?"

Oops. Had she put her foot in her mouth? "I, uh…well, you're missing out on the biggest part of the season. Then you have to inspire a bunch of kids who look up to you, all while worrying about your injury and your career."

"How'd you get into my head?"

She lifted one shoulder into a shrug and set the ingredients down on the countertop and then leaned against it, watching as Ryan set up the popcorn maker. "Doesn't take a rocket scientist to figure that out, just empathy."

"You'd be surprised how lacking that is in most people." There was a soft line between his brows, as though he was trying to figure something out.

This seemed like the perfect opportunity to try

another step in the friendship-making playbook.

2. Get to know the other person by asking questions.

Ryan seemed open, so why not?

"So, uh…why did you start playing baseball, anyway?"

A happy expression drifted over his face, like he was remembering something nice, and it totally transformed him. He lost the hard intensity in his eyes for a moment, lost the tightness in his jaw, and even his stance softened, so that he leaned against the counter in a way that was sexy and relaxed and so damn touchable that Sloane had to will herself to keep her hands on the countertop and not on him.

"Dad always loved the sport, and I guess he saw some natural talent, because he put me into little league before I'd even started school."

"Wow, he saw something in you that early?"

"Is that a chicken and egg thing, though? He believed in me from the beginning, so I had the confidence to pursue what I wanted, and then my skills developed."

"Yeah, but you wouldn't be making the majors without a huge amount of natural talent."

"Talent doesn't mean anything without the right mindset and support and hard work to back it up. I think people have the idea of 'natural talent' on a pedestal, but I've seen plenty of talented players piss their chances up a wall by not having their head in the game."

"I bet it's intense in your head," she teased.

"You're so…serious."

"Is that a bad thing?"

"No." She shook her head. "I think a lot of people who excel in their career are serious."

"But you still think I should loosen up?" He raised an eyebrow.

"Maybe a little."

"And how would you recommend I do that exactly?" There was a liquid heat to his voice. A sensual, silky smoothness that coated his words in invitation.

This is a friendship experiment, not a date.

How many times was she going to have to repeat that to herself? Ryan Bower was the epitome of *wrong* for her.

The day she went to college to start her life as an adult, she promised herself she would never end up in the kind of relationship like her parents had, where one person was at the mercy of the other person's job. Where love came second to work. Where she would have to pack her bags and move to a new place with little notice, needing to start over and make new friends all the time.

Ryan had the kind of job that demanded everything of a person. He was ambitious, driven. If he was traded, he'd have to move without a second thought. If he had a big game on, he'd have to miss family events and birthdays and whatever else happened.

His life was the polar opposite of what she wanted.

"Well, a movie night is a great start. I *was* thinking C-grade dinosaur movie for a 'so bad it's good' viewing experience." She wrinkled her nose in mock seriousness. "But your case is worse than I suspected."

He smirked, clearly amused by her antics. "What do you suggest, doc?"

"D-grade at a minimum, but I think we may need to scrape the bottom of the barrel. So bad it's *terrible*." She sighed. "We may need to watch the worst dinosaur movie of all time."

"I'm not sure I like the sound of this."

"Me, either. But this is a very dire situation." Behind her, the popcorn machine started popping, the kernels bursting in increasing frequency. "Your seriousness could be…terminal."

"Terminal?"

Sloane nodded, hamming up her mock sadness. "If we don't make you laugh soon, your sense of humor may never recover."

"I laugh," he protested, folding his arms over his chest. "In fact, in the clubhouse I'm the funny one."

She wasn't buying that for a second. "Who are you really lying to, Ryan? Me or yourself?"

"You're ridiculous." He rolled his eyes, but the edge of his lip twitched like he was holding back a smile.

"Ridiculousness is the best medicine."

She turned and peered at the popcorn machine as the last few unpopped kernels swirled around, destined not to meet their potential. She flicked the off switch and pulled the bowl out from under the spout, then uncapped the little container of her secret sauce and drizzled it over the bowl of popcorn. Local honey, butter, salt, and chili flakes mixed with the warm popcorn and filled the kitchen with an inviting smell that had Ryan leaning in closer to take a whiff.

"That smells amazing." He tried to grab a handful, but Sloane swatted him away.

"We have to get the movie going first, or else you'll make the remote greasy." She carried the bowl to the couch, and he followed with their drinks.

"What are we watching?"

"It's called *Theodore Rex*. It came out in the nineties."

Ryan settled into the corner of the couch while Sloane set up the spread—popcorn, cookies, chips, salsa, and some lime-salted nuts. His big body filled the couch, his arm extending along the back and his legs spreading enough to show that he owned the space. Sloane tried not to look at the way the soft sweatpants spread across his muscular thighs and pulled taut at the crotch.

Oh boy.

"Never heard of it," he said after some thought.

"There's probably a reason for that," she said. "It never made it to theaters despite having a thirty-million-dollar budget."

Ryan cocked his head and watched as Sloane made all the snacks look perfect. "You seem to know a lot about it for a movie that's supposedly the worst dinosaur film ever made."

"I watched it once, and it was so bad I had to know everything about it." She dropped back onto the couch and held her hand out for the remote. Ryan made a snorting sound but handed it over without argument. "Whoopi Goldberg starred in it, and she tried to back out once she knew how bad it was going to be, but the producer sued her, and so she ended up doing the movie."

"Sounds awful."

"It is."

Sloane gestured for Ryan to dive into the snacks, and he went straight for the popcorn, his face screwing up with delight as he made the most delicious-sounding moan ever. "This is so good. What did you put on it?"

"It's a secret." She grinned. "Maybe if you're a good boy, I'll share the recipe with you."

"A good boy, huh?" He munched happily, looking more relaxed than she'd ever seen him. And possibly the hottest, too.

"Yeah." Her mouth was dry, but she dragged her eyes away.

They took a few minutes to figure out where they could stream a film that nobody wanted to watch, and within five minutes, they were both groaning—and not the good kind. Twenty minutes later, they were Googling facts about the movie and chatting rather than watching.

"This is bad." He reached for some more

popcorn, downing the handful and wiping his hands on a paper napkin. "Like, so bad I wonder how it even got made."

"There's a whole play-by-play somewhere online," Sloane said, digging her phone out to look it up. "See?"

Ryan leaned in closer, peering over her to look at the phone screen. Soon they were reading bits aloud to one another, sharing other awful movies they'd barely been able to watch and laughing over funny anecdotes, while the movie played in the background, ignored.

"God, this is exactly what I needed tonight," Ryan said with a content sigh. "You give good movie night."

"Do I?" Sloane's heart lit up, and she couldn't help the big, goofy smile that stretched across her face.

"Has no one ever told you that before?" He gestured to the coffee table and TV in front of them. "A+ snack game, Z-grade movie selection."

She knocked his arm. "On purpose."

"I bet your friends always make you organize get-togethers."

Way to punch me in the feels, bro.

Of course, Ryan would have no idea what a nerve he'd hit. How would he? A guy like him had people following him wherever he went. Everybody wanted to get close to him, and she knew for a fact it wasn't just because of his athletic prowess and fame. Pat had known Ryan and both his brothers since they were all kids, and she said the boys were always popular in school.

How nice that would be. Her mind flicked to the article about making friends.

3. Be open. You have to let people in if you want to make friends.

Was this too awful a thing to admit out loud? Would Ryan look at her like she was a freak? Probably. But wasn't that the whole point of the practice run? To try things out. She'd never *ever* told anyone about her fears before or that despite her finding the perfect town and the perfect home and the perfect job…her life was still missing something pretty darn important.

"Here's the thing," Sloane said. "I have a confession to make."

"Okay." Ryan stretched the word out, as if unsure exactly where the conversation was going.

"I don't have a lot of friends here. Or like…any friends. At all."

Ryan snorted. "Yeah, right."

She folded her arms across her chest and burrowed back against the couch, feeling stupid for even saying anything. Ryan looked at her like he suspected she was yanking his chain. "I'm being serious."

"Sorry, I thought you were making a joke." He frowned and shook his head. "I mean you're…"

She raised an eyebrow that told him to tread carefully.

"Everyone loves you," he finished. "Seriously, my

mom said you were one of the best things to happen to the library system here."

Sloane took her glasses off and cleaned the lens with the hem of her T-shirt. Then she popped them back on her nose and adjusted the arms that curved around her ears. It was a nervous habit, something to keep her hands busy any time she felt vulnerable.

"I'm good at my job," she replied with a nod. "But that doesn't equal friendship."

If only.

"Are you *sure* you don't have friends?"

Sloane shot him a look. "I think I would know."

"People here are down-to-earth and friendly, and you're the perfect person to fit right into that."

"You think?"

"Yeah." He smiled at her and reached out to touch her arm. "Anyone who doesn't want to be friends with you is missing out."

The words filled Sloane's chest with a warm, fuzzy feeling—the kind of feeling that could have been a friendship feeling, but also could have been something else. All she knew was that in that moment Ryan had made *her* happy. Happier than she remembered being in a long time.

And that was very dangerous indeed.

CHAPTER TEN

"They *are* missing out," Sloane said. "But everyone is busy with their own lives, and they don't have time to take on a new friend. A *real* friend. Not just someone you can chat with in line at the coffee shop, you know?"

He knew. The kind of friends she was looking for were few and far between, and not exactly the kind of thing you could advertise for, either. It took timing and chemistry and a whole host of other things outside a person's control, something he could tell bothered Sloane.

She was a woman who liked to have a hand in things and wasn't passive in her own life.

"I totally understand," he said.

"Do you find it hard, living the life you have? Always travelling and knowing you could get traded and move cities again? Like you're...untethered."

Damn if that question didn't make him curious about her. "Someone wise once told me a person's questions reveals much of who they are and what they care about."

She raised an eyebrow. "And what does that say about me?"

"That you want stability in your life." He cocked his head. "It also explains why you were so insulted when I insinuated that you were a bad influence on the community that day I came into the library. You take your role here very seriously."

"Who would have known the grumpy baseball player was harboring an inner Dr. Phil?" Sloane looked at him like she was seeing him with fresh eyes. And it appeared that she was as intrigued by him as he was by her.

"I'm right, aren't I?"

Her eyes searched his, lashes touching delicately as she blinked. Something streaked across her face, vulnerability flashing like lightning. "Yeah, you are."

"Military brat?"

She shook her head. "My mom was a consultant, whatever the hell that actually means. I never knew how long we would stay anywhere or even if we were moving until the day it was time to go."

"Wow."

"We were comfortable, because she earned a lot, but…" She sighed. "I barely ever saw her. She took trips frequently, and I always had the suspicion she wasn't going exactly where she said she was going."

Ryan's brows shot up. "You think she was a spy?"

"No. I don't think we would've moved around with her if that was the case, but…it was something secretive." Sloane shrugged. "I've wondered at points if maybe what she does isn't exactly legal."

"Fascinating."

"It sounds like it. But when you're a kid and you want to have a movie night with Mom and Dad, but one of your parents is never around and the other one resents it constantly…it doesn't make for the best childhood." She pulled a face. "That makes me sound whiny."

"Tell me more." The words slipped out before Ryan could think about what it really meant—but Sloane had given him a peek behind the curtain, and he was hooked. His sassy little librarian was hiding something complicated behind her cutesy outfits and ballsy personality.

"I guess there isn't much more to say, other than all that upheaval made me really want a place of my own. A *permanent* place."

"Why Kissing Creek?"

He couldn't really understand it. Sure, he loved his hometown and he loved visiting family, but he remembered being a kid desperate to get out and explore the world. To go to a big city with a giant sports stadium and build himself a shining career.

Kissing Creek was never an option for him.

"I wanted somewhere smaller, but not too small. Kissing Creek is perfect. People know each other here, and they'll hand back a five-dollar bill if you drop it." She got a dreamy look on her face, like she'd slipped off into fantasy land.

He wondered if this place looked different to her than it did to him—like the trees were greener and the sky was bluer and the sun shone that much brighter. What had been a shackle on his wrist as a teenager desperate for the next step was a safe, happy space for her.

Like you need proof this is nothing more than a happy interlude from the real world.

Well, he wasn't about to waste an opportunity to indulge in a sexy distraction by delving too much into his feelings. This was never supposed to be about feelings, despite the fact that Sloane was a prickle in his brain.

"How did you make friends when you moved to Toronto?" she asked.

How did he even answer that? When he was traded, friendship was the last thing on his mind. He wanted to make a good impression on his managers and the coaches and the other players.

He couldn't have given a rat's ass about friendship.

"A few guys I met introduced me around to their circles, and it grew from there. It usually takes one person."

"I need to find that one person." She bobbed her head. "Honestly, after a few failed attempts here, I got performance anxiety about the whole thing. I'm really good at the first introduction and then after that…"

Sloane blew a raspberry, and Ryan laughed. "Well, I don't know if you were *that* great at my first introduction."

"That's all on you, buddy!" She huffed. "And, yes, maybe the book is a little dirty."

"If you call chapter sixteen only a *little* dirty, then I want to know what the hell you've been up to."

"You really want to know?" Her lips curved into a sinful smile. She looked delectable as sin snuggled into the big couch, her shapely legs encased in tight Lycra and her eyes peering at him over the top of her chunky black-framed glasses.

It was like some kind of sexy librarian/nerd girl mashup, and he liked it very much.

"Would you tell me if I did?"

"Nope," she replied huskily. "I don't kiss and tell."

She was close to him on the couch, one knee bent up and the other dangling over the edge, her foot not touching the ground. The big, sprawling sectional had been bought for a family of six-feet-tall men—the dark gray fabric chosen to guard against hot wings and beer—and Sloane looked like a colorful little fairy by comparison. Her dark hair was loosely tied back and her T-shirt hung right on the edge of her shoulder, exposing the delicate bone structure of her collarbone area and a light dusting of cinnamon freckles on her chest.

"Never been tempted?"

"I save that for my reading material." She cocked her head. "What about you?"

Maybe it was reading *Stormy Pleasures*. Maybe it was being home and realizing for the first time in a long while that there was life off the field. Maybe it was part of his existential crisis.

Or maybe it's latent onset horniness.

Whatever the reason, Sloane was exactly what he needed right now. A woman with spark, with an attitude, with a healthy dash of irreverence. A woman who wasn't afraid to show him something *real*. A woman who'd taken his first impressions and set them alight, like touching a match to gasoline-soaked fabric.

"I'd need to be kissing in order to tell anyone about it."

The words were off his tongue before he could think about why they were too much. Too telling. Too vulnerable. Ryan *didn't* do vulnerable. He'd learned from an early age that confidence was paramount—vulnerability had no place on the field.

And off the field? That had no place in his life at all. Dammit. Sloane was messing with his head, tempting him with things that didn't normally tempt him.

But right now…Lord, he was tempted. And then some.

"Too focused on work?" she asked. "Or the right woman hasn't come along?"

"A little of both."

She looked up at him with those sparkling eyes. Her lips parted and glistening, gray-blue eyes wide and unblinking behind the lenses of her glasses. He couldn't stand the barrier between them, so he reached out and gently tugged them down her nose and slipped the arms from her ears. He didn't want her sympathy. Her pity. He didn't even necessarily want her understanding, because it didn't matter what she thought.

What he wanted was something else entirely.

She opened her mouth as if to speak, but instead she drew in a deep, shaky breath. Her cheeks were flushed and her lashes touched as she blinked. God, she was beautiful.

"Am I your distraction tonight?" she asked softly.

"You shouldn't be." But there was no denying the want that roared inside him like a lion let out of a cage for the first time. "And it's not distraction. More like…escape."

"Escape?"

"I could get lost in you."

He expected her to tease him, to rally a smart-ass comeback. She didn't.

"I've never been anyone's escape before." She swallowed. "It feels good."

And with that—with those few, softly spoken words—she knocked out a brick from the wall around his heart. Just one brick. Just one small thing. But it was enough for her to get past his defenses, to break through the careful line he drew around himself, so he'd never forget what was number one.

He skimmed his hand along her jaw, unsure what to say in response, and his thumb brushed the edge of her lips. He'd never wanted to kiss a woman more in his entire life than he wanted to kiss Sloane now. He shifted closer on the couch, and she met him, leaning forward and meeting his lips, hands curling into his T-shirt and pulling him closer. Her lips were soft and her tongue met his in glorious contact.

Heat surged through him, tightening his body

like a coil. Hardening him. Making him ache for her.

She snaked her arms around his neck in an effort to get closer, but it wasn't enough. The heat from her body was like standing in front of an open fireplace — it was soothing and thawed his heart.

"Sloane," he moaned against her lips.

Her tongue slid against his, her hands still grasping his T-shirt as though she needed to tether herself to him. "More," she gasped.

He hauled her into his lap, and she came willingly, knees digging into the cushions on either side of him. Her leggings left little barrier between them, and when she lowered herself into his lap, it was heaven. He cradled her head with one hand, feeling her silky hair slide through his fingers, and his other hand travelled down her back, finding the perky curve of her ass and filling his palm with it.

She rocked against him, tilting her pelvis so her heat brushed against the hard length of him. She was a firecracker in his arms, an explosive device ready to detonate. There was no hesitation in her kiss. Her lips were firm, demanding, and they moved in a way that made his body feel like a tiger ready to pounce. In a way that made the whole world blaze with possibility.

He wrapped both arms around her and held her tight, lips moving against her skin. Trailing a path down her neck to the loose neckline of her top. Her collarbone was exposed, and he tugged the fabric aside, finding the sloping curve of her shoulder and the soft pink satin of her bra strap.

He kissed her skin, scraped his teeth along it, and all with Sloane pressed against him. Needy. Wanting. Demanding.

Ryan brought a hand down to the hem of her T-shirt and slipped it under the loose fabric, finding bare skin at her belly, and pressed his mouth back to hers. Searching, he skimmed his palm farther up, over her rib cage, until he cupped the firm weight of her breast. The bra had a touch of lace, and it rubbed tauntingly against his skin.

"Yes," she gasped.

"You feel like heaven." He buried his face into her hair and sucked in the sweet, sweet smell of her.

His fingers found the tight bud of her nipple, and he rolled it against his palm, his brain almost melting at the soft, whimpering moan Sloane released into his ear. Her lips brushed his neck, hands gripping his hair. Tugging. Pleading. But the sound of an engine rumbling outside made them both freeze like teenagers caught necking in the backseat of a car. One car door slammed and then another. Footsteps.

Sloane scrambled off Ryan's lap and launched herself into the opposite corner of the couch. The soft bickering of his parents got louder, as did the jangle of keys, before the lock turned and the door swung open.

Ryan glanced at Sloane, who looked guiltier than a thief in church. Her glossy, dark hair was in slight disarray, and she smoothed a palm over it to try and tame the mussing he'd done to it a second ago. But her cheeks were still pink, her lips swollen, and the endless black of her pupils gave her away.

She looked at him, eyes pleading with him not to say a word.

Damn.

"Hey, you two," his mother said cheerily as she helped his father through the front door. "No need to stop on account of us."

Sloane's eyes widened. "Oh, uh…we weren't—"

Ryan shot her a look, and she snapped her mouth shut. "What happened?"

"My back is playing up again," his dad grunted, hunched over, and Ryan went over to help him. "I sat down in one of Jim's chairs and couldn't get back up."

"Took three of us to get him to the car," his mother said, allowing her son to take over. "I told him it was too soon."

"Come on, Dad. Let's get you laying down." He helped his father shuffle slowly past the couch, but before he left the room, he caught Sloane's gaze.

Her eyes were dark and smoky, her hands folded into an innocent parcel in her lap. This wasn't over. He'd had a taste of Sloane, and now he wanted more. More of her lush lips, more of that petite, curvy body, and more of the sound of her coming undone.

"I have to get going." Sloane pushed off the couch and quickly stuffed her feet into her sneakers.

His mother frowned. "It's still early. And look, you've got all this food spread out."

"Please, enjoy it." Her car keys jingled as she

pulled them from her purse. "I totally forgot I have…a thing."

"A thing?" Ryan raised his eyebrows as if to say, *You'll have to do better than that.* "Really?"

"Yes, a fundraising thing. Sorry. I'll see you soon." And she was out of the house quicker than Ryan could spell his own name.

Who was embarrassed now, huh? *That* was a surprising turn of events. But if she thought she could scuttle away like a scared little crab and avoid them dealing with what happened, then Sloane was going to find out just how serious Ryan could be.

CHAPTER ELEVEN

Two days later, Sloane was wondering what the heck she was supposed to do about Ryan Bower. She'd kissed him. Actually freaking put her tongue in his mouth, crawled into his lap, and kissed him.

You mounted that man like a biker throwing a leg over a Harley.

"Ugh!" Sloane let out a sound of frustration, which raised several heads around the library. Cringing, she held up her hand in apology and went back to her work.

But she couldn't concentrate. This morning she hadn't even been able to remember the name of the author who wrote Captain Underpants when someone had asked. Unforgivable. That was the effect Ryan had on her.

This was supposed to be a friendship dry run, not a…

Her mind wanted to make an inappropriate joke about a wet run, but that was hitting a little too close to home. After she'd fled his house, feeling like a naughty teenager making out with a boy behind the bleachers, she'd gone home and had the mother of all cold showers. And that was only from a kiss.

Lord only knew what might happen if she got

more than that.

"You won't. Not now, not ever," she muttered.

But Sloane had a problem. She needed to get things back on track with Ryan soon. They were already in the second week of October, and the Halloween parade was happening at the end of the month regardless of whether Sloane dealt with her inconvenient crush on Kissing Creek's most famous sports star.

And the float materials were at his house.

And he'd arranged for his brother and some friends to come around tonight and help them build the damn thing.

And she really wanted to see him again.

This was really inconvenient. She hadn't been kissed like *that* in…God, had it been since college? She wracked her brain, trying to remember the smattering of kisses she'd had in her life. Since moving to Kissing Creek, she'd been extra careful about who she kissed, because this was her forever home and she couldn't mess it up by getting involved with the wrong guy.

She'd had a single date with an optometrist, which resulted in a chaste peck by her doorstep… emphasis on chaste. His dry lips had been in dire need of some balm, and the whole thing had been less appealing than day-old squid. Then there was the mechanic who was cute but painfully shy, and after throwing many signals in his direction, she'd given up after a brush on the lips so light she wasn't even sure it could be counted as a kiss.

Neither of those guys had made her feel like she was made of popping candy. Nor did they make her feel like she was going to come apart at the seams.

But Ryan did.

Gah! Why did her spark have to come from Ryan, a guy who was so wrong for her she should have forgotten him the second they met? He was a guy who could stir up all her worst fears—being forgotten, relegated, discarded. His life was the exact *opposite* of what she wanted. The exact opposite of what she'd been working so hard to achieve.

She had to get this back on track. No more swooning over an unavailable guy. Ryan was officially being put *back* in the friendship zone where he belonged.

Her thoughts were cut off when the man in question strolled through the front doors of the library. Like last time, he immediately caught her attention with the way his worn jeans hugged strong thighs and a fitted, long-sleeve T-shirt stretched across his chest.

He looked like a man who'd come to claim a prize.

Ryan was carrying a coffee in each hand, the white cups printed with a hot pink lip print and Kisspresso Cafe's signature, script font. "Thought you might be in need of some caffeine."

He came right up to the front desk and set one down. Sloane looked from the cup to him and back again, trying to figure out what his end game was. The scent of vanilla wafted up from the inside of the cup, making her nostrils twitch.

"Tall vanilla latte with an extra shot." He nudged it along the desk, toward her. "Your usual."

Oh, he was smooth, this man.

"Is this a peace offering?" she asked suspiciously.

"Why would it be a peace offering?" He sipped his own coffee, leaning against the counter in a way that brought him close enough to send Sloane's senses into a frenzy. It wasn't only his incredible eyes and sharp jaw and dark stubble that tempted her. It was the smell of him—crisp, autumnal air and shampoo and something woodsy, a scent she'd sucked in by the lungful as they'd made out on his mother's couch.

Stop thinking about that.

"I don't know. Last time you came here, you insulted my work." She looked at the coffee cup again. The creamy, vanilla-flavored coffee was calling her name, and she was trying as hard as she could to resist, at least until she knew his intentions.

"And last time I saw you, you kissed me and then ran away."

"Shh." She stomped out from behind the counter, grabbed the coffee with one hand and Ryan's wrist with the other, dragging him into an empty aisle.

Sloane only realized her mistake when it became clear that Ryan's large, athletic frame took up most of the narrow space, and she was now standing with her back wedged against a bookshelf in a way that looked *far* too much like the dream she'd had last night.

Only in the dream, her skirt had been up around her waist, rather than draped modestly around her knees. The only option now was to go on the defensive. "*You* kissed *me*."

"That is *not* how I remember it, Dirty Rainbow Bright." He took a long sip of his coffee, as if trying to tempt her to do the same. The cup warmed her hands, and her fingers twitched around the pink waffled-cardboard sleeve. "I remember you looking at me with those great big doe eyes and asking if you were my distraction in a way that would melt the North Pole."

"I didn't see you melt," she said, looking up at him with a stubborn set to her jaw.

"I didn't have a chance. You were in my lap quicker than a squirrel up a tree." His expression was equal parts amused and…enticed. "You were the one driving it, Sloane."

"I was not." With a huff of annoyance, she caved and took a long sip of her vanilla latte. Sugar and caffeine flowed through her system, and she almost sighed in relief. But when she peered back up at Ryan, he was looking smug as hell.

Shit.

"Taste good?"

"You know it does." She took another sip. "Why are here? To taunt me? To make fun of me running away like a scared little chicken because your parents almost caught us making out?"

"Actually, I wanted to make sure you were still

coming tonight," he replied.

"Oh."

"One little kiss shouldn't stand in the way of your parade float dreams." His blue eyes searched hers. Something told her those eyes weren't to be trusted— who needed such pretty eyes anyway? It was clearly a ruse.

"I'll be there," she said with a nod.

Ryan watched her for a long moment, and she became aware of the metal bookshelves pressing into her back, the warm takeout cup in her hands, and the way his dark hair gleamed under the library lighting.

"Are we going to talk about it?" he asked eventually.

"The float?"

"The kiss." His eyes had her locked in place, like they were shackles around her wrists and ankles.

"What's there to talk about?" she asked, glancing over her shoulder to make sure no nosy people had crept into the aisle behind them. The front desk was clear, but she couldn't stay here forever. "Your parents came home. What did you expect me to do?"

"Invite me back to your place." His eyes searched hers, and there wasn't a hint of humor in them.

Sloane's breath caught. She knew what that meant, but it had been so long since a guy had propositioned her. Well, a proposition she was interested in taking up, anyway. She'd *had* offers, but they were the sexual equivalent of spam mail. Unwanted and quickly disposed of. But Ryan's offer...

You're not interested.

Oh, but she was. She was very, very interested.

"That's…presumptuous," she replied primly.

"How so?"

"Well," Sloane started, praying her brain would quit scrambling and come up with something useful. "Just because I kissed you doesn't mean I wanted to take you back to my place for sex."

"Who said anything about sex?" he replied with a wolfish grin. "I was talking about more kissing."

"Sometimes what we don't say is more telling than what we do." Sloane sipped her vanilla latte as if she didn't have a care in the world—or a job that she was supposed to be doing right now.

Pat was due in soon, anyway, and Sloane couldn't let Ryan think he had the upper hand.

"And what do you think I'm not saying?" He leaned a little closer, and her brain short-circuited. It would be an actual, honest-to-God miracle if the words *technical malfunction, please stand by* weren't scrolling across her forehead.

"I think you're not being honest about what you wanted an invite for." Implication hung heavy in the air, and the tension crackling between them was so thick, Sloane would need a cleaver to cut through it. "I mean, if a guy asks to come back to my place, it's not for milk and cookies, is it? No. They want one thing."

The second the words were out of her mouth, she wanted to take them back. Because it made Ryan sound like a sleaze, and he wasn't.

"You think I'm only interested in convincing you to jump into bed with me?" He looked hurt.

Shit. That was a mean thing to say, but she tended to get her spikes out when she was on the defensive. She tried to cover her insecurities by acting like she didn't care. Acting like nothing mattered.

The sad fact was that she cared a lot. Too much, usually.

"I don't think that," she admitted, choosing to let down her walls for a second. "But that wasn't why I came over, you know. I wasn't there for kissing."

"Just into the snacks and bad movies, huh?" His eyes crinkled at their edges.

"I enjoy your company." This was bad, very bad. She had to shut it down now. "But you're not my romantic type. No offense."

Part of that was true—the travelling, pro-athlete, married-to-his-career part. But the rest of him—the broad shoulders, cheeky smile, brilliant eyes, teasing and taunting part of him—absolutely was.

"I call bullshit...no offense," he said with a hint of sarcasm.

"Not everybody likes athletes, you know." She went to walk away, but his hand was still there. She could have easily ducked under it, but something held her there. The delicious tension, maybe. The desire swirling like a mini-tornado in her belly. "Some of us prefer brains over brawn."

"Archaic stereotype incoming." He rolled his eyes.

"That's for assuming librarians should be old."

"Fair. But I don't think you're lying simply because I believe I'm God's gift," he said. "I think you're lying because it's written all over your face."

"I'm *not* lying."

She was totally, absolutely, 100 percent lying.

"Prove it." He inched closer, lowering his head into that tempting, anticipatory "pre-kiss" space.

The air in Sloane's lungs stilled, and a protest lodged at the back of her throat. Her lips parted, and something along lines of "uh, get over yourself" should have slipped easily off her tongue. But logic and good sense and responsibility all packed their bags and took a one-way ticket to another dimension.

And she tilted her head back a little, just enough to show every freaking card in her hand.

"Just what I thought." His hand came up to brush a strand of hair that had escaped her ponytail and tuck it behind her ear. "For the record, you don't act like you're not interested. Not at all."

"Maybe you're not good at reading signals." She resolutely kept her eyes forward, not giving him an inch. Not leaning into him the way she desperately, desperately wanted to.

"Or maybe I've got you totally pegged and you can't stand it."

"More like you can't stand the thought of striking out with a girl."

"I *throw* strikes, Sloane, I don't swing at them. Remember that."

The tables had well and truly turned—Ryan

might have left the library on the back foot last time, but he'd flipped them around with ease. And the smug, cocky smile on his face said he knew it, too.

"Enjoy your coffee," he said. "I'll see you tonight."

She didn't say a word as he strolled away, jeans hugging his ass in a way that had all the moms in the library almost giving themselves whiplash.

"I feel you, ladies," Sloane said, sagging back against the bookshelf. "He's got me, too."

So much for her article about making friends. Turned out she'd made a giant, inconvenient crush instead.

Two hours later, Sloane finished up at work. Pat was doing the second shift and running the parenting book club, which was a blessing because babies were *way* over Sloane's head. Pat had three grown kids of her own and twice as many grandkids, with another on the way, so she was much better suited to run the club meeting and Q&A session.

Besides, Sloane had bigger fish to try. And dinosaurs to build. And a hunky, six-foot-four professional pitcher to put back in the friendship bucket.

Stepping out of her car at the front of the Bower's house, Sloane let the crisp, late-afternoon breeze brush across her cheeks. Her body temperature had been noticeably higher since her personal coffee delivery, and that was unacceptable. This afternoon was about working on the float and nothing more, and she'd even made a point of going home to change into something totally practical and not-at-all cute for the occasion.

No more skin-tight galaxy leggings for her.

It was ugly tan pants (that were originally part of a Dr. Alan Grant costume) paired with a Paleontological Society hoodie, *and* she'd scraped her hair back into a strict bun, without the little floaty bits she usually left to frame her face. She'd even forgone her usual pink lip gloss in favor of some clear balm.

Yep. There was no way any sexual sparks could fly when she was dressed like this.

"You're here to work, not flirt," she reminded herself as she walked up the driveway. "Work, not flirt. Work, not flirt."

She knocked on the door, and a second later, it swung open. Ryan's mother, Gaye, was standing there, a big smile on her face.

"Sloane! Come in." Gaye stepped back. She was wearing a gardening apron over her outfit. "We've got everyone here ready to help."

"Thank you so much." Sloane forced herself not to look at the Bowers' couch as Gaye led her through to the backyard. The last thing she needed was to see Ryan again with the memory of his kiss swimming so close to the surface. "I really appreciate everyone jumping in to help."

"Considering how much you do for our town, it's the least we can do in return."

Outside, the backyard was in full float-production mode. Somebody had wheeled the base of the float through the back of the garage, and the buzz of an electric saw cut through the air as wood beams were sliced. Ryan stood over a beam propped up on a workbench, spreading green paint along it in sweeping back-and-forth motions. It was one job that wouldn't put too much strain on his knee. When he saw her, he put his brush down and moved toward her.

Sloane's breath caught in the back of her throat—Ryan was wearing old jeans, a buffalo-plaid shirt with the sleeves rolled up to his elbows, and a pair of work boots. He had a smudge of the green paint on his thigh and a fine smattering of green dots in his mussed, dark-brown hair.

He looked *so* sexy. Good-with-his-hands, knows-how-to-use-power-tools, makes-all-her-hormones-sing-like-a-canary sexy.

"Hey." He smiled, and she nearly melted into a puddle.

You need to get control over these reactions. Now.

"Hey," she croaked back.

"Let me introduce you around. This is my sister-in-law, Mandy." He gestured to a woman with short copper hair and big brown eyes, who was standing next to a tree trunk of a man who looked like could have snapped the beam of wood in two, rather than using a saw. "And this is my brother, Mark."

"Nice to meet you both," Sloane said with a wave. "Thank you so much for pitching in."

"Any excuse to get out of the house these days," Mark joked. "And I know the boys will love the parade."

"We've got twins," Mandy said. "They're four."

"Adorable."

Mandy beamed. "Archer is going to be so excited for this float in particular. He's having a real dinosaur phase."

"Some of us never grow out of it," Sloane joked.

There was another woman in the yard, working on the chicken-wire sign that Sloane and Ryan had started the night after their trip to the supply store. She looked to be in her late twenties, maybe early thirties, with light brown hair and a petite frame.

"And this is my friend Trudy," Ryan said. "She's a Kissing Creek local from way back, but she's been living on the other side of the country for a few years."

"Nice to meet you," Sloane said. "How long have you been back?"

"A couple of months." The woman tried to smile, but there was something shaky about it, like she'd had a rough landing coming back into town. "Never thought I'd be back here, to tell you the truth. But life likes to throw a curveball now and then, right?"

"Curveball, sure." Ryan snorted. "More like a ninety-mile-per-hour fastball to the face."

Trudy laughed. "Amen to that."

"Well, thanks so much for coming along to help

out." Sloane nodded. "I know it's going to mean a lot to all the kids here."

"Of course! I'm happy to be part of something." Trudy nodded, and this time the smile reached her eyes. "It's nice to be reminded how many good people there are here."

"I was thinking," Ryan said, nudging Sloane with his elbow, "you should take Trudy to that thing they have at Mille Baci. The ladies' night thing."

"I would love that." Trudy's eyes lit up.

Sloane couldn't help but grin in response. "I would love that, too."

Trudy went back to working with Gaye on the chicken wire sign, slathering a small section with glue and then twisting bits of tissue paper into the gaps to create the colorful Olympic rings. Sloane followed Ryan across to where he was painting the freshly cut beams that would frame the sign and provide somewhere for them to secure the advertisements on the back.

"Did you just set me up on a blind date?" she asked, taking a paintbrush and dipping it into the can, being careful to wipe the excess off before she pulled it back out.

"It's not a blind date if you meet the person beforehand." Ryan had his head down as he inspected the edge of one piece of wood, but Sloane saw the hint of a smile even with most of his face obscured. "And as cute as you are, you're not Trudy's type."

"You called me cute." Something fluttered in her stomach.

What happened to work, not flirt, huh?

Technically, he started it.

Yeah, real *mature.*

"I did." Ryan looked up, and his blue eyes locked onto hers, taking that subtle fluttering feeling and turning it up to eleven. "Want to talk about it?"

"Nope!"

Ryan's smile twitched, but he didn't push the subject. "Trudy's had a rough time. She followed a guy to California, but it didn't work out, and her family is still mad because they saw it coming. They're taking some pleasure in the whole 'I told you so' thing. She could use a friend, and it sounds like you're looking for one of those. Seemed like a good match to me."

The kind gesture socked Sloane in the chest. Not only had Ryan gathered his whole family here to help with her parade float, but he was trying to help her find a friend, too. She blinked at him, unsure what to say, because it was so damn…sweet.

"Thank you," she said.

"No sweat." He grinned that sexy, crinkle-eyed grin of his. "And you better get to painting, or else you're going to drip green all over your pants."

Sloane brought her brush up to a fresh piece of wood that was balanced on the other side of the tarp-covered table. She could feel Ryan's gaze on her, like a warm, constant touch. Despite her initial impressions, he was humble and down-to-earth and kind. He seemed to genuinely care about his family and the town, and he took it upon himself to help those around him. He was exactly the kind man she hoped she'd find one day—all wrapped up in a package hot enough to fuel dirty dreams for the rest of her life.

Seriously, no man should look *that* good in paint-splattered jeans and a plaid shirt.

She dared a glance up at him, and he caught her, the edge of his lip lifting into a satisfied smirk. Dammit. Keeping Ryan Bower out of the flirting bucket was going to be much harder than she thought...because right now he was already climbing out of that one and straight into the "take me to bed now" bucket.

Which was a problem.

If she and Ryan crossed that line, there'd be no going back.

CHAPTER TWELVE

The dinosaur float was coming together, and Ryan had to admit, the idea was fun.

His mom and Trudy had made a significant dent in the Olympic rings sign for the back of the float, and Mark had measured and cut all the pieces to frame both the sign and the base. Sloane had the idea to create a tri-level podium similar to the style they used to present medals to athletes. And his dad, frustrated with not being able to help, had sat outside and made sure nobody was cutting corners.

The *survival of the fittest* idea was taking shape.

But now it was approaching dinner, and everyone had paused to grab a drink and admire their hard work. His mom had left to pick up the twins from their godmother's house, and his father had retired inside because the chill was making his back ache. Everyone else stood around, bundled up against the rapidly cooling air, drinks in hand.

"So, Ryan tells me you're a librarian," Trudy said, pausing to sip her coffee. Her hands were wrapped around the mug, which had pictures of different types of dogs printed on it.

"And she runs a smutty book club," he quipped.

"You do *not* want me to give you a lecture on

how society has historically denigrated anything created for or by women. Besides," Sloane said, turning a teasing, saccharine smile toward Ryan, "you seem to be enjoying the latest book club pick."

Mark's eyebrows almost launched off his head. "*Stormy Pleasures*?"

Dammit. Did everyone know about this?

Ryan narrowed his eyes, but there was no getting out of this one. Sloane had officially dropped him into it. Never mind the fact that he kept the book tucked away in his drawer so that his mom wouldn't see it if she came into his room for any reason.

His little game with Sloane was supposed to be their thing. A secret. A private joke.

"How do you know which book they're reading?" Mandy raised an eyebrow at her husband.

"My dispensary tech was reading it in our staff room. She's in the book club," Mark added. "And I made the mistake of asking her what it was about."

Trudy frowned. "What's it about?"

"Yeah, Ryan," Sloane teased. "What *is* it about?"

"It's about two very flexible people." He grunted. "Seriously, how do you even get the hip mobility to do some of that stuff? Chapter twenty-one is setting people up for a dislocated joint."

Sloane burst out laughing. "I can totally picture you drawing the positions out as you're reading to see if it could work."

"Lucky Mom hid her vintage Beanie Baby collection," Ryan fired back. "Or else I'd have some of them reenacting it to prove my point."

Mandy and Mark exchanged amused glances, and Ryan got the distinct impression he was going to be the subject of conversation later that night. He'd never brought a woman home—ever.

You're not bringing Sloane home. You're doing your bit to contribute to the community. Big difference.

Tell that to the fingers that had been itching to touch her all night long. And the more southern part of him that was very much wanting to get in on the action.

"I am *so* lost right now." Trudy laughed.

"It's a steamy story," Mandy said, and this time it was Mark's turn to raise his brow. "From what I've heard."

"It's about two people who don't know who they are," Ryan elaborated. "They've both been emotionally used by those around them, and for most of their lives, they felt as if they only existed for public consumption. She's an actress and he's a politician—but they've been in those public roles for so long that neither one of them knows who or what they would be without it."

Sloane blinked. "Whoa."

"Am I wrong?" he asked. "English was never my best subject at school."

"No, you're absolutely right. I never even thought about the themes like that." Her mouth hung open in a sweet little *O* shape. "These characters only know how to be themselves with an audience, and when they're together, it's like they're trying to learn who they are…as people."

"Yeah." Ryan raked a hand through his hair, feeling a little self-conscious all of a sudden. All jokes about the contortionist sex scenes aside, he related a hell of a lot to the characters in *Stormy Pleasures*. That had taken him by surprise.

But he knew the feeling of everyone wanting a piece of you. He knew what it was like to chase something with everything you had, knowing that at some point it had to come to an end whether you wanted it to or not. And what it was like to fear the future, because once your dream's expiration date hit, you had no idea how you would cope.

Or who you would be.

He never talked about this with anyone, because it would make him seem like the most ungrateful person in existence. What he'd been able to do in his life…well, that was a privilege. One he'd worked hard for, of course, but still a privilege. Complaining about his problems would make him look like a jerk. So, he struggled alone, most of the time. Occasionally, he vented to one of the other veterans on the team. But that was it.

He had a feeling Sloane would understand. That she wouldn't judge him.

"Hang on, hang on. I need to circle back to the hip mobility thing," Mandy said with a laugh.

"Or maybe you need to read the book." Mark slipped an arm around his wife's shoulders.

"Oh really, and why is that exactly?" She looked up at him with barely concealed amusement.

"We might be able to make use of it now that the twins are getting older."

Ryan held his hands up to his mouth like a megaphone. "Get a room!"

Everybody laughed. Mandy looked at Ryan's brother with such love in her eyes, with such warmth and affection and care, that it was almost like an electrical jolt. He knew they were in love, academically. He'd been co-best man with Ace for their wedding. And he'd come home to visit when the twins were born.

He'd seen their love before. And in all those other times of witnessing their love, Ryan had never thought about what it might be like for someone to look at *him* like that. Not once had he envied them. Not once had he coveted what they had.

But he did now.

The stress of the injury is messing with your head. You know *what you want, and it's not a wife and three-point-two kids.*

"Look who Grandma found!" His mother came through the back door, a little boy in each hand.

Their chubby fists gripped onto her as they navigated the back step, dressed almost identically in jeans, and sweatshirts with cartoon characters on the front, and tiny little Converse sneakers that looked like they were small enough to belong on a keyring.

A chorus of *awwws* erupted as the boys ran

toward their mother and father, almost tripping over their own two feet. Mark swung Danny up onto his shoulders and Archer stood by his mother, shyly surveying the strangers in the backyard.

"I should get going," Trudy said. "My sister is coming by tonight to drop off a few things I've been storing at her place."

He could hear the tension in her voice—she wasn't anticipating the visit to be an easy one. But he smiled as Sloane went over to her and they exchanged numbers, the potential for a friendship blossoming. They both seemed eager, if a little nervous, but Sloane's eyes sparkled behind the lenses of her glasses, and that made him know he'd done the right thing introducing them.

You're getting corny and sentimental as you get older.

Maybe. But that was going to remain his little secret.

"We should get you boys fed so we can go home and have a bedtime story," Mandy said, leading Archer inside. Mark followed with Danny still on his shoulders, and Trudy was close behind, waving as she went.

"I should probably get going, too." Sloane glanced back to where the float was propped in garage, with the back door still open and light spilling into the yard. "Thank you for organizing all this."

Ryan was suddenly aware how quiet the yard was. His parents had gone to help get the family fed, and that left him and Sloane alone outside. It was almost dark now, with little more than a hazy purple-and-gold line striping along the horizon. The air was crisp and carried the scent of damp earth, and dry leaves, and the barest hint of Sloane's perfume right up to his nostrils. Somewhere, insects chirruped, and the rumble of a car engine sounded in the street.

"It's nothin'," he said.

"It's not nothing." Sloane's voice was soft, and she stuffed her hands into the front pocket of her hoodie, the breeze whipping the dark strands of her hair around her face.

God, he wanted to kiss her. Again. Over and over and over.

Her light eyes were sparkly and bright, like stars glimmering against the growing dark. He wanted to haul her against him and see if she tasted even better than last time. To see if her body was warm and pliable in his hands.

Her gaze swung to the house. The sliding door was open, and light filtered out along with the sound of laughter and the excited squeal of one of the twins. He could already smell something delicious and the booming voice of his brother carrying out into the night air.

"You have a wonderful family," she said. Then she shook her head like she hadn't meant to say that.

"Why don't you stay for dinner?"

"I don't want to intrude."

His mother poked her head out of the house at a perfectly convenient time, which indicated she had most definitely been eavesdropping. "Ryan, why don't you take Sloane one of my casseroles? I had one ready to go for tonight, but you know the boys refuse to eat anything with broccoli in it."

Sloane's lip quirked up, but she ducked her chin into her hoodie to hide it. Obviously, she could see through his mom's attempts to play matchmaker, since his mother was subtle as a sledgehammer. Usually, something like that would annoy him, and he'd make a crack about her already having grandkids, but tonight...well, tonight he was happy for the excuse.

"What do you say?" he said to Sloane. "Want some home-cooked dinner away from all this chaos?"

"Sure," she answered, a soft smile on her lips. "But give me ten before you come over, okay? I left the house in a bit of a mess today because I was running late for work. I'll text you the address."

Ryan nodded and followed Sloane into the house—her cheeks flushed and possibly not from the cold—as she said goodbye to everyone, thanking them for helping her.

You have a wonderful family.

The pain in her voice was like a punch to the guts, loneliness echoing long after the words were spoken. He did have a wonderful family—loving parents, two loyal brothers, adorable twin nephews who looked up to him.

Did it make him a bad person that he left all that behind to chase his dreams? That he spent most of the year away from them, only accessible via text and the occasional Skype call? He had the very thing that Sloane clearly wanted, and in truth, he took it for granted.

It doesn't matter what she thinks about your family situation.

The front door closed, and Ryan looked at his family all gathered around the table. His father was making faces at the boys, who giggled and tried to imitate him. Mark was nuzzling Mandy's ear, no doubt whispering something dirty about *Stormy Pleasures*, and his mother stood at counter, dishing food into a row of bowls, looking over the rest of them like the proud and powerful matriarch she was.

He'd never wanted this life, never saw the value in it. Never thought it was worth staying put in a small town for. But seeing this through Sloane's eyes, even briefly, he understood how lucky he was.

Twenty minutes later, Ryan walked up the driveway to Sloane's house, holding the casserole his mother had insisted he take. God, he felt like… He didn't even know. An awkward teenager on a first date? Or worse, a way-out-of-practice, thirty-something guy who wouldn't know a first date if it smacked him in the face like a wet fish.

When *was* the last time he'd been on a date?

"This *isn't* a date," he muttered under his breath.

But all signs pointed to him being wrong. One, he'd showered before coming over *and* splashed a little cologne on. Not much, but enough that if she got close, he'd smell good. Two, he'd looked forward to this the whole time he'd been showering and changing his clothes. Looking forward to it with a jittering sensation inside him that felt a *lot* like how he felt before his first game of the season.

Anticipation.

He wanted to be here. He wanted to see Sloane. He wanted...

Ryan paused on her doorstep and shook his head. Maybe it was the stupid book he'd agreed to read, filling his head with ideas of relationships and passion and other crap he didn't need in his life. Or maybe it was the effects of focusing everything on his career and nothing on his love life. Because it felt a whole lot like he wanted...*her.*

Don't be ridiculous. She's a small-town girl with flowers in her garden and a hand-painted mailbox. She's set down roots here.

Besides, the second the playoffs were over, he was heading back to Toronto to put the blinders on again. He was passionate about one thing and one thing only—his career.

Ryan jabbed at the doorbell and waited, shifting from one foot to the other as he tried to tamp down the excitement of seeing her again. Jeez. When she opened the door, he blinked. She'd changed out of her work pants and hoodie into a pretty red dress with a line of small buttons down the front. It wasn't revealing, but the fabric was thin and the breeze pushed it around her legs in the most enticing way, allowing glimpses of the warm light from within her house to shine through. Her silky dark brown hair tumbled down over one shoulder, unrestrained and gloriously free.

"Wow." The word popped out before he even had a chance to control his reaction. "I mean, I don't think I've seen you in something without dinosaurs on it before."

"I figured I'd wear something 'normal' and spare myself your endless teasing." Sloane's cheeks warmed, and she rolled her eyes, holding the door open for him. "So much for that plan."

He saw behind that little comeback the second the words flew out of her mouth. She'd changed. For him.

Maybe she wore it for herself, caveman.

His throat tightened as she took the food from him and headed toward the kitchen. The inside of her house was more modern than he'd expected, with bright white paint and some interesting, abstract prints hanging on the wall—dino-themed, of course. A cozy blue couch was decorated with mismatched pillows in shades of cream, dusty pink, and navy, and the kitchen was mostly pale wood and white granite, making it a perfect backdrop to that mesmerizing red dress.

There was something about the loose hair and the bare feet and the so-thin-you-could-rip-it-with-your-teeth fabric of her dress that had him rooted to the spot.

"You've got some nice digs here," he said.

"Thanks. I've been thinking about getting a pool for the backyard." Sloane set the dinner tray down onto the marble countertop. "It's a small space, but I love swimming in the summer."

Great. Now he had visions of Sloane wearing some scandalous triangle bikini.

"It's a lot of upkeep considering how long the cold lasts here."

Are you trying to sound exactly like the curmudgeon she accused you of being?

How did she do that to him? Every time her idealistic, whimsical side showed, he resorted to being some stick-up-his-ass, stiff-upper-lip kinda guy.

Better than stiff something else.

That would also be a problem if he kept staring at how good she looked in that dress.

"Lots of things that are hard work are worth it," she said breezily, her eyes glinting with mischief. "I'm sure your family says the same about you."

"I'm going to need to up my medical insurance with these burns you keep dishing out," he joked, and Sloane burst out laughing.

"That was a bit mean, wasn't it?" She grinned. "You leave yourself wide open, Ryan. And I have excellent aim."

"Shouldn't you be nice to me, since we're float-making colleagues and all?"

"I'd like to think we're friends now, too." A teasing smile pulled her shapely lips into an enticing curve. "I mean, I wouldn't put up with your shit if I was *just* your colleague."

"You've got it lucky, Sloane. Most colleagues wouldn't put up with *your* shit, either."

"What do I do that's so bad?" She wandered over to the oven and pressed the pre-heat button.

"You've got an opinion about everything," he said, leaning against the countertop and watching her.

"I'm *informed*."

"You trick people into doing what you want."

"I have the ability to motivate others," she corrected, removing the cling wrap from the casserole dish.

"You're a bad influence," he said, knowing it would press her buttons.

Sloane paused and looked over her shoulder with an incredulous expression. "I am *not*."

"Chapter twenty-one."

"Have you finished it yet?" Her eyes twinkled.

"No. I'm finding it tough to get through."

Liar, liar. And they both knew it. He'd already experienced more dirty dreams in the past few days than all his horny teenage years combined. *All* of them had featured a sexy, pushy—and yet sweetly vulnerable—librarian.

The things Sloane had done in his head…

"Bullshit. One, you perfectly articulated the book's themes earlier," she said smugly. "And two, unless you have the curiosity of a doorstop, you're enjoying that book."

"How are you so sure of yourself?"

"Because you want to know what all the fuss is about." The oven beeped, and she picked up the casserole dish. "Admit it, you're intrigued."

"I'm really not."

"Like I said, BS. Total and utter—" *CRASH!*

Ryan's mother's casserole shattered all over the tile floor, sending brown goop splattering the pretty white cupboards and Sloane's bare legs. There were big chunks of glass around her bare feet, and she wasn't wearing shoes. Thankfully, the dish had missed her foot by a few inches or else they might have ended up with a trip to the ER.

"Don't move," he said. "Where's your trash?"

"In there." Sloane pointed, and then she groaned. "I don't know what happened. I had a good grip on it, and then it slipped out of my hands. I'm so sorry."

"Accidents happen." He tossed the biggest chunks of glass into the trash and tried to wave Sloane's help away, but she wasn't having it.

"It's my fault, okay? I can pick up some glass."

"Don't move your feet. There might be smaller pieces you can't see."

"You really do have the hero thing going on, don't you? Maybe you should come as Batman for Halloween." Sloane's defenses were shooting up around her. Clearly, she was feeling a little embarrassed and vulnerable. "Or Captain America. I could see you with a shield."

"I told you, I'm not dressing up."

"We'll see about that," she said with a heavy sigh. "I can't believe I dropped it. Now we have nothing for dinner, and after your mom was so kind and made us something, too."

"She literally has an entire freezer full of casseroles in the garage. It's fine."

For a moment, Sloane got a faraway look in her eyes. "She's a real storybook mom, huh?"

Ryan frowned. "What do you mean?"

"She loves feeding people, and she's all friendly and warm and loving." She sighed. "My mom wasn't like that."

"What was she like?" he asked. The hints she'd dropped about her childhood painted an interesting picture. That coupled with the way she looked at his family told him that perhaps her years globe-trotting for her mother's job were not happy ones.

"Career-focused. Permanently attached to her laptop. Worked all hours of the night. I knew she loved me, but…it was a different kind of love. Family wasn't her top priority. Work was."

"I can identify with that," Ryan replied with a nod.

Sloane nodded and continued trying to clean up her mess, muttering something under her breath about staying away from trouble. Ryan decided it was easier to pretend he hadn't heard anything, so he fetched the paper towel roll from the countertop and crushed several sheets into a thick wad. But as he was about to wipe the mess off the floor, he caught Sloane holding her hand up. Blood oozed from her fingertip.

She looked at him, her brow creased. "Yes, I cut my finger, and no, I don't want a lecture. Can you grab the first-aid kit from up there?"

She nodded to a cupboard higher up.

"Let's get it under the water," he said. "You need to make sure there's no bacteria lodged in there."

Sloane looked down at the ground, where several more glass shards glittered on the tiles. Ryan hadn't taken his shoes off—too distracted by Sloane and her pretty dress when he'd walked inside. Bad manners, but perhaps a saving grace now.

"Come here."

"I'm playing *right* into this damsel-in-distress thing, aren't I?" She sighed and then reluctantly held her hand out. Blood gathered around her fingertip, and he ripped off a few more sheets of paper towel for her. "Thank you."

"Was that an actual thank-you? Not a screw-you masquerading as a thank-you?" He gasped comically, and Sloane laughed, shaking her head.

He took a step closer to her, feeling something crunch under his foot as he lifted her up and removed her safely from the kitchen. He carried her only as far as he needed to, setting her down on the safety of the floorboards near the dining table. She clutched the paper towel around her finger, and there was already some red oozing through. He'd need to have a look and make sure it wasn't deep enough to require medical attention.

"Where's your bathroom?" he asked, taking his

boots off to make sure he didn't track glass through the house. "Let's deal with the finger first and then we can clean up in here."

"This way."

He followed her into the bathroom, where she carefully removed the paper towel and inspected the cut. It was still bleeding. Ryan turned the tap on and checked the temperature. "Give it a quick rinse, then we'll bandage you up."

She winced, pain flashing brightly in her eyes as the water connected with her wound. "Oh God, that really stings."

"Is it deep?"

"I don't know." Her words came out a little strangled. "I'm not great with blood."

Uh oh. He'd seen his share of blood over the years. Came with the territory of growing up in a house of rambunctious boys. As far as baseball injuries went, though, blood was usually the least of their worries. He'd seen a catcher take a foul tip right in the nuts and that was *not* pretty.

"Don't look at it."

"Too late." She clamped her lips together like she might be worried about vomiting. Or maybe it was because she was holding her breath. Either one wasn't good.

"Here." He reached for her finger. The cut wasn't deep enough to require stitches, but it was more than a surface scrape, and with all the nerve-endings flinging out pain signals, he needed to make sure

Sloane didn't pass out on him. "Hold the paper towel on it for another minute to stem the flow. Then we'll put some cream on and bandage it up."

Sloane followed his instructions, but her breathing was shallow and her usually warm, glowing skin was looking a little pale. "The blood thing is…so silly. I know in my head it's going to be fine."

"It's nothing to be ashamed of." He found the antibiotic cream he was looking for and pulled the cap off. He needed to get a little dab of that onto her, then some gauze and a little flexible tape to hold it in place. Then, after they'd gotten something else for dinner and sat for a while, he could check and make sure it wasn't worse than it looked currently. "I've seen plenty of people lose their lunch, and yours is still firmly in your stomach, so I'd call that a win."

"I don't know if I'd say firmly," she said with a weak smile. "But it seemed like vomiting on you might *really* make you dislike me."

He chuckled. "Okay, I'm going to take this gauze off so I can put a little cream on the cut to make sure it doesn't get infected. Then I'm going to put a piece of gauze on and tape you up so we can give the blood time to congeal."

"Thanks, Doc." She smiled up at him, her gray-blue eyes luminous with the tears that had sprung out of shock at the pain. But she didn't spill a single one.

"You're a tough cookie." He gingerly removed the first piece of towel and contemplated whether or not he should warn her that the cream would sting like a bitch. Probably better not to worry her. "Ready?"

She nodded. When he dabbed it on, she gasped and her body jolted, but he had a firm grip on her wrist and managed to get her patched up even while she wriggled like a caught fish.

"That hurt." She hissed between her front teeth as Ryan released her from his grip. "You could have warned me."

"A little pain now to save a lot of pain later." He shrugged and swept the little bits of packaging into the metal bin hidden inside her cupboard. "And warning you would have only made you more difficult."

"You've got the bedside manner of a cactus."

He straightened up, suddenly aware of how close they were. Her bathroom was no bigger than a postage stamp, and it was like the walls were pushing them together. Boxing them in. The air was charged with little electric sparks, a sizzle and pop of energy that made his breath run short.

"You okay?" he asked, seriously this time.

Sloane nodded. "A cut finger is the least of my concerns right now."

What did she mean by that? He looked at her, trying to glean more information in her body language. But the only thing he saw swirling in the depths of her pale eyes was heat. Or maybe that was nothing but a reflection of what was roaring inside him.

This is a bad idea. She's a small-town gal who

wants it all—the house with the vegetable patch, the family. A man who wants all those things, too.

He knew that—knew it down to his bones because he could see how much she loved this place. How much care she'd taken setting her life up here. And he was the opposite of all that, a guy who'd only returned because something had gone wrong and treated his hometown like a waiting room.

He swallowed back a healthy dose of guilt.

But all that logic was drowned out by the need screaming inside him, pent-up desires and unfulfilled cravings all contributing to the haunting sound in his head. His eyes tracked over her face, cataloguing her details—the gentle slope of her nose smattered with freckles. Full lips, naturally rosy. High cheekbones and hair that gleamed with shifting shades, from deep chestnut to espresso to almost-ebony.

He wanted to kiss her so bad. He wanted to taste her, to feel her. To see if she needed this as much as he did. In the tornado of doubt that was his life right now, *this* felt good. It felt right.

He touched her wrist, running his fingertip up the side of her hand to where the gauze capped her pointer finger. She had a mole right next to where her wrist bone jutted out slightly, and he traced over that little dark spot. When he brought his finger down the inside of her wrist, over the taut, sensitive skin there, she shivered.

"Ryan…" Her lips parted, then closed, then parted again.

What are you doing? You're supposed to be hiding away from life right now. You're supposed to be wasting time until the new season starts.

But nothing could stop the tidal wave of attraction crashing into him—nothing except Sloane herself.

"If you're going to do it, then do it already," she said, her voice breathier than normal. Huskier. A little rough and perfectly sexy.

"Do what?" His heart hammered in his chest, as if there was a fist trying to punch its way out.

"Kiss me."

It was like some red flashing light in his head suddenly turned green. He drove his hands into her hair, the slide of silky strands heaven against his palms, and he bowed slightly, bringing his head down to hers. Their noses brushed and her breath hitched, the moment of no return dancing in front of them like sprites. Was he really going to kiss Sloane, the woman who was totally and utterly wrong for him, all over again?

Yes.

He brought his lips down to hers, slowly. Deliberately. Telling her with his body exactly what he planned to do, and almost hoping she might stop him. Stop this. But instead, her lips parted, her head tipped back, and her eyes fluttered closed. She fisted her hands in his T-shirt, pulling him closer.

"Hmmm, yes," she whispered.

"I thought I wasn't your type," he said. "I only

like boring-ass vanilla, lights-off, race-to-the-finish-line missionary sex."

She let out a laugh. "I really said that, huh?"

"Yeah, you really did."

"It was…a hell of an introduction." She blew out a breath. "And maybe when I said you weren't my type, I wasn't exactly telling the truth."

That was enough to stoke the fire deep in his belly—so she *had* noticed that snap and crackle between them. There were times he wondered whether it was all on his side. Whether it was in his head.

Knowing that she felt it, too…

"Don't tease me, Sloane," he rasped, brushing his lips over hers. "I'm not playing right now."

"Good." She crushed her mouth to his, her breasts pressing against his chest and her lips warm. She tasted like citrus and joy.

He kept one hand in her hair, tangling his fingers in her curls, and slid the other down her back. The red dress offered little resistance between his palm and her warm skin, and he could feel everything underneath—the strap of her bra, the elastic of her underwear. He cupped her backside and drew her closer, his cock stirring against the fly of his jeans. He was hard in an instant, and she gasped into his mouth as she rubbed against him.

How had he intuitively known that Sloane would be a firecracker like this?

She had a spark to her that leaped right out at him. A hint of temper that drove him wild. A stubbornness and sense of challenge that called to him. He kneaded her ass as he kissed her, his tongue sliding into her mouth and dragging another moan from deep in the back of her throat. He couldn't get enough, didn't want to stop. Was totally and utterly unable to see reason.

He leaned against the vanity and pulled her with him, until she stood between his open legs, her arms wrapped around his neck as though he was holding her afloat at sea. Her lips moved hot and demanding over his, power flicking back and forth between them in an intoxicating way. One minute she was in the driver's seat, pushing him for more…until he wrested it away from her, melting her under his touch.

He cupped her cheek and pulled away, both of their chests rising and falling with quickened breath. Her eyes were darker, lashes touching softly with each blink, and her cheeks were pink. For a moment, neither one of them said a thing, as if daring to speak might shatter this perfect bubble they'd created.

And right now, he wanted to stay in this bubble forever.

CHAPTER THIRTEEN

Ryan looked like pure sex and sinfulness, and Sloane was acutely aware of how dangerous those things were when paired together. Because she couldn't fall for someone who would put his career before her. Who would expect her to pack up and move whenever the job called for it.

She'd worked *so* freaking hard to be part of this place. To build a solid foundation under her feet where she could set down roots and grow a life. A life that was safe and stable and grounded in comforting sameness.

But the second he'd set foot into her house, Sloane couldn't seem to find her anchor of sensibility. And no, it wasn't the sex that had knocked her for a loop. For all her joking about "chapter twenty-one," Sloane needed *more* than physical stamina and a hot body and excellent hip mobility. She needed more, even, than true crackling chemistry.

She needed connection.

And being his arms…she felt connected to him. Tonight, working on something together, she felt connected to him. Laughing with his family and friends, she felt connected to him. It was like the universe was telling her she was meant to be here, in this moment, with him. Touching him, kissing him, wanting him…and well, it felt as natural as the sun rising.

"Why did you stop?" she whispered, looking up at him.

"I'm making sure you're okay."

She sucked in a breath. "I'm not delicate."

"I've never once seen you as delicate," he said with a warm smile. "You're like a tiny rainbow hurricane."

"I'm not *that* tiny. You're just absurdly tall for a human being," she teased.

"Absurdly tall, huh? Do you like tall men?"

"I do."

Hell, putting aside his single-minded career drive, she had a weakness for *all* things Ryan Bower. His stature, the sculpted muscle all over his body, his intense blue eyes, and the way his cheek got the tiniest little dent in it when he smiled.

She was weak for it all.

"And do you have a weakness for dino nerds with dirty reading habits?" she asked.

"I never expected to have a weakness for anything or anyone. That's not how I got to where I am." With those few words, Ryan's joking tone was gone, replaced by smoldering heat and that razor-edged intensity that she'd already come to crave. "And yet I find myself thinking about the ways you drive me wild."

"Tell me."

His lips brushed over her skin. "How you're so vibrant and full of life. How you like making an impact on this place. How you really want to be a good friend."

The words warmed her deep inside—because they weren't the obvious, outward things. Sloane had always made herself memorable with her clothes and her bubbly personality and her quirkiness. But he mentioned the other, truer things that were below the surface. Which meant he'd been looking closely.

She wasn't sure what else to say—because the right thing would be to say *stop*. Ryan wasn't her dream man. He didn't fit into her dream life, and she didn't fit into his. But walking away now would be… impossible. Because that connection she felt with him was shiny and new and wonderful. It was unique. How could she possibly *not* explore it?

She looped her arms around his neck and pulled his head down to hers, kissing him like her life depended on it. Like her very existence depended on it. Like the rotation of the earth and alignment of the moon and the oxygen in the air depended on it.

He turned them so Sloane was backed up against the bathroom counter, wedged between hard granite and harder man. His hands pinned her in, strong arms keeping her delightfully captive. But Sloane was no passive participant—she arched against him, tugging at his hair and rubbing her body against his, secretly thanking her past self for putting on some nice underwear.

This wasn't what she'd been hoping for, but she would damn well enjoy it.

And the consequences?

None. She wouldn't let there be any.

Tomorrow they'd go to the scheduled committee meeting and pretend like nothing had happened, and this would be a happy little memory for her to keep in her back pocket for whenever she felt lonely at night. It was an indulgence, like a slice of rich blueberry cheesecake.

"I…" She tried to think of the right words to say, of how to get it out in the open. "I want you to know that I understand what this is."

He frowned. "What do you mean?"

"That this isn't…" God. Why did she say anything? "You're not…"

Ryan cupped her face with his hands and looked her right in the eyes. "Just because I'm going home in a few weeks doesn't mean this is simply about sex. If I wanted a warm body, I could find one with ease. But I don't want just anyone, Sloane. I want you."

The words tempted her. But it was a promise of disappointment masquerading as a promise of more. There *wasn't* more.

"You're not looking for a relationship," she said, shaking her head. "I don't need you to make this out to be more than it is for the sake of my feelings."

"You're right," he admitted. "I'm not looking for a relationship. My career is number one, and it will always be number one. That will never change. But right now, being here with you…"

Her heart skipped a beat.

"There is nowhere else I'd rather be." He brushed his lips over hers. "In another life…"

"I'm happy with this life," she whispered.

"Then let's make the most of it."

The lines were drawn, boundaries clarified. Tonight's pleasure was simply that—making the most of their chemistry in the moment. Nothing more.

Because she would never be someone's second priority.

"Touch me," she said. "Make me feel good."

Her mind blanked as Ryan's hand slid up over her rib cage up to her breast, the dress and the soft-cup bra offering little resistance. Her nipple peaked as he stroked her with his thumb, and she moaned into him. God, it felt good. It had been so long that she'd forgotten the thrilling rise of her pulse and the deep, needy ache between her legs. She'd missed them. Missed feeling something so strongly it blocked everything else out.

"These dresses you wear," Ryan muttered as his lips graze her jaw, then down her neck. "I lose my head every time."

"That's why I didn't wear one earlier." She gasped when one of his hands found the slit of fabric at her knee. "I was trying to look boring so I wouldn't flirt with you."

"You could never look boring." His palm was sliding against her inner thigh—he had the slightly roughened hands of someone who used them often. Working hands. Competent hands. And the extra friction ratcheted up her senses until her body sang like a harp wire.

"You're a siren."

"Luring you to your untimely death?" She let out a throaty chuckle.

"To my demise, at the very least."

His hand skated higher, higher, higher. But he worked slowly, drawing out the moment she was waiting for, the touch she was desperate for. Who would have thought Ryan had some capacity for patience after all?

"Please," she whimpered, not even sure how that sound had come from her own mouth.

Her body was so tight with anticipation she worried her heart might crack from the pressure. He barely moved a fraction of an inch, but he was still pressing hard against her and she felt his erection swell. He was torturing them both. Warm skin to warm skin, hot breath mingling as their lips grazed… she was heady with the rush of it all.

"Are you frightened, Ryan?" she teased softly, grabbing the back of his neck and holding him close. Or was she hanging on?

Ryan's throaty laugh sent raw, naked heat barreling through her. "Of a rainbow tornado of woman with a tongue like a razor blade? Any man who isn't afraid of you is an idiot."

Fair point.

He inched his hand higher, stealing her ability to think of a snappy comeback by grazing his knuckles along the front of her underwear. Or maybe he didn't even touch her and it was air she felt. She was so primed, so ready, that even the merest of breezes was enough to have her shuddering.

He pressed his lips hers, coaxing her open and sliding his tongue into her mouth for a deep, searching kiss. When he cupped her between her thighs, his palm hugging her most sensitive area, Sloane's eyes rolled back in her head. She braced herself against the countertop with one hand and looped the other around Ryan's neck in case her legs gave out. The way he touched her was...everything.

He took his time, applied the perfect pressure to have her panting but without even getting close to pushing her over the edge. His fingers toyed with the edge of the elastic on her underwear, his knuckles rubbing against her bare skin. Sloane's eyes clamped shut, and it felt like her whole world was bursting with color and light. The heel of his palm ground against her and Sloane's muscles tightened, anticipating the rush of endorphins, and she craved them with every cell in her body.

"Kiss me," she gasped into his ear.

His mouth found hers, and she shattered, quaking against his hand as he muffled her cries with his lips. Overwhelming satisfaction rolled through her. It was like being lowered into a warm bubble bath, the tightness leaching out of her body the second her orgasm subsided. She was liquid. Melted. Sub-human.

Ryan removed his hand from her underwear. "My god, you're beautiful."

She almost couldn't look at him. Having someone

witness her at her most raw was unnerving. Sloane never let people see her like that—what everyone got was a carefully assembled replica of her true self, with all her insecurities covered up and hidden away under dinosaur prints and quirky outfits and smiles.

"Sloane." Ryan said her name in such a way that she couldn't *not* look at him. "Don't shrink away from me now."

"I'm not shrinking," she said, fighting the need to do exactly that. "It was just…"

"Intense?"

"Yeah." Her hands went to the buckle of his belt—the tan leather worn with a scratch in one place. She ran her fingertip over the imperfection.

"But it was good."

"You asking or telling?" A smile crept over her lips.

"Telling," Ryan said with a dash of his trademark confidence.

"It *was* good." She ducked her head.

"Don't be embarrassed. It's hot." He pressed a soft kiss to her temple that was so sweetly in contrast to the words coming out of his mouth that Sloane couldn't help but look up at him with a smile. "But we should probably get you naked now so you don't ruin that pretty dress."

She brought her hands to the top button, which held the modest V-neck closed. "Ryan Bower, fashion conservationist."

"I do what I can," he said, pressing a hand to his chest in mock humility.

She pushed one small button through the buttonhole and then another, watching as Ryan's eyes tracked the widening *V* of skin as she exposed herself to him.

By the time she got to the last button, Ryan had jammed his hands into his pockets as if trying to physically restrain himself from touching her. She found herself enjoying being able to put on a show. With a shrug of her shoulders, she let the open dress flutter to the floor and pool around her bare feet. Then she reached behind herself and felt for the clasp of her bra—tugging it open and slowly removing it.

"I like it when you look at me like that," she said, slipping her thumbs into the waistband of her underwear and rubbing them back and forth. Payback was sugary sweet.

"I'm incapable of looking at you any other way," Ryan rasped.

He reached forward and gently grabbed her wrists, easing her hands down so that she took the underwear with her. He sunk to his knees at her feet, sliding the red elastic and lace over her thighs and knees and calves, then he held onto her hand as she stepped out of the growing fabric pile and he pressed a kiss to the inside of her knee.

From this angle, Sloane felt like a queen. A gorgeous, sexy man at her feet, pleasures untold awaiting her.

"Your turn," she said, tugging him up. "Strip."

He pulled his sweater and T-shirt up and over

his body. Muscles flexed—his abs starkly defined and his shoulders broad and strong. Sloane's mouth ran dry, and she tried to swallow. His work kept him in incredible condition.

"You're staring," he said, toying with his belt buckle. The click of metal on metal echoed in the quiet house. When he gave his belt a yank, jerking his hips forward a little, Sloane felt her eyes float even further down to where the hard length of him pushed against the denim of his jeans. He was outlined to perfection, long and strong and hard.

Hell yeah, she was staring.

"Aren't I supposed to be staring?" She was acutely aware of how naked she was, the gentle brush of cool air tightening her nipples and her skin tingling with anticipation.

Ryan shucked his jeans and underwear and took a step toward her. He was glorious naked—all finely honed muscle and smooth skin and generous dustings of hair on his legs and arms, and just a sprinkle across his chest.

Ryan seemed totally comfortable without anything at all on his skin. The man was confident in himself no matter the situation.

"No second thoughts?" he asked as he came closer, sweeping her loose hair back over her shoulders so it trailed down her back, tickling the top of her butt.

"I probably should," she admitted, trailing her hand along his chest, admiring the dusting of freckles along his shoulders and the smooth, flat discs of his nipples and the little white scar near his bellybutton. He had those muscles that cut a perfect *V* into his midsection, drawing her gaze—and her touch—farther down. "But I don't. We're going to be okay tomorrow, right?"

"No regrets."

"No regrets," she echoed.

Sloane kissed him hard, as if using her mouth to quiet any doubts that might dare slip into her mind. As if action and pleasure erased the risk of what they were doing. Deep down, she knew it wouldn't. But right now, Sloane was so far gone she didn't care. She deserved a little indulgence once a while, and Ryan was perfect for that.

He ground against her in a way that made her groan.

"Condom," he rasped.

"Bedside table." She had a box stashed in the back of her underwear drawer that still had the seal on it.

She grabbed his hand and led him, pulling him into her bedroom then releasing him only to dig out a little foil packet from the back of her drawer. It was incredible to see him—all hard, honed man—against the soft girlishness of the room. She had a pretty throw on her bed and pillows in pale shades of gold and pink.

Ryan took the packet from her and opened it, taking a moment to sheath himself before his hands were on her again. Instead of lying her down on the bed, he hoisted her up onto her vanity unit.

"Plot twist," she said, laughing.

"You've already dented my pride by assuming I'm a boring-ass vanilla sex guy." His lips trailed a line of heat along her neck. "So I couldn't dump you on the bed now, could I?"

The wood was cool against her heated skin. She could see the reflection of him in the full-length mirror on the other side of the room—the long line of his back and curve of his ass an enticing view. He stepped between her legs, parting her wider with his hands at her knees.

The vanity had her at the perfect height, and Ryan rubbed against her.

"Now." She didn't even recognize her own voice anymore. She was wanton and wanting and willing. She was his. "Please."

He pushed into her, slowly as though he wanted to feel every single inch. Sloane dug her hands into his back, letting her nails sink into muscle and flesh, pulling him closer. Bracing one hand against the mirror behind her, Ryan drove all the way in, seating himself deep. The feeling of fullness was so foreign that Sloane gasped, momentary discomfort slicing through her pleasure.

"Easy," he crooned, kissing her. "Give it a minute."

But her mind was a pendulum swinging from too much to not enough and back again. That's what he did to her—he spun her around. Turned her inside out.

After a few seconds, her body relaxed, and Ryan moved inside her, stroking her with a sensual roll of his hips. Sloane's head fell back, landing against the mirror with a dull thud while her eyes drifted skyward. Ryan wasn't in a hurry, at least not yet, and the lazy strokes filled her body with fizzing, sparkling energy.

But then his thumb found her clit and strummed the sensitive bundle of nerves as though he knew *exactly* what she wanted. What she needed.

"Oh, Ryan." She groaned as he circled the pad of his thumb over her, applying more pressure. More friction. More…everything. "I'm so close."

He brought her right back to the brink in an instant, her belly tightening and the muscles inside her contracting around him.

He swore under his breath. "If you keep that up…"

"I can't help it," she panted. "I'm…I'm going to…"

Release broke over her like fireworks—it was big and brilliant and bright, triggering a series of smaller explosions in quick succession. She gasped, rocking against him to wring out every drop of pleasure. Ryan's hands were in her hair, his mouth hot on hers.

"Yes," she demanded as she continued riding the high. "That feels so good."

His fingers tightened at her hips as he thrust deep for the last time, shouting her name so loud she was sure it rattled the foundations of the house. The sound seemed to echo around her, eventually muffled by the thumping of her heartbeat and the first tendrils of worry creeping into the edges of her mind.

Would they be okay tomorrow? Would she ever be able to look at Ryan Bower the same way again?

CHAPTER FOURTEEN

One week later…

Ryan watched a seemingly endless parade of green roll by as his brother drove them deeper into a wooded property.

"How's the knee?" Mark asked out of nowhere. Trust his big brother to wait until there was no means of escape before bringing up a sensitive topic.

Ryan grunted. "The knee will be fine."

"And the man attached to the knee?"

"Also fine."

Mark was a weightlifter—could have gone pro when he was younger, but instead he chose to get a degree and settle down for small-town life with a wife and kids. But he still trained and was still built like a brick shithouse. But his job as the town pharmacist played to Mark's softer, more caring side. He was a gentle giant for sure.

And never the person to let Ryan dodge a question.

But Ryan didn't want him to worry. And he certainly didn't want to talk about his existential "I'm getting old" crisis. It seemed ridiculous to be thirty-five and feeling over the hill, but that was the life of an athlete. And pitchers had more time than most. The youngest Bower brother, Ace, was nineteen and away at college on a scholarship for swimming. His peak days would be done before he reached twenty-five.

"Is it really fine?" Mark asked, brows furrowed. "Because I would expect you to say it sucks a giant bag of donkey dicks, so now I'm worried."

Ryan snorted. "What do you want me to say? Yeah, I was set to have the biggest championship run of my career, and I ruined my knee on a routine play. It's not exactly sprinkles and sunshine, but I'm coping."

"Coping like that time you let Jimmy McBride hit a homer off you in the last game of the season in middle school?" Mark glanced over at him and grinned. "I remember someone coming home and putting a ball through the bedroom window."

"First of all," Ryan said, "Jimmy McBride should have been out on that third pitch, and you know it. Mrs. Kirkman had a pitch zone wider than a freight truck. Second of all, putting the ball through the window was unintentional. Sweaty hands."

"Mom never forgave you for that. You knocked Ace's first swim meet trophy over, and she had to put it back together with superglue."

"That's because Ace is the favorite, and she's not supposed to play favorites." Ryan chuckled.

The conversation moved away from Ryan's injury as they reminisced about old times and eventually arrived at a small house nestled between towering trees, a riot of gold, burnt orange, and red foliage contrasting against the crisp, blue sky. Ryan stepped out of his brother's truck, his boots immediately crunching down on a thick layer of dead leaves. The bang of two car doors closing echoed through the trees, and after the sound faded, there was glorious, peaceful nothingness.

"It's…perfect." The air smelled cleaner out here, fresher. Damp earth and decaying leaves and a hint of smoke from a wood-burning fireplace somewhere close by.

The trip to his brother's work-in-progress couldn't have come at a better time. Ryan and Sloane had been awkwardly tiptoeing around each other ever since their night together. He'd forgotten how strange that dance was after you slept with someone who was in your orbit. And Sloane was most definitely in his orbit.

She'd been coming around to his parents' place most days to work on the float with him, and usually his dad hung around trying to be helpful but ultimately making things kind of…weird.

Sloane was clear she didn't want to talk about it, but Ryan wasn't sure he felt the same. What he'd shared with her was something, that was for sure. Something wonderful. Something unique. Something…something.

No wonder she doesn't want to talk. You're about as articulate as a pile of bricks.

Ryan shook off the self-criticism. The whole point of coming here with his brother was to clear his head. No point thinking about how she well and truly rocked his socks. It was a great way to blow off steam, and nothing more.

Mark came around the front of the car, looking every bit like the kind of guy who was renovating a house with his own two hands. He had on boots and dark jeans, the collar of a flannel shirt poking out the top of a hand-knit sweater that his mother-in-law had made him. His five o'clock shadow was verging more into beard territory by the day, though he made some effort to keep the edges neat.

"The neighbors are actually closer than you think, but these trees make it feel like we're all alone out here." Mark sighed happily. "We've got access to the lake right on the other side of the building, and a little jetty. I'm planning to teach the boys to kayak as soon as they're old enough."

"You mean as soon as Mandy thinks it's safe," Ryan teased.

Mark snorted. "If I left it up to her, I'd be waiting until they were forty-something to teach 'em how to do anything more dangerous than tying their shoes."

"She's a mama bear."

"That she is."

Mark led Ryan up to the front of the building that would become a weekend getaway and opened the front door. Inside was barely more than a few walls and a floor. There was a big, empty space where the kitchen should be, and save for a little bar fridge wedged into one corner and a microwave sitting on top of what looked like an old bedside table, the place was a blank canvas.

"It's…how do you say? Rustic?" Ryan grinned.

Mark laughed. "At the moment, it's a shell. I've got a friend who's going to do all the kitchen cabinetry for me, and we're almost done with the wiring."

Ryan walked toward a huge window overlooking the view at the back. If someone had told him it was a painted mural instead of a window, he would have believed them. Outside, the lake stretched into the distance, surrounded by more fall-toned beauty.

"We should be able to get some good ice-fishing out there in the winter," Mark said.

"Since when are you the outdoorsy lumberjack type?"

"Mandy would certainly like that." Mark waggled his eyebrows, and Ryan punched him in the arm like he used to when they were kids shit-stirring each other. "I've had this itch the last few years, ever since the boys were born."

"An itch?"

Mark smoothed a hand over his burgeoning beard. "It's my responsibility as a dad to make memories for them."

Ryan looked back at the view, watching a leaf drift to the ground, swinging back and forth and turning a bit in the breeze before settling with its fallen brothers and sisters.

"And I don't necessarily want the same memories we had growing up."

That surprised Ryan. "What was wrong with our childhood?"

"Nothin' was wrong with it. But…" Mark stuffed his hands into his pockets in what the family teasingly referred to as his "thinking stance." Ace used to joke that he kept his brain in his pockets. "Almost all I can remember about us being young is car trips to sporting tournaments and waiting around to find out if I'd done enough to make the whole thing seem worth it."

Ryan frowned. It was strange how they could both look at the same memory with completely different eyes.

"I mean, wherever we went for you or Ace, it was expected that you'd dominate," Mark said. "I had to live up to that."

"I had no idea." The sad thing was, Ryan could barely remember any of his brother's sporting events. When they were kids, Mark had been into track-and-field. He'd quickly realized he was stronger than the other kids, rather than faster, and transitioned to lifting weights in his teens. But as for specific events…nada. "I have fond memories of us all piling into Dad's old station wagon," Ryan said. "Remember Blue Betty?"

Mark groaned. "Blue Betty with no A/C and Dad playing that same damn country music album over and over and over? Yeah, I remember that low-level form of psychological torture."

"You, me, and Ace all sitting in the back and taunting one another until Mom threatened to take the snacks away." Ryan laughed. How could his brother not look back on that and smile?

"I'm not trying to say we didn't have good times.

But when I think about Mom and Dad having to cart us all over the country for things, always waiting for one game to finish and another one to start…that's not the kind of life I want for Mandy and the boys."

A question hovered on Ryan's tongue—what other kind of life *was* there? He knew that said more about his love of competition than it did about the memories themselves. Sure, there'd been some brutally long road trips and a lot of standing around in the rain and the odd night in a shitty motel that smelled like mold and polyester duvets. But the fact that they were all there as a family, pushing to make each other better, supporting one another…wasn't that what family was all about?

"I can tell your head is basically about to explode while you try to relate to what I just said," Mark quipped drily.

"Yeah, a bit." Ryan looked at his brother as if he didn't quite know the man next to him as much as he thought he did.

"I don't want my boys growing up thinking the only way to get through life is by thinking you have to perform all the damn time. I don't want their life to be endless competition. I want them to get dirt under their fingernails and spend all day on a boat, not catching a single fish, but still having a great time because they've been watching the clouds shift overhead."

"You want them to spend a whole day *not* achieving the thing they set out to do." Ryan blinked.

"Is this…have you been hitting the stash at work?"

Despite the serious tone of the conversation, Mark shot his brother an amused smile. "I'm sure to you, Mr. Competition, it must sound like I'm smoking something."

"It sounds like some crunchy granola hippie stuff, to be honest."

"I guess I want to them be kids. To be messy and to make mistakes and do all the stuff that we seem to have lost along the way of forcing them to sit through hours of homework and after-school activities and every other bit of pressure we pile on them to make sure they have a chance in life. I want things to be… simpler."

Ryan stared out at the water, watching the boat putter around in slow, sweeping arcs. "Life isn't simple."

Lord knew he understood *that*.

"It's not simple because we complicate it every step of the way," Mark replied. "I'm trying to create a haven here away from all that. When we come out to the lake, I want it to be peaceful and relaxing and… high-quality family time."

The love Mark had for his wife and his twin boys radiated. He'd always been a family guy, but now when Ryan looked at his brother, he could see how far their paths had diverged. Ryan hadn't come home as much as he should have in the last few years. Too busy training and doing everything he could to win a World Series. In that time, it was almost like he and

Mark had become different people.

"This place certainly is a haven," Ryan said.

"I take being a dad seriously. I want my boys to grow up understanding what's truly important—that it's the people and relationships that make our lives whole, not accolades or chasing the next gold star."

"You mean not a life like mine."

"That's not what I meant." Mark shook his head.

"Yeah, it is." Ryan nodded. "And that's fine. This life *isn't* for everyone. Hell, I'd say it's not for most people."

"Are you happy?"

The question took Ryan by surprise, and he could only answer with the words that were programmed into him. "Of course."

But if he thought about it a little longer, dug a little deeper...*was* he?

"I mean..." He sighed. "Maybe not right now, with everything that's going on. Knowing I'm about to face a contract renewal while injured is stressful as hell."

"But in general, when you're at full capacity?"

For the first time, Ryan wasn't sure. Was he proud of all he'd achieved in his career? Yes. Was there still more work to be done? Absolutely. But was it also hard to keep sacrificing things like family time and relationships and normal-people things?

Yes.

He swallowed. Coming home had stirred up some of those doubts he'd tried so hard to ignore— like that maybe he'd sacrificed too much somewhere along the way. But thinking about that was pointless.

Only...he *had* thought about it last week, with Sloane in his arms. After they'd defiled her vanity, he'd picked her up and carried her to bed. They'd made love again, lazy and slow, and then she'd been snuggled into his side, her hair draped all over him. The way she'd looked up at him, big gray-blue eyes sparkling like drops of dew on a clear spring morning, had filled him with a sensation he'd never known before—contentment.

Who wanted to be content? Being content meant stagnation and stillness and stalling. It meant inertia. It meant...not achieving.

Yet, Ryan had felt none of those things with her. In fact, being with Sloane, stroking her hair and finding all the little details of her—like the cluster of freckles on her shoulder that looked like a constellation and the way her eyes had a thin rim of navy around the edge if you looked real close—was anything *but* inertia. It was like finding the pieces of a puzzle that finally made you able to see the big picture coming together—it wasn't a final piece, necessarily. But it was an important piece.

That's not *how this is supposed to feel. Sex isn't an important step toward your future.*

Though he'd be lying if he said it had been only about sex. What he shared with Sloane was as much about the before and after as the act itself.

"You're not going to answer that basic question?" Mark asked.

"I don't need to prove my happiness to anyone," Ryan replied, more than a little peevishly.

"Only yourself, big brother."

Did he need to prove it to himself? Or could he believe that he was truly happy?

"Anyway, you're welcome here any time." Mark slapped a hand down on his back. "Seriously, once we're up and running, whenever you need to get away from it all. My house is your house."

"Thanks, man."

He couldn't help but be unsettled. It was like Mark had found some little chink in his armor and was poking at it with a stick to see whether it would hold. That was Mark in a nutshell. He was a deep thinker. A ponderer. Someone who wasn't satisfied to look only at the surface of a thing.

Right now, Ryan wasn't sure he wanted to look beneath the surface of his life, because from his vantage it looked mostly calm and still. His injury was a ripple, for sure. And yes, contract negotiations were complicated by his injury. But he'd get back to Toronto soon and get on with chasing his career dreams in no time.

If he looked closer, though, if he broke through that mostly calm and still surface, he might find a tangled web of things underneath. Doubts and fears and thoughts he wasn't yet ready to acknowledge.

Signs that could lead him to the fact that he wasn't as happy as he claimed.

• • •

Sloane had changed her outfit more times for this catch-up than for any date she'd ever been on. Was she too dressy? Too casual? Too many dinosaurs? Not enough dinosaurs? Should she go with the cute shoes and hope the ground wasn't too muddy from the day's rain or be practical?

In the end, she settled on a pair of sturdy tan boots that laced up tight. But she made them look cute by pairing them with black tights, a pleated check skirt in autumnal shades, and a sweater she'd found at a thrift store years ago, which was black and had an adorable pterodactyl on the front.

And yes, pterodactyls *could* be adorable, especially since this one had a little gemstone for its eye.

At the last minute, Sloane threw on a trench coat and stuffed a knitted hat into her bag in case the temperature dropped. She parked her car and walked up the street toward Kisspresso Café, her heart pounding.

She was having coffee with Trudy. They'd exchanged numbers at the Bowers' house, and when Trudy had messaged yesterday to ask Sloane if she wanted to meet up, Sloane couldn't type YES! fast enough.

Maybe that was poor form. Was making friends like dating—were you supposed to play a little hard-to-get? Did she seem desperate? She'd never been too good at playing games. But knowing what it was like to be left out of social events and gatherings, Sloane never looked a gift horse in the mouth.

The path was littered with gold-toned leaves, and she carefully avoided the slippery bits. The sun had almost set, with only a band of orange against the horizon, and the dim, dusky light made the warm glow coming from the café look even more inviting.

She wiped her hands down the front of her skirt. Why was she so damn nervous?

It felt like a big deal. Because friendship was a core piece of the puzzle for her life in Kissing Creek. It was a core piece of the puzzle in her dream life. Yeah, a romantic relationship would be nice, of course, but she knew that would come eventually. It shouldn't be rushed. Besides, didn't most people meet their spouses through friends anyway?

So that was a later problem. The friendship thing was what mattered now.

"Go inside and stop being a chicken," she said under her breath.

She pushed open the door to Kisspresso Café. The pink-and-red decor was cheery and welcoming, and they even had little pink ghosts drawn on all their chalkboard menus. Sloane's gaze roamed the café until she spotted Trudy sitting at one of the tables on the far side of the room.

She was tapping at her phone, her expression a little tense. But as Sloane approached, Trudy looked up, and a smile blossomed on her lips.

"Hi!" she said, jumping out of her seat. She leaned in, as if to give Sloane a hug, and then froze. "Uh, I'm a hugger. Is that okay?"

"Sure." Sloane reached out and embraced the other woman, catching a whiff of some light perfume—something warm and inviting. "I'm a hugger, too."

"Oh good." Trudy pulled back and laughed, cringing a little. "Sorry, that was kind of... I don't know why I'm being awkward. I'm nervous. Is that silly? It's silly, isn't it?"

Her words came out with a flurry of headshakes, and Sloane could only smile. "I was a bit nervous, too. I changed my outfit several times. More than several."

Trudy's shoulders dropped a little, as if she'd let go of some tension. "I like your sweater."

"Thanks. It's a pterodactyl. Well, not really. Pterodactyl is kind of a misnomer. These types of dinosaurs are actually called pterosaurs, which means 'wing lizards.'"

Okay, maybe don't go in too heavy with the dinosaur facts.

"Cool." Trudy's eyes lit up. "I don't know much about dinosaurs, but I always enjoyed visiting that section of any museum."

They left their belongings at the table so they could order coffee at the counter, and a few minutes later, they were seated back at the table, beverages in hand.

"So, you've only come back to Kissing Creek recently, right?" Sloane said as she cradled a pink mug with gold detailing between her palms. The sweet scent of her vanilla latte curled into the air.

"Yeah." Trudy nodded. Her gaze dropped for a second before coming back up. "I got engaged and moved to California with a guy I thought was *the one*, and he turned out to be…not that."

The pain in her voice made Sloane's chest clench. "I'm sorry."

"Don't be. Better that I figured out sooner rather than later." She sighed. "I guess it would have been better if I hadn't burned so many bridges on the way out of town."

"Can I ask what happened?"

"He was a guy with big dreams, which I found attractive. He wanted to move to L.A. to become an actor, and I was happy to follow him. I thought I loved him…" She sighed. "My family and friends had all tried to warn me from the beginning. I assumed it was because they didn't want me to leave, so we had a big fight about it. I felt like they weren't supporting me."

"It sounds like they weren't," Sloane said.

"Don't get me wrong, in reality I should *never* have followed him there. He was everything they said about him—a liar, a cheat." She brought her mug to her lips and sipped. "But I'm still an adult who needs to live my own life and make my own decisions, even if that means making mistakes."

Sloane nodded. "Sometimes telling someone not to do something is the quickest way to get them to do it."

"So true." Trudy sank a little farther into her

chair, as if she'd finally, fully relaxed. "But when I said I was coming back, I got a whole lot of 'I told you so' from my mother. My sisters weren't much better, and the friends I'd had since high school are too busy with their happy lives to see me much. It's been...lonely."

"That's rough."

Trudy nodded. "I want a fresh start. So I'm changing jobs and living in a new part of town and trying to rebuild my life."

"By making new friends?"

"Exactly."

A moment of understanding passed between them. Owning up to mistakes was difficult. Starting over was even worse, and it only seemed to get harder with age.

"Have you ever made a mistake like that?" Trudy asked. "Something so stupid you look back on it and wonder if an alien had taken over your body?"

She thought about it for a moment. "I honestly don't know if I have. I guess the way I see it is that all mistakes have led us to where we are now, which is where we need to be."

Or maybe it was more the fact that while Sloane *thought* she put herself out into the world, it was more a front than anything else. She could easily hide the true, tender part of herself behind her quirky outfits and sense of humor. Maybe that's why friendships had been hard to come by, because she was too afraid to let people get close. Too afraid that, if they did, they wouldn't like the real her.

If you keep doing that, then how do you expect to ever make real friends?

She thought for a moment about how Ryan made her feel—like she could be herself, be at ease. That's what she wanted in all her relationships—friends, family, and otherwise.

"I, uh…" She sucked in a big breath. "I think I haven't made a mistake like that because I've never put myself out there enough to get hurt. You got hurt because you were willing to give something a try. You were brave enough to take a chance."

"I never looked at it like that before." Surprise streaked across Trudy's face, and for a moment, she looked a little emotional. "Thank you. Everyone else I've spoken to criticized me for following him. You're the first person to say something positive."

"You're welcome," Sloane said with a tentative smile.

Trudy nodded, and a big smile lit up her face. "I'm glad Ryan introduced us."

Something warm and hopeful lit a spark inside Sloane's chest. Something that felt like the beginning of a special relationship. "Me too."

CHAPTER FIFTEEN

Book club day was always the highlight of Sloane's week. The library ran several different book clubs—a nonfiction one targeted at parents, the Big Little Book Club for kids under twelve, the Cliff-Hangers for teens, and the adult fiction book club, Believe in Your Shelf. That made for about one book club every week, and Sloane always made it her mission to decorate accordingly.

Since it was time for the members of her club to gather 'round and chat about *Stormy Pleasures*, Sloane had dug deep into her box of tricks. Each chair was draped with a red feather boa, and she'd made black masks from craft paper and tied them with pieces of silky red ribbon. On the snack table, she had the usual coffee urn with paper cups, bowls of chips, and a tray of donuts from Glazed and Confused, which she'd paid for out of her own pocket. Somehow, her usual flavor choice—Frenching Vanilla—felt even more appropriate than ever.

She hadn't been able to help buying a bag of penis straws from the party store—the kind usually seen at bachelorette celebrations—to go with the jugs of orange juice and iced tea. For a minute, she'd worried if it might offend someone, but then she figured that if they'd read *Stormy Pleasures*, they probably weren't too concerned about miniature plastic dicks.

"Look at all this!" Pat poked her head into the room they used for book clubs, among other events, and grinned. Today, she had a bright orange-and-green silk scarf knotted around her neck and gold hoop earrings that were so big they almost touched her shoulders. "Maybe I should've brought my hot date to book club."

Pat and Hot Grandpa were already onto date number three, and Pat had practically been floating in and out of work each day. Maybe that was how it felt when you were dating someone who was looking for the same things you were.

Sloane, on the other hand, had been doing this awkward dance with Ryan every time they were in the same room. On one hand, she had to restrain herself from wrapping her arms around his neck and dragging his mouth down to hers every single time she set eyes on him. On the other hand...they were both acting like it never happened, which made it hard to look him in the eye.

Because any time she did, all she could remember was that night. The rattle of the vanity as he thrust into her, the hard grip of his hands at her thighs, the softness of his lips on hers. The way he held her afterward like it meant something.

It doesn't mean a thing.

Sure, her head might say that, but her heart mightily disagreed.

"You're welcome to join us," Sloane replied. "I'm sure the rest of book club wouldn't mind if you brought Hot Grandpa along."

Pat chuckled. "I really need to stop calling him that or it's going to come out at the wrong time."

"Hot Grandpa, do me harder!"

It was at that moment, as Sloane was doing her poorest *When Hally Met Sarry* impression, that Ryan walked into the room. His dark brows were crinkled in confusion, but the edge of his lip was most definitely ticking up into an amused smile.

"On that note, it's my cue to leave." Pat was out of there so fast, there was only a Pat-shaped cloud of dust where she once stood.

"Coward," Sloane muttered.

"I don't know if I walked in on that conversation at exactly the right moment or exactly the *wrong* moment," he said, laughing.

"Depends on your preferences."

"Like yours...for hot grandpas?" He leaned against the back of one of the chairs that had been set up in a circle for book club, looking unfairly attractive. A soft black sweater hugged his broad shoulders and muscular chest, and it looked so cozy and touchable that her hands almost ached to reach out to him.

Instead, Sloane busied herself by making sure that every single chip bowl was filled to the exact same height.

"You know damn well what my preferences are," she said, lowering her voice. Ryan came up next to her, and she sucked in a breath, the nipped-in waist of her skirt feeling like a vise.

She'd curled her hair that morning, carefully wrapping each strand around her wand until they all fell in perfectly uniform, loose, and springy spirals around her shoulders and back. Ryan reached for one, tugging on it playfully.

"D-grade dinosaur movies?" he teased.

"And sexy novels." She rolled her eyes. It was easier to pretend like he didn't affect her than admit the truth—which was that every single night since they'd slept together, she'd thought about him. That she'd picked up her phone to text him so many times but kept chickening out. "What are you doing here, anyway?"

He held up the copy of *Stormy Pleasures* she'd loaned him.

Her eyebrows arched. "You finished it?"

"Stayed up late last night because I wanted to see what happened. Are you proud of me?" His smile crinkled the edges of his eyes, and Sloane almost swooned like a Jane Austen heroine.

A man who got excited about reading was her ultimate weakness.

"What did you think?" she asked, holding out her hand to take the book from him.

"Shouldn't I save that for book club?" He held it out of her grasp.

Sloane raised an eyebrow. "You're staying for book club?"

"Sure am."

"You know your mother is in this book club." She could barely hold back a laugh—especially since his mom reading the book was the entire crux of how they'd met.

"She can't make it, unfortunately."

"Oh no!"

"She'll be okay. It's a migraine, but when she gets hit with one of those…" He shook his head, worry forming a crease in the middle of his brows. "Only a dark room and a bed will help her."

"And you're taking her place?" Sloane glanced around the room, an evil little laugh bubbling up in her chest. The thought of Ryan wearing a feather boa and drinking orange juice with a penis straw…well, *that* would make it a book club to remember.

"I figured you wouldn't mind me filling in."

"Only if you participate fully," she said, doing her best to keep a straight face.

"You're not going to scare me away, Sloane." Ryan leaned forward, his bright blue eyes laser-locking onto hers. "I already know you're all sizzle and no steak."

Her mouth popped open. "What's *that* supposed to mean?"

"You act all tough, but when it comes down to it, you're a soft, little kitten." His smile turned from teasing to wolfish, like he thought he'd gained the upper hand.

Out of the corner of her eye, Sloane could see the

book club members trickling in. But if she shushed Ryan now, he'd only think she was embarrassed, and that would mean he'd won. So she held her tongue. Held his gaze. Held on to control with every shred of her willpower.

"After we had sex on your bedroom vanity, you've barely been able to look me in the eye."

It was true, things had been mega awkward, but not because Sloane regretted sleeping with Ryan. Not at all. The only thing she regretted was how much she wanted it to happen again. How much, if it wouldn't get her fired as well as giving her a criminal record for public indecency, she wanted to push him to the ground and do it again right now.

"We'll have to continue this conversation later," she said, gritting her back teeth as the room started to fill and one of the older members wandered up next to them at the snack table.

Mrs. Nellie Silverman was a five-foot-nothing speed knitter with gray hair and a permanent smile. She had a raspy voice, even though she'd given up smoking years ago, and had kind brown eyes that were always crinkled in laughter. Sloane had momentarily forgotten she was part of the book club, because she'd been away for a few months, visiting her grandkids in Cape Cod.

"What's this? Fancy straws?" She reached for a straw and brought it right up close in front of her face. "I forgot my glasses again."

Sloane had a moment of panic, thinking maybe

she'd gone a little too far with the decorating theme. Had anyone in the library system been fired for using penis propaganda before? Ryan's eyes almost bugged out of his head as the older woman brought the tiny, phallic object right up to her face to inspect it.

"It's, uh…" Sloane glanced at Ryan, and he shrugged.

"Oh, it's a penis." The older woman cackled and made a motion by crooking her little finger. "So small, like my first husband."

Ryan snorted so loud he had to turn away from them and compose himself for a minute.

"Oh, come on," Nellie said, shooting them a look as she popped the straw into a glass and poured herself some iced tea. "Don't tell me you youngsters get all uptight about human anatomy. You know you weren't delivered by a stork, right?"

"That's a good point," Sloane replied, her cheeks aching from suppressed laughter. It wasn't at Nellie, but at the fact that Ryan's cheeks were red as anything. "Do you know Ryan Bower, Mrs. Silverman?"

"Gaye and Alfie's boy, of course." She reached out and patted Ryan on the arm. "So nice to see you, dear. Would you like a drink?"

Ryan looked like he wanted to shoot daggers at Sloane, but of course he'd been raised too well to be rude. "Juice would be great, thank you, Mrs. Silverman."

She plucked another straw and popped it into a cup for Ryan before pouring the bright orange liquid into it. "Here you go."

Curiosity had drawn more of the group toward the snack table—though whether it was because of the fun decorations, the lure of sugar and salt, *or* because they had a famous MLB pitcher in attendance, Sloane wasn't quite sure. Ryan waded the straw through his drink as though not quite sure what to do.

"Stop playing with it," Sloane said. "Get to sucking."

His lip twitched as he moved aside to let the other book club members get to the food. Sloane grabbed a drink for herself and followed him.

"Now, how would you feel if I said that to you?" he asked, his voice low and rumbly. "That's not very gentlemanly."

"Good thing I'm not a gentleman."

"You most certainly are not." Ryan brushed his gaze over Sloane from head to toe in a way that made her feel like she wasn't wearing a cute pink top and pleated check skirt and high-heeled boots. Oh no, the way he looked at her was as if she was wearing nothing at all.

"Right!" Sloane clapped her hands together to get the attention of everyone in the room—and hopefully shake herself out of whatever spell Ryan was putting on her right now. "The October meeting of Believe in Your Shelf will start in a few minutes. Please help yourself to some snacks and drinks, and then grab a seat in the circle."

Ryan leaned in toward Sloane and kept his voice low. "It's kind of hot when you get all Miss In-Charge."

"You like that, huh?" She raised an eyebrow.

"Nothing like a woman who knows how to command a room." He winked.

"I would have figured you prefer being in charge, being such a Type-A high achiever and certified grumpy pants."

"Certified? You think I went to the Grump Association of America to get these skills? Nuh-uh. That's all natural talent, baby." He waggled his eyebrows, and she laughed.

Dammit. Why did Ryan have to be so charming and funny underneath it all? It would have been much safer for her heart if he really *had* been a heartless grump.

As the rest of the book club took their seats, she had to tear herself away from him so she could do her job. Mrs. Silverman was patting the seat next to her, and Ryan obliged, folding his long body down onto the empty plastic chair and talking to the older woman like she was a long-lost friend.

Sloane took her position at the head of the room. "I can't wait to hear how you all enjoyed this month's book club pick, *Stormy Pleasures*."

A titter went through the room, and several heads were nodding enthusiastically. Ryan sat back and watched Sloane, his piercing eyes holding her prisoner while a sexy smirk lifted one corner of his mouth.

"Who wants to start us off with some initial impressions of the book?" Sloane asked. "What were you expecting going into it, and what did you get out of it? Maybe you could start us off, Ryan?"

Sloane stifled a smile as all heads swung in his direction, and he stilled, the penis straw caught between his lips. She had to force herself not to laugh, because she didn't want to discourage anyone from speaking up. But if Ryan thought he could sit there and unnerve her with his sexy, broody stare, then she was going to fire right back at him.

He set his glass down on the floor by his feet and then crossed one long leg at the knee, resting his ankle on the opposite thigh. The pose made Sloane's throat tighten. It was such a commanding pose, such a masculine pose, and he had the attention of everyone in the room.

"You know…at first I thought I wasn't going to be a fan of this book. I assumed it was all about shock value and the sex was only there to titillate," Ryan said thoughtfully.

"It titillated me!" one of the female members of the group piped up. She was a woman in her sixties and a friend of Ryan's parents. Her friend, who was sitting next to her, nudged her in the side with a sharp elbow. "What? We might be getting old, but we're not dead."

"Hear, hear!" Marcia Wagner, a retired schoolteacher and grandmother of ten, clapped her hands. "I'm sick of everybody thinking that sex is only for young people. Where do you all think you came from, huh? Why, my darling Rufus and I do it three times a week like clockwork. If you don't use it, you lose it!"

Okay, *now* Ryan looked like a deer in headlights. He'd probably known all these people since he was a little kid. Maybe they were friends of his parents, or grandparents to his old classmates.

"Although, I have to say," Marcia continued, "we need to talk about chapter twenty-one. How is that even *possible*?"

"Right?" Ryan threw his hands up in the air. "Who has that much flexibility?"

"Well, dear, if *you* can't do it, then what hope do the rest of us have?" Marcia shook her head. "I had my hip replaced last year, and I can tell you now, my body can't make those kinds of shapes anymore."

The group dissolved into a passionate debate about the accuracy—and, thus, replicability—of chapter twenty-one. One of the women tried to enact a demonstration with her friend, which caused the whole room to dissolve into laughter. Sloane couldn't remember the last time the group had been quite this animated over a book.

"Okay, okay," she said, motioning for everyone to sit back down. "Now that we've got that out of our systems, can we talk about the book and not just the steamy bits?"

"I believe Ryan was going to share his opinion," Marcia said. "Sorry I derailed the conversation."

"That's okay," Ryan replied graciously. "The biggest thing I took from this story was that it's possible to be more than one thing."

"What do you mean?" Sloane asked.

"Rita is an actress, right? And she's only ever been an actress, right from when she took her first job as a child. Her whole life has been about performing for an audience and playing a role—that's all she knew. She needs to learn who she is *outside* all that. It takes her secret affair with Jonathan to show her that it's possible for her to have more in her life than her work. And same goes for him."

"You're right." One of the book club members close to Ryan nodded. "Jonathan spent his whole life clawing his way to the top of the political food chain, and he ruthlessly cut out anything that didn't align to that dream. But being with Rita showed him that he'd sacrificed so much. Behind closed doors, he was…"

"Lonely," Ryan supplied. There was a soft resonance to his words, like the distant echo of a church bell.

It sucked the breath from Sloane's lungs, because she knew—deep down to the very marrow of her bones—what loneliness felt like. She knew how it made you ache, like a deep, damp cold you couldn't shake. She knew how it haunted you, lurking in the shadows and waiting for a moment where you felt okay before it revealed itself.

"If he'd continued down that path, when his career was over, he would've had nothing," Ryan added. "He would've given up everything for his work. For *that* version of himself."

"The only version he thought existed," Sloane said with a nod.

"But it wasn't the only version," he said. "With her, he become the whole person he knew he could be. Not just this two-dimensional part."

"That's insightful."

"Yes, great job, Ryan," Nellie Silverman said encouragingly. "Here, you get to wear a feather boa for the rest of the meeting."

She plucked the fluffy red boa from the back of her chair and handed it to Ryan, who simply nodded and draped it around his shoulders like the good sport he was. "Thank you."

"It looks fabulous on you, dear." She patted him on the arm. "Red is your color."

They looked at each other across the library meeting room, something passing between them that felt like a fist around Sloane's heart. Her whole life she'd thought it was paramount to be remembered. But in that moment, she realized that wasn't quite correct. It was paramount to be understood. To be known.

And to have someone in her life she could know and understand back.

Right now, she saw Ryan in a deeper and more meaningful way than she'd ever seen another person. He'd bared part of himself in sharing this insight, and it felt a whole lot like he'd entrusted her with something special.

CHAPTER SIXTEEN

By the end of the book club meeting, Ryan found himself laughing with the other members and feeling more at home than he'd been in a long time. In fact, he wasn't sure he'd *ever* laughed so much as he had in the last couple of weeks. It was almost like a stone block had started lifting from his shoulders, and with each genuine heave of his chest, it got a little lighter.

Sloane was right. When he'd first arrived in Kissing Creek, he'd been a grumpy asshole. He'd always been a serious guy—contentious, hard-working, driven. He'd carried the weight of the world as though it was a normal part of life. As though that crushing pressure was the norm. But maybe he needed to make room in his life for pleasure.

Maybe he needed to make room right now.

Sloane stood around talking with some of the book club members who hadn't yet trickled out of the library. She looked radiant, dressed up in her quirky style and smiling at everyone, no doubt making them all feel special and unique in that way she had a talent for.

He hung back, waiting for her to finish, and as the last person left the library, her gaze drifted to him. She gathered up the remaining penis straws and feather boas. Ryan had kept picking at the little bits of red fluff stuck to his pants, and he was sure he'd be finding it for a week.

As if sensing his thoughts, Sloane came over and rose up onto her tip toes, stretching her arm out to extract another small red feather from his hair. "You look like you got attacked by a Sesame Street character."

"Or a stripper."

"Nah, not enough body glitter for that." She winked. "How was your first book club?"

"I have to say, I was impressed." He stuck his hands into his pockets. "They got all their dirty jokes out in the first few minutes, and then it was a very thought-provoking discussion."

"I guess I was asking for it, putting these on the snack table." She waved the straws in a way that made him laugh. "I try really hard to make each meeting as fun as possible. This is my favorite part of the job."

"Yeah?" He helped her pack up, discarding the empty donut boxes and moving the chairs and tables back into their usual positions.

"Totally. I get paid to sit around and talk about books for a few hours with people who are equally as passionate about reading as I am. What could possibly be better than that?"

Her genuine enthusiasm for her work was contagious. "That's how I feel about my job most days. When I'm tossing the ball and standing outside with the sun beating down…it's like all my childhood dreams come true."

She looked at him with a curiosity that made him burn on the inside. It was like a question hovered on the tip of her tongue, but she wasn't ready to ask it yet. He only recognized that in her because he felt the same. He had a question he wanted to ask, too. Several, in fact. But one circled in his head louder than the others.

"Do you want to grab a drink?"

He noted the warmth in Sloane's face, the flare of interest in her eyes, and the sparkle of excitement zipping across her face. She felt it, too. So why had she been avoiding him all week?

"I…" She tore her gaze away for a moment, as if trying to figure out what to say. "Do you want to come to my place? I'm pretty sure I have a bottle of something gathering dust that we could drink."

"Well, when you put it like that…" He laughed, and she blushed. "That sounds great."

Fifteen minutes later, Ryan was sitting at Sloane's dining room table. She wasn't kidding about the "something gathering dust" back home. There was a bottle of vodka that she'd liberated from the back of her cupboard and had brought to the table along with two shot glasses.

"When I said let's grab a drink, I didn't mean let's get wasted on potato juice," he said with a laugh.

Sloane snorted. "Potato juice, I like that. And what's wrong with shots?"

"Maybe I'm a cheap drunk?"

It wasn't true. Despite laying off the liquor every season to keep himself as healthy as possible, the Bowers knew how to hold their own. He and both his brothers could drink anyone under the table while still walking a straight line with ease.

Sloane raised an eyebrow disbelievingly. "Why do I feel like that's a ploy to throw me off the scent?"

"The scent of what?"

"You." She plonked the glasses down and then opened the vodka. "You're tricky like that."

"How so?"

"Well, you led me to believe you were this prudish grump."

"Uh no, that was your assumption. A *false* assumption."

"But," she said, holding up a finger, "it was a trick. You're not like that at all."

"No, I'm not. I can suck on penis straws with the best of them." He grinned.

Sloane poured two shots, filling the small glasses right to the brim. Ryan wasn't quite sure where this was going—he'd have settled for a beer somewhere. But Sloane inviting him back to her place had lit a flame of hope inside him. Of anticipation.

He wanted her again, with a hunger unmatched even by the first time he came here. Because now he knew how good they were together, how compatible.

How combustible.

And for the first time in as long as Ryan could remember, he wanted to feel something that had nothing to do with his work. He wanted to be someone other than Ryan Bower, starting pitcher for the Toronto Blizzards. He wanted to forget all about his injury and the uncertainty of his future and the weight of his own expectations. He wanted to be a regular guy with a crush on a girl and the hope it might lead somewhere.

And he did hope it would lead somewhere—to bed. But also, somewhere beyond that.

"I was thinking we could play a drinking game." Sloane carefully slid the shot glass along the table. "Truth or dare."

He looked at her leaning over the table so that her top showed a hint of cleavage, a saucy sparkle in her eye. Her glossy hair hung in loose spirals over one shoulder, and faded pink lipstick stained her lips. Temptation hung heavy in the air. She was weaving a spell on him, that was for damn sure.

"Why not?" he said casually. Though Ryan should have been anything but casual right then—because Sloane could have asked him for the moon, and he would have done anything in his power to give it to her.

Coming home to Kissing Creek was only supposed to be an escape from his problems. Yet, staring into Sloane's beautiful face, he was starting to think he'd stumbled on something else.

Something that felt a whole lot like everything.

• • •

There was playing with fire, and then there was jamming a bunch of fireworks into a cardboard box, pouring some gasoline over it, and taking a flame-thrower to the whole thing. But when Ryan asked her to go for a drink—a sexy, hopeful, utterly disarming smile on his handsome face—how could she possibly resist? Now she was pouring vodka shots under the guise of playing truth of dare, when really, what she was trying to do was loosen herself up. Any *why* would she need to do that, exactly?

Because I want something to blame my bad decisions on. I want to do the wrong thing and say, "Oh, that silly vodka, always a bad influence," and go on my merry, hungover way.

"You go first, since it was your idea," he said, with a gentlemanly gesture of his hand. "Truth or dare?"

"Truth," she said, staring at the vodka in front of her. She only had to drink if she didn't want to answer, so there was a chance this terrible plan might backfire anyway.

Ryan rubbed a hand over his jaw as he thought about what to ask. "What's the best thing that happened to you this week?"

Sloane didn't even need to think about her answer. "I had coffee with Trudy after work the other day."

Ryan's face lit up, and the happiness was so genuine it made Sloane's stomach do a backflip. "That's great."

"We went to the Kisspresso Café and chatted. But before we knew it, we'd been there for three hours and the staff were trying to clean up so they could close for the night." It made her feel warm and fuzzy just thinking about it.

Trudy was lovely. She was thoughtful and perhaps a bit damaged, which Sloane totally identified with. But she had a wickedly sharp sense of humor, and they'd talked about everything from funny things about the town, to books they were currently reading, to dream travel destinations, and even some of their hopes and plans for the future. They were *real* conversations, and it felt like the beginning of a *real* friendship.

"I knew you would get along well with her," Ryan said with a confident nod of his head.

How was it even possible for Ryan to know something like that about her? Something…deeper than her quirky outfits and bright smiles? Something true?

"What made you so sure?" she asked.

Ryan shrugged. "Trudy's a no-BS person. She faces things head on, like coming home even though she knew it would be hard."

"And you think I'm like that, too?"

"You sure faced me head on. And you're not a person who sits passively on the sidelines, because you're always working to make things better and putting your hand up to help out."

She *did* always try to make things better—whether it was broadening the horizons of the book club or suggesting new fundraising ideas at the volunteer committee meetings. Even when it came to her own life, she was always trying to make improvements like building relationships with her colleagues and finding new and interesting educational videos to send to her half-sister.

"Okay, well…" She was feeling a little shaken by Ryan's kind words. "Your turn now. Truth or dare?"

"Dare." He didn't even hesitate.

"Drink your shot with no hands." Sloane grinned with all the unrepentant wickedness of an evil supervillain.

"You think you got me with that, smarty pants?" Ryan shoved his chair back and stood, making a cocky snorting sound. "You forget, I went to my share of frat parties in college."

"Ah, of course. College jock." She leaned back in her chair to watch him.

He put his hands behind his back and leaned forward so he was closer to the shot glass. Ryan's piercing blue eyes captured hers over the top of the glass, and her breath caught in the back of her throat. She loved him like this—playful, fun, up for anything. It was like he'd let his walls down with her. He'd checked the serious, guarded part of his personality at the door and now the real Ryan was out to play.

He wrapped his lips around the shot glass and steadied himself. Sloane pressed a hand over her mouth to try and stifle a laugh. Either he was going to master this or he was going to end up with "potato juice" all down his top.

Ryan tossed his head back, taking the shot glass with him and downing all the liquid in one easy gulp. Not a single drop escaped his lips, and he remained splatter-free. He plunked the glass down on the table and pumped a fist into the air.

"Show off," Sloane grumbled, reaching for the bottle of vodka and topping him up.

"Truth or dare?"

"Dare," she replied, stretching the word out slowly. "Don't make me regret choosing this."

"Talk like a pirate."

Sloane groaned. "Seriously?"

"Or you can drink your shot. Which you made me do, I'd like to point out." He dropped back down into his chair. His knees fell apart in a way that said he was taking ownership of the space, and it was the sexiest thing she'd ever seen.

He felt comfortable here. Comfortable with her.

"Argggh, me matey." She cringed at her terrible rendition of a pirate. "I'm Captain Jack Sparrow and I like rum. Umm…treasure and ships and scurvy and stuff."

Ryan burst out laughing. "Scurvy, really?"

"Vitamin C deficiency is a serious topic, Ryan." She planted her hands on her hips. "It was a problem for a lot of men of the sea."

"Fine, I'll pay it." He grinned. "Dare."

"Another dare? You are a glutton for punishment." She tapped a finger to the side of her cheek. "Show me your best dance moves."

"No way." He reached straight for the shot and downed it.

Sloane gasped. "Are you a terrible dancer? No! I have to see!"

"I drank the shot." He shoved it forward so she could fill it up again.

"But—"

"No buts." He shook his head, unwilling to move. "I have two left feet and the approximate dance-floor coordination of a newborn giraffe."

"Party pooper." She rolled her eyes. "Fine. Truth."

"When was your first kiss?"

She scrubbed a hand over her face. Could she even tell this story? It was so mortifying. "A game of spin the bottle when I was fourteen, and I had a piece of lettuce stuck between my teeth. I spent the rest of the year being known as Lettuce Breath."

Ryan's eyes went wide. "No."

"Let's not dwell on it, please."

"But—"

Sloane held up her hand. "Moving right along."

He chuckled and shook his head. "Fine, truth."

"No! I was going to ask you to dance again."

He folded his arms across his chest. "I know. And I don't feel like getting wasted that quickly."

"Now you're encouraging me to come up with some really deep and personal truth questions." She rested her elbows on the table and dropped her chin into her palms so she could watch him closely. Sloane wasn't sure when was the last time she'd had so much fun.

Hell, she couldn't remember the last time she'd gotten to know someone the way she was getting to know Ryan.

"What's the biggest lie you've ever told?"

His face turned serious for a moment, and she could see things ticking over in his mind. The drink remained untouched. If he had to think about it that hard, then he probably didn't have much in the way of lies. Usually, if people had something big to hide, it would show on their face immediately.

"I told my younger brother once that I thought one of his friends was a better athlete than he was," Ryan replied solemnly. "But it wasn't true. Ace was the best, and I was being mean."

"That's it? Your big, juicy lie was that you were mean to your younger brother one time." Sloane made a derisive sound and reached for Ryan's shot glass. "I'm not sure you even deserve potato juice."

"What?"

"That's nothing."

He shrugged. "I'm an open book."

"You are *not* an open book."

"Maybe not with most people." The rest of his sentence hung in the air, the unspoken words like a promise of things to come.

But I am with you.

Sloane removed her hand from his glass, feeling a

strange tension building in the air. Truth or Dare was meant to be fun and an excuse to get a little tipsy so she could shrug off some responsibility. But it felt like they were learning something real about each other.

"I'll forgive you for that boring answer if you dance for me," she said, a smile curving on her lips.

"Hard no."

"Not even a little bit? Like, five seconds?"

Ryan shook his head, looking mighty pleased with himself that he had something to hold out. "It's not my fault you don't like the answer to my question, either. Suck it up, Buttercup."

"You did not just say that to me."

"I surely did. Now, truth or dare?"

She narrowed her eyes at him. "Truth."

"What's the biggest lie *you've* ever told?" He leaned back in his seat, his eyes capturing her in a way that made her heart thump in her chest.

For years, she'd craved being known. She'd craved having someone be interested in her beyond the superficial. Now she had an amazing man—a good man—in front of her with curiosity radiating from him. It was too good to be true, she knew it.

Too good to last. But her stupid little heart still fluttered.

"I told my father I wasn't upset when he uninvited me from Thanksgiving," she said, the words slipping out of her so quick and so clear that she didn't have a snowball's chance in hell of stopping them.

"What do you mean he *uninvited* you?"

Ugh. Way to suck the sexy fun out of their little game. "It's nothing. He's got kids with his second wife, and they're all going to her sister's vacation house. It's logistics. Not enough bedrooms."

Ryan's face didn't show anything at all. His eyes were placid and clear as a lake on a cloudless day, and the hard line of his jaw didn't move. She felt compelled to fill the silence.

"I was a bit upset, but I'm over it now. He suggested I host a Friendsgiving type thing."

That's when she saw that Ryan *was* moving. There was tiny little tick in his jaw, almost like he was biting something back. "How nice of him, suggesting that someone else include you when he didn't see fit to do the same. That's convenient."

Well, yeah. It *was* kind of a dick move, although she knew her father hadn't meant it like that. "He's a good man, he's just…"

Sleep-deprived. Distracted. Focused on his real family.

"I'd love to hear how you justify why he's not really an asshole for doing that," Ryan said.

"He's not." She shook her head. "It's…"

There really was no way to justify it.

"You deserve to be included, Sloane. Nobody should be left out by their own damn family."

"We're playing Truth or Dare, not Truth or Dr. Phil." She offered a shaky smile, but the fact was she agreed with Ryan. Being uninvited had really hurt her feelings.

It had been like salt in an already very open, very *raw* wound. A wound that had never felt like it was healing...until now.

"Maybe I'll ask Trudy if she'd like to do something," Sloane said. "Anyway. Truth or dare."

"Truth."

"You really don't want to dance, do you?" She laughed.

"No. Unless you're just trying to get me drunk?"

"Now why would I do that?" She toyed with the edge of her shot glass, still full from the first round.

"I have no idea, but I do know I'd rather answer any truth question than risk scarring you for life with how terrible my dancing is."

"You can't be *that* bad."

"Trust me, I'm that bad."

"You'll answer any question at all, no matter how personal?"

"Bring it on."

She drummed her fingers against the tabletop, not willing to break his stare, not willing to be the first to flinch. It looked like she was going to do this, *without* the adult beverage courage.

"What's your current sexual fantasy?"

She fully expected him to take the shot. Ryan was a hot guy, but he didn't seem like the kind of guy to be *too* honest about deepest, darkest desires, despite his commitment to answer anything. Hell, if he wouldn't even dance in front of her...

But to her surprise, the drink remained untouched.

"You, reenacting that scene from *Stormy Pleasures* where she sneaks into his penthouse while he's showering." Ryan's gaze from across the table was molten hot.

"The one where she strips naked and waits for him like a birthday treat?"

"Yes, that one."

Sloane swallowed, her throat suddenly a little tighter and the spot between her legs pulsing with tension. "You answered that question pretty quickly."

"It's top of mind." He raked a hand through his hair. "Truth or dare?"

"Truth."

"Did you think of anyone specific while you were reading that book?"

Yes. From the second Ryan set foot in the library, he was the one she thought about late at night. It was his face, his body in her fantasies. And now that she'd slept with him, it only made the fantasies stronger and more vivid. They were fueled with memories as well as her imagination.

But Sloane wasn't sure she wanted to admit that. Because the fact was, sexy as her fantasies were, she'd never put a real person into them before. Usually, it was some nameless, generic, hot guy with a rockin' bod. Making Ryan the literal star of her dreams was worrying.

She reached for the shot glass and knocked the vodka back. It burned a little on the way down, because she didn't have the good stuff. She placed the glass back on the table.

"Interesting. So, either it's me and you don't want to admit it, or you're thinking about some other guy and don't want me to know."

Was that...a hint of jealousy in his voice? If only he knew.

"Truth or dare?" she said, keeping her face from revealing anything of the wild, swirling thoughts in her head.

"Dare."

He said the word with reverence, like there was a weight to it. Like he wanted something to come from it. Sloane had two options—get him to take another drink by daring him to dance or...dare him to do what she really wanted. Her brain was screaming at her to stop, but her heart was urging her on, urging her to stop worrying so much and take the plunge.

"I dare you to kiss me," she said breathlessly.

Maybe it was a weak dare, since they'd already done plenty more than kissing. But she wanted an excuse to touch him. To taste him. To be with him.

Ryan rose from his chair like a god about to claim the spoils of victory, looking powerful and magnificent and magnetic. He walked around the table, trailing his fingertips along the surface of the wood in a way that was so unexpectedly sensual that Sloane's breath caught in the back of her throat.

Damn. This was one fine man, inside and out.

"Did you set this whole game up just to get me to kiss you?" He held out his hands and helped Sloane from her chair. She looked up at him, tilting her face toward his. "Because I don't need vodka and games to convince me, Sloane."

"Then what do you need?"

He reached for her glasses and carefully slipped them down her nose, so he could place them on the table. The gentle brush of his fingers sent a shower of sparks through her, because as giant as Ryan might seem, he treated her as though she was a precious crystal bowl.

"Absolutely nothing at all," he said huskily. "Wanting you is inevitable."

Whoa.

Sloane couldn't find it in herself to respond— there was too much feeling inside her. Too much hope. She wanted to blot it out with the physical. She curled her hands into Ryan's sweater and pressed up on her tiptoes, eyes locked onto his. It felt like an eternity for his lips to lower to hers, but when they did…oh boy.

Sloane melted into Ryan's chest, his arms coming around her body and holding her tight. His fingers tugged at the end of her hair, pulling her head back so he could kiss her more deeply. The taste of him, the scent of him—so warm and inviting—was everything. His tongue swept into her mouth, and his body was a hard wall beneath her fingertips.

When he eased back, breaking their kiss, his eyes were like blue fire. "Truth or dare?"

"Truth."

"Do you want this to stop at a kiss?"

"No." She clung to him, feeling like if she let go then she would float away forever. "I...I want to try out that fantasy idea you had."

Ryan made a harsh sound as he swore under his breath. "The *Stormy Pleasures* scene?"

"Yeah." Sloane's whole body was warm yet tightly coiled. There was an itch beneath her skin, a desperation. For him, because of him.

"You make me wild," he whispered. Then he brought his lips down to hers once more.

"Same."

For better or worse, Sloane *knew* this would crash and burn. Their lives were incompatible, their goals were incompatible. Their futures were incompatible. But no matter how much she knew it to be true, nothing would stop her from having him now.

CHAPTER SEVENTEEN

Sloane laid on her bed, exactly like the heroine had done in *Stormy Pleasures*. She listened to the sound of rushing water from the bathroom and imagined what Ryan would look like working the soap over his body. She was tempted to join him. *So* tempted.

But the anticipation of waiting here for him, naked as the day she'd been born, made her feel hot and achy.

The whole thing with Ryan had thrown her for a loop. Here was this guy who, by all accounts, was so far from her type he might as well have been another species. And yet he'd broken into her heart this afternoon. Turning up at the book club, his insightful thoughts on the story, being angry on her behalf about the Thanksgiving thing…

Well, it'd punched her in the feels.

Don't go thinking you'll get anything from Ryan because he's going to be out of here so quick the dust won't settle for eternity.

She knew it, she really did. But that didn't stop her body and her heart responding to him like there might be an alternative. Like there might be something more than sex between them. Ryan made her feel good about herself. He encouraged her and gave her a shove when she needed it.

But his career would always be number one, and she'd promised herself she'd never beg for second place ever again.

The taps squeaked, startling Sloane out of her thoughts. She imagined what Ryan looked like, beads of moisture smattering his broad shoulders and clinging to the light dusting of hair on his muscular thighs. She fought the urge to get out of bed and confirm whether fantasy met reality. But he wanted her here, laid out like a spread.

She flushed at the thought. Knowing he could walk in any moment and see her…wow. Would he know that *he* was the only man in her mind? The only man in her dreams?

"That's even better than I thought it would be." His deep voice caused her eyes to fly open. One of her towels was wrapped around his waist—it was a bright pink and much too small for a man his size. She snorted, and he swaggered forward, clearly unperturbed by a tiny pink towel.

"It's a good look on you," she said.

"Pink is totally my color." He grinned.

Frankly, she could have given him a loincloth made out of glittery purple cheetah-print fabric and it *still* wouldn't have stolen the show. The towel hung low on his hips, enhancing the defined muscles of his abs and waist. His hair was damp and darker from the water, and his blue eyes seemed to glow like twin flames. Sloane was sure she'd never been as attracted to another man as she was to Ryan Bower.

"God, Sloane." He let out a breath. "You're magnificent."

Her breath stuck in her throat as he stalked forward—all grace and sleekness, despite his size— and she could only watch. The bed squeaked when he lowered onto the edge, his knees pressing into the soft duvet. He reached down for the knot at his waist and undid the towel, revealing the rest of him.

"Don't let your eyes bug out of your head."

Sloane sniffed, playing along. "Your ego is next level."

He tossed the towel to one side, and it hit the pink velvet chair in the corner of her room with a soft *thump*. "You love it."

The air left her lungs. Ryan's cockiness did it for her in a way she'd never even known before. Maybe it was because he seemed so clean cut and responsible out in the world—forever the good influence. Forever the Golden Boy.

And yet in here…he was something entirely new.

"I don't," she lied, her voice quaking.

"Don't try to fool me. I can see in your eyes how turned on you are, even if you're too stubborn to admit it." He made the final distance across the bed, parting her thighs with his strong hands. "See, my mouth is big, too."

"You *do* talk a big game."

"Only for you, my little dinosaur."

A lump unexpectedly formed at the back of

Sloane's throat. *Only for you...* Words she'd longed to hear, words telling her she was important. That she was cherished. That she was home.

But Sloane was not one of those gullible people who turned a situation into what they wanted it to be by seeing things that weren't there. She was logical. Experienced. She'd been through enough disappointment to know how to protect herself.

She might be his "only" right now...but this was just a moment in time.

"Little dinosaur, huh?" She pulled back the covers. "Are you trying to set up a joke about bones?"

"Busted." He got underneath the covers and then pulled her beneath him. His body was warm, hard. And it felt so, *so* good. "You've got my number, Sloane. I can't get anything past you."

She looped her arms around his neck, bringing him down to her. But instead of kissing her, he rested his forehead lightly against hers, his eyelashes brushing over her skin. Damn him. Why did he have to be so charming and hot...and sweet? She hadn't expected sweet. She hadn't prepared for it.

"Shhh." She pressed her fingertip to his lips. If he did anything else...who was she kidding? Her heart was already going to burst into a million pieces when he walked away. Damage control was pointless now. "Enough talking."

The way he smiled at her sent something shimmering and warm through her veins. It made her feel like they were the only two people in the world. She was about to reach for her drawer to grab a condom, but Ryan moved slowly down her body, lips blazing a trail across her breasts and her stomach, over her hip bones and down to her thighs. Her knees immediately fell open in invitation.

"That's how you're planning to keep your mouth shut?" She reached down for his head and ran her fingers through his hair.

"Well, my mouth won't be *shut*." Running his hands up the insides of her thighs, he leaned forward. At the first brush of his lips against her sex, she gasped. "That wouldn't be much fun."

She let herself sink back against the pillow and sighed happily. This man. This utterly perfect, intoxicating man.

He blew cool air across her flushed skin, and a tremor ran through her. Sloane was already on edge, and his warm breath made her breathing come shallow and quick. Every time he touched her, she turned more and more liquid. There was no hesitation when he brought his lips to her sex. Ryan knew exactly where and what and how. It didn't take long for the waves to ripple through her, and her cries filled the room as she came hard and fast against his mouth.

He traced circles on the inside of her thigh as she came down from the edge of bliss. The touch was gentle, loving. And when he looked up at her, it was with such clarity and sincerity that Sloane realized her heart had *already* broken in two.

"You undo me," he said softly.

"Come here."

She retrieved a condom from her bedside table and tore the packet open so he could protect them both. When he pressed into her, moving slow and deliberate, her body turned liquid. He was a master of anticipation—stretching time like warm toffee until she wasn't sure whether they'd been together for minutes or hours.

For some stupid reason, it felt like forever.

"You undo me, too," she said, looking up into his eyes.

He kissed her slow while his hips rolled languid and unhurried against hers. "You're everything I had no idea I wanted."

This was it. *This* exact moment. Fantasy had weaseled its way into reality—tempting her with false promises and a sugar-coated vision of the future. It made her want desperately to believe that this could work. That they could work. That this could be... *everything.*

You're not his one and only. This is just because you feel good together.

But even as she tried to get her brain in alignment, he scrambled her thoughts again with a kiss. Sensibility was like a flock of birds scattered to the wind. Logic dissolved like cotton candy on her tongue.

She wanted him. All of him. Every single thing.

"Ryan," she gasped. "I'm so close. I want...I need you..."

His fingers tangled in her hair, thumbs brushing her cheekbones as he kissed her like it meant something. Like it was real. The pressure built inside her, the want and desire and hope swelling like a bubble. Then the feeling burst as if pricked by a needle, fracturing as she found release in his arms. A second later, he followed her.

In the quiet moment after, Sloane felt moisture gather in her eyes, but she blinked the tears away. She wouldn't cry, even though she knew this was all over before it began.

It was going to hurt like hell.

$$\bullet \bullet \bullet$$

Ryan lay in Sloane's bed, feeling strangely at home in the small space with her body curled into his. Her glossy, brown hair was fanned out every which way, and her lashes cast crescent shadows on her cheeks.

Did it sound corny as hell to say that he could spend all day watching the rise and fall of her chest as she breathed? And no, not because she had amazing breasts.

Outside her house, Sloane was…a lot. Bold outfits, a take-charge attitude, and her energetic, upbeat personality. Not to mention a razor-sharp comeback or two. She demanded people's attention in a way that made him wonder what drove her to stand out. Because inside her house was a different story. When Sloane was at home, she seemed still. Relaxed.

Less…intentional, but in a good way. Like she wasn't trying so hard to be an extreme version of herself.

She was an enigma, this woman. A beautiful, sparkling enigma.

"I think you broke me," she mumbled, stretching in a way that made Ryan's body twitch like he was ready to ravish her all over again. "Woman down. I repeat, woman down."

He chuckled and traced a fingertip along the flat plane of her stomach, swirling around her hip, down, and then continuing a straight line down her thigh. "You look pretty whole to me."

"Whole, but not wholesome." Her pale gray-blue eyes locked on his.

"Not bad for a guy who only likes vanilla sex, eh?"

"You *did* say you were an excellent student." She reached down and pulled the covers up over her, snuggling further into him like a kitten seeking out a warm lap.

For some strange reason, that made Ryan's heart swell, but he decided to chalk it up to being giddy on endorphins after breaking a self-imposed dry spell. "I try my best."

"You really do, don't you?"

Ryan slung one arm over her body, feeling a driving need to have as much of him touching her possible. She felt bare. Almost like he was seeing her without her brightly colored peacock feathers.

"Well, yeah," he said with a shrug. "I picked a career that makes hard work a necessity and failure a public spectacle. Not to sound like a bad motivational speech, but giving a hundred percent is the minimum."

"Is it painful for you to be home now while the team is in the playoffs?"

The question socked him right in the chest. "Yes."

His team had made it all the way to the American League championship series, where they'd be up against a team who'd dominated all season long. They were the underdogs. The wildcards. The team who'd scrapped their way through the last three seasons to go from breaking all the wrong records to being so close to those bejeweled rings they could taste it.

And Ryan was missing out. The ultimate glory moment, the ultimate proof that they were a team who could take the fight all the way to the end...and he had to watch it from the sidelines.

It killed him.

"It's really fucking hard." He swallowed. "This is the last year of my contract, and I wasn't worried about re-signing before. But now with the injury, coupled with my age, they could view me as a risky option...What if I missed my one shot? What if I don't even get the chance because they don't offer me another contract?"

What if I'm worth nothing now?

"Is that a likely outcome?" she asked.

"I don't know." He blew out a long breath. "I don't have all the time in the world left. I'm slower to heal these days. I don't bounce back the way I used to, and I need more rest days between outings."

The team had been required to manage his schedule more carefully this past season, since it'd become obvious that he pitched better with an extra day between games. He was slowing down, and it felt like his body was betraying him.

Time was betraying him.

"What do you think you can do about it?" she asked.

"Nothing."

God, it hurt like a burr in the back of his throat to say that out loud. To admit that the march of time was inevitable. To admit that his dreams had an expiration date.

It was out of his control, and he hated it.

"You know," she said, reaching for his hand and intertwining their fingers, genuine concern radiating through his skin until he felt the ice thawing in his veins. "One thing I learned about moving around a lot was that you may not always think you'll figure things out, but you adapt. You find new things to be excited about."

He turned their hands over, looking at her long, delicate fingers and the shimmery polish coating her nails. "I operate better when I know what's going to happen."

"That's not realistic, though. You have to trust that you'll know what to do when the time comes and that even if it's not all clear, you'll take it step by step until you know exactly what's next."

"How do you know that?" he whispered.

He'd never opened up to anyone about all this because he wanted to be the strong one. The example. For the young players, for his coach, for his family. For himself, in some cases. Acting tough was the only way he could deal with the media and online scrutiny. He wanted to pretend he was invincible and immortal and an anomaly. But each year that passed made it harder and harder to ignore what was coming. He might not want to face his fear, but fear was facing him dead on.

Still, he hadn't shared those vulnerabilities so bluntly with anybody…until her.

Now, this quirky, resilient, sexy woman had slipped past his defenses and started to peek around the walls that protected him. She'd coaxed him out of the shadows and shown him that it was okay to say what he felt. To admit he was scared.

But what was this all for?

They'd drawn the boundaries already. Kissing Creek was home for her, the place she'd carefully chosen. It was stability. A necessity after a lifetime of moving and starting over and uprooting. And he wanted to give his career everything he had—which meant moving back to Toronto at a minimum. The possibility of being traded, of being told one day, "Hey, it's time to go," and having to pack his bags without question.

His life was the opposite of what Sloane wanted. It was the life she'd chosen to leave behind.

"Because I'm starting to know you," she said, smiling up at him. "You're smart and talented and driven. Those qualities together make for a very good chance of success."

"Watch out," he said huskily. "You'll give me a big head."

"I'm not afraid of your ego," she whispered, touching her lips to his chest. "You're a good man."

"You think?"

"I know," she said, turning her beautiful eyes up to him. "One step at a time. That's all anyone can do."

"I know what step I want to take right now."

He shouldn't want it, because it wasn't going anywhere, and as soon as the season was done, he would head back to Toronto and pull himself together. He needed to prepare for contract negotiations, believing he would take the mound next year. Whatever it took, he would fight to prove he still had time left in him.

And now he knew that was going to hurt them both. But he couldn't pull away from Sloane, no matter how much he knew he should. The woman had this hold on him, so gentle he hadn't even noticed it at first—but wasn't that the most dangerous kind of hold? The one you didn't even see coming.

"Tell me." She cupped his face and looked up at him with those big, beautiful gray-blue eyes, echoing his words from earlier.

Yes, this was exactly what he needed to concentrate on right now.

Her eyes turned from thoughtful to smoky, and her palms skated up his chest and curled over his shoulders. She shifted her body, sliding closer so she could rub against him. Ryan moaned, rocking his hips against hers and thrusting his hands up into her hair.

"What do you want to do?" she asked, her voice like a lazy summer's day.

"Maybe we should explore another scene from the book."

"Feeling adventurous?"

"Always."

But even as he rolled Sloane beneath him, parting her soft thighs with his own harder ones and taking her mouth in a searing kiss, he knew *always* wasn't part of the equation when it came to her. She deserved a man who would put her first. Who would sacrifice anything for her.

And Ryan wouldn't put a relationship ahead of his career.

CHAPTER EIGHTEEN

The following week…

The Blizzards made it to the World Series. Ryan had slept through the final game, distracting himself by pulling Sloane into the shower with him and then collapsing onto her bed, where he'd slept like the dead with her in his arms. He'd never considered himself a good sleeper—his brain was far too active for that.

But in the past week, he'd slept better than ever before.

Copious amounts of sex will do that.

Or maybe it was something else. Being with Sloane was soul-soothing. They'd slipped into a comfortable routine where they worked on the float in the evening, ate dinner with his folks, and then came back to her place after. He'd spend the night exploring her body and they'd talk until the wee hours, waking to do it all over again.

It was easy. He craved seeing her. She made him laugh so hard tears came to his eyes; her jokes were silly and irreverent and curious, a total balm for his more serious personality. But five minutes ago, he'd woken to a flurry of texts and DMs from pretty much everyone he'd ever met. He'd done the right thing and called around some of his closest friends on the team to congratulate them. It was a big deal.

The *biggest* deal for a baseball player's career.

This was the final stop—the pinnacle. All they had to do was win this seven game series and they'd be champions for the first time in decades. They'd be heroes. Legends. Gods.

They would be…but not him.

Ryan leaned against the kitchen counter in Sloane's place, staring into her backyard. It was dark out, and rain streamed across the glass in great big rivulets. An orange leaf was stuck against the pane, getting battered by the wind and rain, and it clung on for dear life, taking the beating like a champ.

Didn't his life feel like that sometimes?

He was clinging desperately to his career, pushing through injuries and mental pain because he still had more to achieve. He didn't want to be done. And yet the resistance was getting stronger and stronger, and sometimes he didn't know for how much longer he could hang on.

"Ry?" Sloane shuffled sleepily into the kitchen, and he couldn't help but smile.

Her dark hair stuck out in all directions, and she was wearing a quilted blanket like a robe. She blinked owlishly without her glasses, but there was still a hint of a satisfied smile on her lips from where he'd brought her to the brink over and over.

"Come here," he said, his voice rough and low. She obliged without hesitation—which was how he'd learned she did most things—and when she rested her head against his chest, he felt his muscles relax.

"I heard you talking on the phone." Her voice was gravelly from her nap.

"Yeah." The rest of the words stuck in the back of his throat, and that made him feel like a Grade-A jerk. He *was* happy for his teammates and the coaches who'd worked so hard, but dammit, it felt like he'd been robbed.

She curled her arms around him and squeezed tighter. She knew. He didn't even need to say a thing because she already knew.

"I'm sorry," she whispered, her lips brushing his bare chest.

"Nothing to be sorry about," he rasped. It felt like there was a fist around his throat. "The team worked hard, and they deserve to be there."

"I'm not a journalist, Ry." She hugged him tighter. "You don't have to say the right thing to me."

"It sucks not to be there."

She flinched at the pain in his voice, tightening her arms further. She was like a sleepy, sexy little vise. Or a barnacle. It was nice to be held.

"I feel like I'm being punished for absolutely nothing." The words came out of him in a rush. Inside, it felt like there was lava in his veins, the frustration bubbling to a fever pitch, and yet...

And yet when Sloane stood there quietly, letting her care and understanding seep into him, for the first time in months Ryan felt like he could manage it. The *fear*, the anger, the resentment. All of it.

"I feel like I've wasted all the sacrifices that my parents made, all the time and money they spent. I feel like I've wasted all my own efforts, all the sacrifices *I've* made over the years." He slouched back against the countertop so he could rest his chin on her head. Sloane wriggled against him, opening the blanket to envelop him inside her fluffy cocoon. Underneath, she wore a pair of underpants and that was it.

"But it's still worth it, right? Because you haven't stopped yet."

Her question felt weighted down with rocks. No, he hadn't stopped yet. He *wouldn't* stop until there was literally nothing more he could do. Which meant…

He'd be leaving soon.

His flight was already booked, in fact. He'd scheduled it before he left Toronto, telling himself that he was going to come back the second the season was over and start mentally preparing for the following year. Kissing Creek was a temporary diversion. An escape from the real world.

Sloane hadn't broached the subject, so neither had he. Despite them spending every day together and him practically living out of her adorable little house, they both watched the oncoming freight train in absolute silence. It was like, if neither one of them admitted it, then it wouldn't happen.

But it would.

Ryan was leaving, and Sloane had made a life here. She'd hung out with Trudy a couple of times now, and they were getting along like a house on fire. Sloane was getting even closer with his Mom and Dad, because they were helping her out with the float each day.

He'd *helped* her to put even more roots down here, to be even more engrained in his hometown. Where did that leave them?

Somewhere in the mushy middle.

"I haven't stopped yet," he finally replied with a sigh. Outside, the rain beat down and the wind thrashed a branch against the window—it scratched and clawed like a monster wanting to get inside and ruin their perfect, sexy bubble. "I have to keep going."

Sloane nodded. For a while they stood, neither one of them saying a word, but then eventually his stomach growled, and she laughed. "Come on. Let's re-heat that dinner we got too distracted to eat."

"It seems to be a habit with you. We always skip right to dessert." He tipped her head back and leaned down to capture her sweet lips in a kiss.

"It's my favorite bit," she whispered, sliding her hands up his chest.

"Mine too."

• • •

Sloane waddled across her bedroom, arms outstretched and her balance a little unsteady. She took each step carefully, peering through the mesh that covered her eyes and making a mental note to walk as straight as possible so she didn't bump the little potted plant she'd recently purchased on the other side of the doorway.

"Are you coming out?" a feminine voice called from the living room.

"Just a minute." Sloane squeezed through the doorway. "Ta-da!"

Trudy gasped and clamped a hand over her mouth, and then she burst out laughing. "That. Is. Magnificent."

"Right?" Sloane did her best to twirl, but the tail on her blow-up T-Rex costume swept precariously close to a glass on the coffee table, and Trudy made a quick grab to save it.

This had become something of a weekly habit for them now, although this was only the third time. But three weeks in a row was enough to qualify as a weekly habit, right? They hung out every Thursday night, ordering dinner in from one of the good takeout places, cracked open a bottle of wine, and chilled.

Tonight, Sloane was showing off her Halloween costume.

"I've ordered one for everyone who's going to ride on the float, and we'll have them all dressed as different types of Olympic athletes. I managed to find a tennis racket at the charity shop, so one of the guys can channel their inner Sharapova."

Sloane made a few attempts at a forehand, grunting in the style of the famous Russian tennis player.

"Very convincing," Trudy said. "But you should probably stop doing that unless you want to knock over a piece of furniture."

"Agreed." Sloane sighed. "I was really hoping to be on this float, but it looks like I'll need to be accessible in case something goes wrong with the parade. Such a bummer."

"Management never gets to partake in the fun." Trudy patted the T-Rex head.

"I'm thinking I'll keep one of these for my trick-or-treating outfit." Sloane smoothed her little dinosaur hands over the front of her costume. "What do you think? I'll scare a few kids."

"I don't think you'll scare anybody. You're going to get mobbed for photos."

Sloane changed out of her costume and into something a little more human. They'd gotten pizza — the good, woodfire kind — from the Italian restaurant, Mille Baci, and settled onto the couch with an open bottle of Sangiovese.

"How did things go with the family dinner last night?" Sloane asked, reaching for a slice of the pepperoni pizza.

"It was okay. My older sister is still being... difficult." Trudy sighed. "She takes a swipe whenever she can."

Trudy's family sounded like a bit of a nightmare — her sisters, all four of them, were highly competitive. Her mom and dad sounded equally challenging, with her mother wanting to control every aspect of their lives and her father being emotionally unavailable.

For the first time ever, Sloane had a friend who

could relate to her own family issues.

"What about you? Did you end up calling your dad today?" Trudy asked, taking a bite out of her pizza slice.

"Yeah." She cringed. "It was messy."

Ever since she'd confessed to both Ryan and Trudy about how her father had uninvited her from Thanksgiving, she'd been thinking about confronting him. Not to cause an argument or a scene, but to explain why she was hurt. For some reason, after years of taking those little snubs on the chin, she wanted him to know how she felt.

"Uh oh." Trudy frowned. She had on a Boston Celtics hoodie over a pair of black leggings, and she sat with her feet crossed like a preschooler on the couch. "He didn't take it well?"

"No," Sloane replied, fighting the wobble in her voice. "I thought he would at least try to understand where I was coming from. But he got on the defensive, saying I was being too hard on him and that it was impossible for him to please everybody. Blah, blah, blah."

Trudy put her pizza slice down and reached over to give Sloane a hug. "Oh man, families suck sometimes."

Sloane laughed, even though her eyes were pricking with tears. "They really do."

The hug was nice, and it made her feel a little better—not because it solved the problem at all, but because Trudy seemed to really understand her.

Sloane never felt judged when she complained about her dad's disinterest or her mom's absence.

"I mean, I *do* understand his position." Sloane sighed. "But I'm still his family. Don't I deserve to be included?"

"Absolutely. I would invite you to my family's Thanksgiving, but that's a guaranteed shitshow, and I don't want to put you through that." Trudy pulled a face. "But I feel like I have to go, because it could be the final nail in that coffin if I'm back and I start avoiding them on holidays."

Sloane's stomach sank a little. There went *that* idea to have a Friendsgiving instead. She didn't begrudge Trudy spending the day with her family, of course, since she was trying to repair that relationship. And it was great that Trudy had something to repair.

Not everybody was so lucky.

"How's things going with Ryan?" Trudy asked.

Oh yeah, *that*.

"Amazing," she said with a dreamy smile. "He's literally perfect…well, except for the fact that he's leaving soon."

Talk about the ultimate deal breaker.

"You wouldn't try the long-distance thing?" Trudy asked.

"It doesn't work." She sighed. "My parents tried it for a little while when Dad got sick of following her around the world. We stayed with my grandma in Michigan, and Mom was…somewhere."

"Why didn't it work?"

"I'm pretty sure he had an affair while we were there. He used to make comments about her, saying she was married to her job more than she was married to him." Sloane took a long sip of her wine and then set the glass down on the coffee table. "It wasn't simply about us being in different places. It's the fact that her job was always number one."

Trudy nodded. "Right."

"I watched my father traipse all over the world, following my mother. He felt neglected and she felt unsupported. They ended up hating one another." She sighed. "Ryan is Mr. Baseball. He's never going to change. I wouldn't want us to go through what my parents went through."

"You're not giving him enough credit," Trudy said, frowning. "Have you tried talking to him about it?"

"He literally said it himself—his career will *always* be his top priority. And really, that shouldn't change, because it's the reason he's so successful. I understand his position." She sighed. "He's a wonderful man and I…"

Love him.

No. She rejected the words as soon as they popped into her head, shunning them like they were proximity mines threatening to blow her apart if she got to close. She couldn't love him. She *wouldn't* love him. Because she'd never loved a man before and her first time couldn't be with someone who was destined to be the one who got away.

"I appreciate that we've been able to have this

time together," Sloane finished, looking at the pizza sitting on the table in front of her. Her appetite had turned to dust in an instant, and now she couldn't even bring herself to pick up a slice. "But I have a life here that's important to me, and he has a career goal that he's been working toward his whole life. Neither one of us deserves to have that sacrificed."

"So that's it, huh? A stalemate." Trudy reached for the wine and topped them both up. "That makes me sad. I think you two would make really attractive babies."

"Freakishly tall like him and near-sighted like me?" Sloane laughed. "If only that was enough to make it work."

"What are you going to do about it?"

They'd been pretending it wasn't going to happen all this time. The closer they got, the harder they seemed to ignore the inevitable expiration date. But that would only work for so long. Eventually they would have to face the facts.

"I'm going to call things off," Sloane said with a nod. "It's the right thing to do. I want a chance to say a proper goodbye and have some closure."

She'd do it on Halloween. It would be a gloriously fun night and a memory she'd treasure for a long time. Wasn't it better to go out on a high than wait for the end to catch you off guard? She might not have forever with Ryan, but the time they did have deserved a proper ending.

CHAPTER NINETEEN

It was parade day.

Ryan had worked his tush off, helping Sloane get everything in order, and now they could see their hard work pay off. Sadly, Sloane was running around and trying to be in three places at once while everyone got set up. So she'd left Ryan and Mark in charge of the Survival of the Fittest float.

"You stand back," Mark said to Ryan, shooing him away with one hand. "Mom put the fear of God into me about making sure you don't aggravate your knee."

Ryan rolled his eyes but chose not to fight.

All the vehicles had pulled into the section of Main Street where they were due to start. They were the third float, sitting behind one representing an accounting guild. Their participants were a group of people dressed as "corporate zombies," which Ryan thought was clever. The first float in the line was for the Harrison Beech Flames, and he could spot Pace the Pitching Prodigy strutting around like a peacock.

Mark crouched, trying to fix a section of bunting that had come loose from the base of the float. It wasn't the most impressive float in the lineup, but Ryan could see how much love and laughter had been poured into it. In some ways, the nights he'd spent working on the float with Sloane and his family and friends had reminded him of what he loved about Kissing Creek.

What he missed about it.

He didn't have much of a community in Toronto—not because the people there weren't great. They were. But there he was a celebrity. A public figure. Here he was more of a regular person, someone who was famous, sure, but also someone who could walk down the street and bump into people who'd known him since he was a kid.

"That's better." Mark stood and brushed his palms down the front of his jeans. "She's ready to rock and roll."

Out of the corner of his eye, Ryan spotted Sloane walking over. She looked more than a little frazzled. Her hair was starting to slip out of her ponytail, and her glasses had slid down her nose a bit.

"All good?" he asked.

"Yeah, it's…a lot." She smiled. "This is the biggest event I've ever organized."

"You got this." He grabbed her shoulders and gave her a squeeze. "You're a leader in this community, Sloane. Everyone here admires you, and you're doing an awesome job."

"You think so?" she asked hopefully.

"I do."

He really wanted to kiss her then—to show her how much he thought of her. It wasn't only attraction that was urging him to connect with her; it was a healthy dose of respect for who she was and what she stood for. She searched his face, something simmering behind the thick lenses of her glasses, like she was trying to solve a riddle. But the moment was shattered when someone called her name.

"Crap. I have to go." She pressed a hand to his chest, and Ryan immediately closed his palm over hers, like he didn't want to be without her.

Which was pointless. His flight was in a few days.

"Go," he said, the word feeling sticky in the back of his throat, like he'd swallowed a spoonful of molasses. "Kick butt."

Sloane smiled before darting back into the crowd. He watched people flocking to her like she was a magnet, drawing waves and questions and interest. She belonged here. He could the see the reputation she'd built in Kissing Creek. Despite her lacking confidence when it came to making friends, she was important to the people here…even if she didn't quite see it the way he did, looking from the outside in.

"Want to explain what *that* was all about?" Mark asked walking up beside him. "For a moment there, I thought I could hear trumpets and crashing waves."

Ryan shot his brother a look. "Trumpets and crashing waves? You might want to get that checked out. Sounds like an auditory hallucination."

Mark dug his elbow into Ryan's ribs. "You know what I'm talking about."

"I don't," he replied stubbornly.

Mark snorted. "You look at a girl like you're star-crossed lovers and then you act like nothing's happening. That's delusion, buddy."

He didn't want his family poking around in his personal life, although it must have been obvious what was going on. Ryan was out every night, not returning until mid-morning the next day, dodging questions like some guilty-as-sin teenager. His parents weren't oblivious, but they hadn't pushed him.

Probably because they were happy to have him out of the house and they could go back to reenacting *Stormy Pleasures*—at least as well as they could with his dad's still-recovering back. His nose immediately wrinkled at the thought of it.

"And now you're ignoring me because I hit a sore spot." Mark scrubbed a hand over his beard. "Curiouser and curiouser."

"You're Lewis Carroll now?"

"Thanks for not calling me Alice."

Ryan laughed. "You'd look great in that blue dress. Definitely got the skinny little chicken legs for it."

"Screw you," his brother said good-naturedly. "And nice diversion tactic. You got it bad for this chick."

Was there any point denying it? Probably not.

Ahead of them, the chaos of the parade went on. The people riding on the Survival of the Fittest float arrived, all dressed up. The collection of blow-up T-Rex costumes was hilarious. Some of them had fake medals around their necks, and one guy was attempting to bounce a basketball with his puffy T-Rex hands.

"I like her," Ryan said simply.

"Nah. There's like and there's...whatever that was. It's more." Mark slapped a hand down on his back. "Trust me, I know that look. I've *given* that look."

"Can you spare the mooning over your wife? The whole town already knows you two are perfect together," Ryan said. The words came out a little more bitter than he wanted them to, and he immediately shook his head. "Sorry. That wasn't cool. I'm happy you have such a great family."

"What's going on, Ry?" Mark's dark eyebrows crinkled in concern.

"Nothin' talking can fix." He sighed.

No matter how much he rolled it around in his head, the facts didn't change. If he and Sloane wanted to keep seeing each other, then one of them had to give up something. Either she would have to go with him to Toronto and leave Kissing Creek behind, which wasn't good for her. Or he would have to come back to Kissing Creek, which would end his career.

As for the long-distance thing...he wasn't sure about that. Some guys in the industry made it work, but it wasn't easy. His closest friend on the team had recently called things off with his girlfriend because of the strain the distance put on their relationship. Jealousy brewed from both sides and trust broke down.

Besides, even if she did follow him to Toronto, between the away games, spring training in Florida, and sponsorship work...all of that would take him away from her. And he wasn't giving up what he'd worked so hard for. But whenever he thought about ending things with her, this part of him would roar *NO* so loudly it made his ears ring.

"Okay." Mark nodded. "Point taken. But I will say this—"

"You're incapable of *not* giving your opinion, aren't you?" Ryan shook his head, because it was easier to tease his brother than admit how difficult this was right now.

"You know me, Mark 'mouthy' Bower." He laughed. "And don't worry, I'm not going to tell you that love is worth sacrificing everything or some unrealistic bullshit like that."

Love? Ryan had never experienced romantic love before. He'd never wanted to. But whatever he felt for Sloane—regardless of the label that could be applied—it meant something. It was important. Ryan had a talent for zeroing in on things. Whether it was a batter's weak spots or the energy of the guys behind him on the field…he could read things before they happened.

And he was reading this situation before it happened—leaving Sloane was going to break a part of him he hadn't even known could be broken.

"Don't let anything go unsaid," Mark replied. "If you're thinking something about her, at least say it. That way you can leave with no regrets, right?"

Ryan nodded. "Thanks, man."

That's where Mark was wrong, because Ryan would leave with a regret. He'd regret getting himself into this situation in the first place—because it never should've happened. He took his eyes off the prize for a flash, and Sloane slipped under his radar with ease. Love was never supposed to be part of the equation. It wasn't on his plan. It wasn't on his list of goals. It wasn't in his vocabulary.

But when he thought about her and all they'd shared…well, he wasn't sure how else to label it.

CHAPTER TWENTY

The parade was officially a smash hit!

All sixteen floats made it down the stretch of Main Street, celebrating the spirit of Halloween, community, and local business. A prize had been awarded to the most creative float. The ladies who ran the local bookstore had an epic Bram Stoker theme with some terrifyingly real-looking costumes and a coffin filled with dry ice and red lights that was about the eeriest thing Sloane had ever seen. They definitely deserved to win.

Douglas Shaw had come over to congratulate Sloane on a job well done. Plus, he'd asked her if she might be interested in a more senior position within the volunteer committee. They were always looking for younger folks with good leadership skills, and he saw people like her as the future of Kissing Creek.

The *future* of Kissing Creek!

When had she ever been the future of anything? Hell, she wasn't even the future of her own family. But today she'd made an impact on those around her. Her work had *meant* something to the people here. Sloane was so giddy she could barely stand up straight.

Floating on a cloud, she headed home to freshen up and change into her trick-or-treating costume. But the second she walked through the front door, it was like all the goodness and light from the day evaporated into a puff of smoke. Coming home and changing her outfit signaled the beginning of the end. She'd made a commitment to herself that she would end things with Ryan tonight. They'd go out on a high.

If she let things drag on with Ryan, then it would tarnish their time together like oxidization. It would destroy the shine and luster of the memories they'd made, and she didn't want to remember him as anything but the incredible man who'd helped her feel valued. Who'd helped her find a stronger foothold in her community. Who'd helped her know that Kissing Creek *was* the place for her to be.

She respected Ryan, his dreams, and his hard work. He deserved to find a woman who could give him what he needed—a woman without the kind of baggage that made Sloane fear being second-best. He deserved someone who was flexible and adaptable and who embraced change and the unknown.

But she wasn't those things.

Here, her life was carefully created, stable, and secure. Predictable. She knew a lot of people would find it boring, but to someone who'd never had the idea of a home base and people who knew your name and a community of potential friends...well, it was everything to her.

By the time she heard the knock on her front door,

Sloane's stomach was tied up in knots. She was wearing her T-Rex costume and carefully made her way through the living room, trying not to knock anything over.

The front door was unlocked, since she wasn't sure if she'd be able to do that with her costume on. The blurry figure of Ryan through the frosted glass panels made her heart thump. It felt like going through a portal. Or maybe it was more like finishing a race that you didn't want to be over. Like the last season of *Game of Thrones*—too short, with wasted potential and the lingering sadness of something that could have been amazing.

"Just do it already," she said to herself.

She managed to get the door open with her clumsy hands, and the sight that greeted her almost made her melt inside her T-Rex suit. Holy smokes. Or should that be, holy smoking-hot man?

"Jonathan, from *Stormy Pleasures*." She let out a breath. "Whoa."

Ryan was dressed in a sharp black suit with a crisp white shirt and Jonathan's signature blood-red tie. His hair was styled, and he even had on a pair of the knotted silver cufflinks that the character wore in the story. The costume was perfect, down to the littlest detail. And it wasn't like he'd picked up some cheap suit that would barely make it through the night, either. It was a proper suit, broad at the shoulders and nipped slightly at the waist, with the perfectly fitted pants making his legs look long and powerful.

"I like whoa." Ryan grinned. He turned on the spot, arms out wide like he was on a red carpet somewhere, not on the doorstep of a small-town woman dressed in a blow-up dinosaur outfit.

"I feel slightly underdressed now," she said.

"Not wearing anything under that suit?" He winked.

Sloane burst out laughing. "Seriously? Is that another one of your weird fantasies?"

"Hot chick naked inside a dino suit? Sure, why not?"

"How did you turn into a kinky fantasy generator, huh?" Sloane shook her head, which felt odd with the oversize T-Rex's head bobbing above her own.

"All it takes is the right influence." He looked at her, those piercing blue eyes catching hers through the mesh on the dinosaur's neck that allowed her to see out. But she refused to get in her own head. Tonight, she was going to enjoy herself, and the end would be a celebration, not a commiseration.

She waddled forward, and Ryan kindly helped her close and lock the door. "If you must know, I have thermal underwear on under this costume."

"Mm, sexy," he replied with a laugh.

"I don't fancy catching hypothermia tonight." She paused. "Now, I felt bad knowing we'd be out when I should be handing out candy. I put some in a little bowl there in case anyone comes knocking. Do you think that's okay?"

"That's perfectly fine. And stop worrying about everyone else for a minute. Tonight is about *you*." He held his arm out, and it looked like something out of a fairy tale...minus the fact that she resembled a viral internet video more than a princess. "I'm going to make sure you have the Halloween to end all Halloweens."

If only he knew how close he was hitting to home right now.

"Teach me everything about trick-or-treating," she said.

"It's important to have a strategy." Ryan bent down and picked up a little bucket shaped like a jack-o-lantern. "And something to carry all your candy in. But since you barely have arms, I can do that for you."

"T-Rex is powerful and strong, but only on leg day." Sloane giggled. "I can't believe I almost forgot something to put the candy in."

"I've got you," he said in a way that made Sloane wish it was true. Because right now Ryan looked like the man she hoped would be waiting at the end of a church aisle one day and sounded like a man who could be her everything.

It wasn't fair. Why did it have to be him? Why did he have to be so wrong...and yet absolutely freaking perfect at the same time?

"Here's what you need to know about trick-or-treating in Kissing Creek," he said as they walked down her driveway and onto the street, where dozens of kids were already running around, hopped up on sugar. "Mrs. Cookson gives out the best treats, but you'd better go early or all the good stuff will be gone. Because of the parade, we've probably missed the boat."

Sloane lived on one of the main residential streets, which had a good number of smaller streets running to the left and right. Ryan pointed to a large corner block with a pretty porch decorated with at least a dozen hand-carved pumpkins.

"Mr. and Mrs. Perez live there. It's worth going to their door to see how amazing their costumes are. Seriously, Mrs. Perez should be working on Hollywood movies, she's *that* good." He then pointed to another house with a tidy front lawn. "That's the Kelly family. Mrs. Kelly makes up her own little bags of candy, but they always have tons of candy corn in them. I recommend passing."

"What's wrong with candy corn?" Sloane asked.

"What's wrong with…?" Ryan looked at her aghast. "Seriously? What's wrong with candy corn? Do you like eating small, flavorless pieces of candle wax? Do you like tiny morsels of pure hatred?"

Sloane laughed so hard her eyes almost watered. Ryan was clearly putting it on to make her laugh, but she suspected he really *did* hate candy corn. "Come on, it can't be that bad."

"Good lord. Next thing you're going to tell me is that you like Peeps!" He made a face of pure disgust.

They strolled down the street, heading toward a house with huge, glittering cobwebs stretched across the windows and a ghostly figure illuminated in the front window. Every few seconds, an eerie red light flickered. People here really had skills when it came to their decorations.

"I tried Peeps one time, not a fan." Sloane wrinkled her nose as they followed a group of cute kids dressed up as Pokémon characters up a driveway. "Although maybe this is horrible to admit, but I also don't love anything Reese's. In fact, I'd go as far as to say peanut butter in general grosses me out."

"Really?"

"Who decides to grind down a legume until a weird paste forms and then says, 'You know what will go well with this? Chocolate.' Uh, no thanks."

Ryan was chuckling as they got to the front door. A woman in a convincing witch costume—right down to the realistic-looking fake wart on her nose—cocked her head. "You're a little older than my usual trick-or-treaters. Wait, is that…? Ryan Bower, my goodness."

"Hi, Mrs. James." He raised a hand in a wave.

"What on earth are you doing, dressing up with the kids?"

"Well," he said, gesturing to Sloane, "this is Sloane Rickman, and she's never gone trick-or-treating. Ever. So I wanted to take her around and show her what it was like, because I figured nobody should miss out on that experience even if they didn't get to do it as a kid."

He sounded so sincere, it made Sloane's heart want to burst. How had she mistaken him for some cold, humorless grump? He had more heart than most people. None of this was necessary. None of this was expected. But that was Ryan—going above and beyond was the only approach he knew.

"Isn't that lovely?" Mrs. James smiled. "How come you never did trick-or-treating as a kid?"

"I spent most of my childhood overseas," Sloane replied. She left out the rest—that the small amount of time she had been on home turf had been so miserable that nothing had dragged her from her room. And, besides, who trick-or-treated on their own?

"Well, here." Mrs. James reached into something that was stashed just inside the door. She deposited some brightly wrapped liquor chocolates into Sloane's jack-o-lantern bucket. "I save these for any parents who come by. They're better than the kids' stuff."

"Thank you!"

"And you, you're such a sweetheart." Mrs. James reached forward and patted Ryan on the arm. "Have fun!"

Sloane almost skipped back down the driveaway, feeling a giddy, child-like wonder wash over her. And it had nothing to do with the sugar—she wouldn't even be able to eat any of her candy until she got out of her costume.

They went to the next door and scored some Butterfinger bars and small packets of Skittles. The next house was set up like a graveyard, and Sloane shrieked at the top of her lungs when Mr. Park jumped out from behind a tombstone. Ryan laughed, knowing full well what the routine was at this house and doing not a thing to spoil the surprise.

As they walked around the neighborhood, he held her hand through the dino suit and kept her candy safe. The air was rapidly cooling, and they walked close. A few little kids stopped Ryan to ask for his autograph once their parents pointed out who he was.

The night air smelled like sugar and leaves and the creamy scent of hot cocoa with marshmallows. There were plenty of kids still out, even as the sky grew inky dark, enhancing the glow from open doors and making Sloane cuddle further into Ryan. Well, as much as her costume would allow.

An achy feeling squeezed her throat. Despite promising herself she was going to enjoy tonight without worrying about what came next, every footstep dragged her closer to it being over. And yet every time she looked into Ryan's eyes, she wanted desperately for it *not* to be over.

She wanted desperately for him to be an ordinary man with an ordinary job and an ordinary small-town life.

But Ryan was far from ordinary, and it was that unique quality he had—his care and effort and work ethic—that made him special and ultimately out of her league. As they approached another house, Sloane's jack-o-lantern bucket so full she would have to donate most of it to the staff room at work, Sloane felt a tear slip out onto her cheek. What the hell was she doing? She had no business sleeping with a man like Ryan. She had no business hurting herself with unattainable desires.

Hell, she was walking her heart right into a bear trap and wondering why it hurt when the damn thing snapped around her. It was stupid. Holding hands and acting sweet was only prolonging the inevitable. Only ensuring that she'd feel his loss as sharply as if someone punched her in the chest.

They approached another house, and it wasn't until she set foot on the driveway that she realized he'd brought her to his parents' house. It was almost unrecognizable. Two skeletons sat in rocking chairs in the front yard, holding hands, surrounded by silhouettes of black cats and crows. A garland of lights shaped like pumpkins wrapped around the porch railings, and a sensor tripped some booming thunder sounds as they walked past the mailbox.

Sloane gasped. "It looks amazing."

"My parents go all out. Mark helped Mom pull it all together this year, since Dad is still being careful with his back." He looked so proud it made her want to kiss him until they were both gasping for air. "Every year they do a different theme."

"What's the theme of this one?" Sloane asked.

"Till death do us part." Ryan snorted. "I thought it was a bit morbid, but Mom says it's romantic."

"It's got a foot in both camps, for sure."

Till death do us part… She knew better than anyone that vows didn't always have longevity. It hadn't worked for her parents. It hadn't worked for Pat first time around. People made mistakes, they chose the wrong person, and no amount of wishing in a white dress could change reality.

Sloane walked on numb feet toward the Bowers'

front door, her eyes drifting to the skeletons in the front yard. It felt symbolic somehow—not of love until death, but of the withering of love. Of the slow erosion of trust and affection until there was nothing left.

"Sloane." Ryan paused outside the front door, something simmering in his eyes. There was a tension to his body, an excited energy that crackled and called to her. "There's something I want to say."

The air left her lungs. She could feel it, the moment racing toward them. He reached for her hand, trepidation in his eyes. Anticipation flickering in the beginnings of a smile. He was going to do something romantic and stupid and beautiful.

Stop leading him on. Stop leading yourself *on.*

"I have something to say, too," she said, the words tumbling out in a rush. "We need to break up."

CHAPTER TWENTY-ONE

Okay, so this was *not* how Ryan had pictured the night going. Momentarily stunned by Sloane's outburst, he was at a loss for words. Which she took as her opportunity to verbal diarrhea all over the place.

"I mean, well…I guess we can't break up if we weren't officially dating. *Were* we dating? I certainly wasn't seeing anyone else and I didn't want to, but we never talked about it, and I know I sometimes rush to put a label on things," she said, her voice getting higher pitched with each rushed sentence. "But if we weren't dating then we probably don't even need to have this conversation because it's a moot point. Moot is a funny word, isn't it? Sounds like an angry cow. I've always wondered—"

"Sloane." He said her name harshly, and it cut through the night air like a blade. She immediately grew quiet and still, almost like he'd frozen her to the spot.

Dammit. He'd been about to cut himself open in front of her. He'd been about to confess all the crazy thoughts in his head that had been swirling around like fireflies. He'd been about to say…

Being with you was the only thing that got me through the past month.

But she'd cut him off at the knees.

"What?" she eventually asked in such a small voice that for a moment he wondered if he'd made the sound up in his head.

"What do you mean we need to break up?"

Had they been experiencing the same evening for the past few hours? Or was his view of things, of sharing a special moment with her and taking a few hours out to revel in the child-like glory of his favorite celebration, something else entirely to her? Was it possible he'd horribly misread this situation and that the emotions and feelings he had running through his body for the very first time were his and his alone?

"I mean," she said, her voice wobbling, "this has been a really wonderful night and I'm going to cherish it forever. But I'm done."

"Done?"

"With you." Her voice cracked, and Ryan was sure there would be tears in her eyes if only he could see them through her damn costume. "With us."

"Am I missing something?" He shook his head, feeling totally and utterly caught out. Off-balance. Rattled.

He couldn't remember the last time something had caught him so off guard. Not even the surprise slugging rookie who'd smacked a perfect fastball out of Tropicana Field last year had caused him to falter.

Not in the way Sloane had now.

"Tonight was amazing. I felt like a little kid again. I felt like..." The giant T-Rex head bowed a little. "I felt like I healed something. It made me think about all the things I wanted back when I first came to this town. It made me remember how lonely I was and how not lonely I am now, thanks to you."

"It's nothing to do with me, Sloane. *You* made your place here. You made people accept you."

"But you introduced me to Trudy, and now I have a real friend. You brought me closer to your family with all the nights we spent working on the float. You made me see what it was like to be with someone who understood me and how it's so much more than great sex."

"I don't understand how any of this is leading to us breaking up." He threw his hands into the air in frustration. "And yes, it is a breakup. I don't care that we didn't put a label on it. You mean something to me, Sloane. This is not a hookup. It's…"

"A lie."

"Why is it a lie?"

"Because it doesn't matter how much either of us wants this to work, and it doesn't matter to us how much the idea that 'love conquers all' is drummed into our heads, the fantasy is a lie. Love only works if you pick the right person."

She thought he wasn't the right person for her? Sloane may as well have whacked him in the chest with a baseball bat. Her words felt like wood splintering on impact with his heart.

"Our lives are…" She sighed. "They're not compatible."

"Because I live in another city?"

"Technically, you're in another country."

He huffed. "That's semantics and you know it. Toronto is an hour-and-a-half flight from Boston, so don't give me this another country crap. It's no different than flying to New York."

"It's not the distance."

"Then what, Sloane? Because from where I'm standing, it sounds a whole lot like you're grasping at straws."

"I'm not grasping at straws. These are legitimate concerns I know will impact the longevity of a relationship. And how do you think we're going to carry this relationship forward? If you're not ready to give up your career, then where does that leave me? Do you expect me to give up everything here and follow you to Canada?"

Well, shit.

He'd be lying if he said he hadn't thought about it—her packing her bags and flying first class beside him. Her standing in front of his apartment's view of Lake Ontario, the possibilities of their life glittering in the water on the other side of the glass. Her in his bed, waiting for him when he got home from a day of training. Her cheering in the stands when he walked up to the mound.

And what about her *dreams, asshole?*

"That's exactly what you were thinking, wasn't it?" There was a sharp disappointment in her voice. "That I would follow you. That I would change my life to suit your career."

"I never said that."

But the protest was weak. He might not have said it out loud, but the thought had been there in the back of his mind, growing and growing. He wanted Sloane and he wanted his career. Wasn't there some way to create a situation where he could have both?

"Then how do you think we'll make it work, Ryan? Because if you have some magical solution, I'm all ears."

He shoved his hands into his pockets and shifted on the spot as a chilling breeze swept past. The streets were quieter now, and he caught the movement of a shadow inside his parents' house. Someone was eavesdropping.

But stopping now would only make it harder to face things tomorrow. To get the words off his chest.

"I'm not going to pretend to have it all figured out, but…" God, was he really going to do this when he couldn't even see her face? "All I know is that the day I walked into the library, my whole world was falling apart. And in the four weeks since then, I've laughed harder and more often than I can ever remember. You bring light into my world. You're effervescent. You're intoxicating. And I can't leave without telling you that this means something to me. That *you* mean something to me."

"You mean something to me, too, Ryan. But I'm not looking to give up everything I've worked for, either. I'm not looking to give up my life in Kissing Creek or the job I love or any of it." She sighed. "I made a promise to myself when I graduated college. I was going to make the home I never had as a kid. I can't give that up."

"So, we look at other options. We don't have to live in the same location. Plenty of people make long-distance work." He could hear the urgency in his own voice, like if he didn't win this battle now, then the whole war would be over. *They* would be over.

"The distance is a challenge. It was the final nail in the coffin for my parents. And honestly…"

"What?"

"We're both walking down a path toward something we desperately want, and if I'm being really, truly honest…I can't see how our paths intersect. You have this amazing career waiting for you, and I know how much it means to you. I know it's everything to you."

How could he argue with that? She was right. His career was everything to him.

"Yes, I have a career that's important to me," he said.

"No, it's not just important," she corrected him. "It's *everything*. It's your single driving force. It's the reason you get out of bed in the morning. It's *who* you are."

"What's wrong with that?"

"I already know someone like that, Ryan. My mom." She shook her head, and the T-Rex head bobbed back and forth. "I know what happens when people like you put the blinders on. You forget everything else. You forget about people and relationships, and you make the sacrifices that are required of you."

Hadn't he done that? Hadn't he lost touch with friends and schoolmates and old teammates as he'd climbed up the ranks? Hadn't he accidentally forgotten to call home on Father's Day because he'd had a big game? Hadn't he missed his brother's birthday every single year because it was right around opening day?

"You're right," he said, finding this throat was dry, and it scratched as though he'd swallowed a glassful of thorns. "I've been an absent family member. I've been a shitty friend. I've been single-minded most of my life. But that doesn't mean I'm not capable of more."

Did she not even want to try? Did she not even trust him enough to give him a chance?

"I *am* capable of more. And fuck, Sloane. I…" Could he lay himself bare? Could he put it all on the line, winner takes all and loser gets nothing? "I think I love you."

"No. No, no, no, *no*."

Okay, Sloane was officially melting down.

"That's, uh…" Ryan let out a long breath. "Wow."

"This wasn't supposed to be about love!"

"Do you think I was looking for love when I walked into the library?" His voice was getting louder now, and twin shadows shifted in the windows. Great. "I was home to hide from my problems. Not create more."

He felt her flinch. Shit.

"That's not what I meant," he said.

"I agree, though. This is all wrong. I had a plan. Find the right town and buy the right house and plant a vegetable garden and make friends and…then find the right kind of love. Find a man who wants the same things I do and who makes everything feel safe and secure."

"And I don't make you feel safe and secure." Ouch.

"No! You make me feel like I'm on a rollercoaster with my arms in the air. You make me feel like I'm about to jump into a pool so deep I can't see the bottom."

He could hear the tears in her voice, the stress. He wanted nothing more than to sweep her into his arms and melt all her pain and fear with his kiss. But he couldn't do that. First, he didn't feel like making out with a Jurassic Park reject. And second, well…he was worried he might not be able to leave if he did that.

"Love is supposed to fit into my plans, not tear them to shreds." Her voice wobbled, but she was doing her best to stay strong. "And you…you take everything I thought I wanted and make me question it all. I don't *want* to question it! I want to build my life here and feel stable. I want what I never had before—roots, a home that stays the same. People who remember my name. I can't make my father's mistakes. I can't let myself love you and then watch it slowly fall apart until I'm back exactly where I started—having nothing and being nothing."

"I won't let that happen," he said through gritted teeth.

"Yes, you will. You won't mean to, but you'll be forced to choose between baseball and me. Between baseball and our anniversary dinner. Between baseball and my birthday. Between baseball and…"

The worst, most painful thing of all was that he knew she was right. The guys on his team who were married were often bemoaning how they'd missed things. Hell, his catcher had missed the birth of his first son last year because he was playing a crucial game and the kid had come a week early.

There was a big chance Ryan would do things like that, too.

Does she really deserve someone who's going to put her second? Think about that for a moment. If you really love her, then is it right to put her in that position?

Ryan deflated, the frustration and passion and anger icing over his heart like first frost. She was absolutely right.

"It's not about us being in different places, Ry," she said softly. "It's the reasons why we're in those places to begin with. It's the goals that brought us there. Neither one of us deserves to give up our dreams."

He nodded, words clogging the back of his throat. He wanted to say so much, but nothing would come out. It was over. The first time he'd ever felt something for a woman, and it had crashed and burned in a spectacular fashion.

"If it means anything at all, I'll be watching every single game you pitch," she said, sniffling. "I know you're going to make it all the way."

It felt like she wanted to say more, but instead they both stared at each other for a long moment. The cold wrapped around Ryan and settled into his bones, making his limbs feel stiff and leaden.

"I'll walk you home," he said.

"It's okay. There are still people out, and it's not far. Besides, nobody would dare mess with a dinosaur."

He handed over the bucket of candy, feeling something gaping and hollow yawn inside him. Everything about this felt wrong. Sloane was special. In their short amount of time together, she'd changed him. Made him see that he wanted more in his life than work. He wanted relationships, love. Laughter.

But none of that was going to happen now.

"Thanks for taking me trick-or-treating." She touched his arm lightly with her puffy dinosaur hand, and he would have laughed if the whole thing wasn't so painful.

He was breaking up with a dinosaur on his parents' doorstep. Utterly ridiculous.

And yet it was easily the most painful day of his entire life.

CHAPTER TWENTY-TWO

Three and a half weeks later…

Sloane tried to put on a brave face as she led the Believe in Your Shelf Book Club meeting for November. It wasn't fair to the members that she was failing in her duties as chief bibliophile. As it was, they'd had to push the meeting back by a week because Sloane hadn't finished the book in time.

She *never* missed a book club deadline.

It was shameful. A severe breach of her duties. A mark on her otherwise spotless reading record.

As she wrapped up the meeting and bid everyone farewell, she tried not to let her smile falter. But that was hard. *Really* hard. Ever since Halloween, she'd felt off-kilter, and that feeling wasn't going away anytime soon. Stupid Ryan Bower and his sexy smile and his beautiful eyes and his caring, thoughtful gestures.

Why couldn't he be a normal guy? Why couldn't he be the kind of man who wanted love more than he wanted career domination?

But then again, would she even have fallen for him if he wasn't the exact man he was now? Probably not. Because the parts of him that opposed her life were the very same parts she admired in him.

Tears pricked the backs of Sloane's eyes, but she

blinked them away. Not that crying would matter too much—it wasn't like she'd bothered to put mascara on in the last month. Or lip gloss. Or any of her pretty dresses.

Without him in her life, it felt like none of those things mattered. She didn't have any reason to dress up, and frankly, she'd spent so many nights tossing and turning that the extra half hour of sleep in the morning was critical. Trudy had been checking on her and was even so sweet as to have some flowers delivered to the library—a big, colorful bouquet in shades of pink, purple, and yellow.

She knew she'd made the right decision ending things with Ryan. Nothing about that had changed— but the pain seemed to be getting worse, not better. The giant Ryan-shaped hole in her heart showed no signs of healing.

Sloane trudged through her front door and let it swing shut behind her. After changing into sweatpants and an oversize hoodie, she settled onto the couch with next month's book club pick. But the words swam in front of her eyes, and it only took a few minutes for her to give up in a huff. Nothing felt right—books weren't holding her attention, TV bored her, all her favorite rewatch-worthy movies didn't appeal.

It was like she couldn't feel joy anymore.

The familiar ringtone of a Skype call cut through the quiet house. Weird. She wasn't expecting a call. Sloane reached for her laptop, which was sitting on the console table across from the couch, and clicked the button to answer the call, expecting to see her half-sister's chubby-cheeked face staring into the camera. Instead, it was her dad. His big bookshelf was cramped as always behind him, and the artificial yellow glow of a lamp highlighted the crinkled lines at the corner of his eyes.

"Hey, Slo," he said.

"Is everything okay?" she asked, frowning.

He raked a hand through his hair. "Yeah, everything's fine."

They hadn't talked since she'd confronted him about being uninvited to Thanksgiving. He'd messaged a few times and she'd replied—because deeply ingrained responsibility made her do it—but she hadn't exactly fostered the conversation.

"I, uh…" He tapped his fingers against the desk, and it made a dull rhythm through the speakers. "I'm sorry about the Thanksgiving thing, Sloane. I didn't consider how it might come across, and then when you called me out on it—rightfully so—I was indignant and defensive instead of listening like a good father would do."

Sloane was taken aback by the surprise apology. Her dad wasn't exactly the vulnerable type.

"Truth is, I've been feeling horrible about it this whole time, but I was sticking my head in the sand. I'm sorry I made you feel excluded, and I'm even more sorry for not listening when you told me how you were feeling."

"Thank you," she said a little stiffly. "I appreciate that."

"I know my relationship skills leave a lot to be desired," he said. "Unfortunately, I think I messed up more with you than with anyone else. Even more than your mother."

Now *that* surprised her. "Why do you think that?"

"Because you never asked for anything, so I allowed myself to believe you didn't need anything."

The words were so simple and yet so startlingly true. They stole the air from her lungs. He was right. She'd never asked her parents for anything. She never asked anyone for anything. Never wanted to be a burden or to face rejection.

Which turned into a deep-seated need for her to rely only on herself.

And that had morphed into a tightly held desire to have everything she wanted without compromise.

"Now I know you needed a hell of a lot more from both of us, but I was too caught up in my broken marriage to see it." For the first time, Sloane saw pain and regret in his eyes when he talked about her mother, rather than anger. "I wish I'd realized this a lot sooner."

"It must've been hard following Mom around the world and playing second fiddle to her career."

Her father frowned. "You think that's why we got divorced?"

"Isn't it?" That was the belief she'd always held, especially after hearing her father complain about her mother's work on *so* many occasions.

"I definitely exacerbated problems, but...no. It wasn't her career moving us around that was the main issue. It wasn't even that I gave up working in my field during that time."

She was well and truly stunned. "Then what was it?"

"Our relationship broke down because of a lack of communication." He reached for something offscreen, and then a glass of something amber-gold came into view. He took a sip, then set the glass down on his desk. "Your mother and I weren't great at sharing. The nature of her work was secretive, as you know, but she was a closed book in all areas of her life."

If she was being honest, Sloane couldn't really tell anyone much about her mother because she didn't *know* much about her. "She's always been an enigma."

"It's part of what I fell in love with," her dad said. "She was a mysterious and worldly woman. I realized that while an enigma is good in theory, being married to someone who never opens up about their feelings or desires is really hard. She shut me out constantly, and I turned spiteful and started shutting her out, too."

A lump lodged in the back of her throat. Her parents were good people—fundamentally flawed, but good. Like Sloane herself. She wasn't perfect, but she tried. She learned. That was the important part.

"I regret how I handled it back then, and I'm trying not to make those mistakes now. But travelling around the world with you and your mother wasn't the cause of our problems. Our relationship would have broken down in the exact same way, even if we'd lived in the same place for twenty years."

She felt like the world was tilting beneath her. This shook her understanding of everything—her understanding of the reasons her childhood had been hard and lonely. The reasons why she'd chased the small-town dream.

"Sloane? Are you frozen?"

"No, I'm still here." The words were tight in the back of her throat, and her lips felt stiff and uncooperative. "Just tired."

Tired and miserable and...lonely.

Well, that wasn't entirely true. She and Trudy had hung out last night, ordering the woodfire pizza Sloane loved and eating it at Trudy's new dining table, talking until they'd barely been able to speak through their yawns. It was the beginnings of a real, true friendship. For that, she was grateful.

But her house was lonely. Her *bed* was lonely. And the thought of having another man there that wasn't Ryan felt...icky and wrong.

"You really think you and Mom would have split up even if you'd stayed in Michigan?"

"I don't think it, I *know* it." He took another swig of his drink. "A relationship needs vulnerability. It needs open, two-way communication. If you have those things, then you can make it work no matter where you are."

"But didn't you hate having to start over all the time? Every time we'd leave a place, people would forget us and then..." She looked at the computer screen, hoping her dad would understand her this time. That he would know what she was asking. "Wasn't it hard starting over every time?"

"Of course it's hard to start over. But as for people forgetting us… I don't know if that's true. Do you think Grandma and Grandpa forgot us when we moved overseas?"

"Well, no." Sloane remembered the international calls on her birthday and on Christmas, and the sound of her grandma and grandpa bickering over who was holding the phone receiver. "But they're family. They have to remember us."

"Fair. But I keep in touch with a few people I met over the years. Remember Mr. Fischer from Munich?"

Sloane had a vague recollection of a man with pink cheeks and a permanent smile who'd helped her father learn German. He'd lived in the apartment next door, and his wife had always baked amazing apple cake.

She nodded.

"We've been emailing back and forth for almost fifteen years now. In fact, I'm planning a surprise trip for Amy next year. We're going to take a family vacation to Europe, and Tobias is going to host us for a few days."

"I had no idea you still talked to him."

"Why would I tell you? All he and I do is share articles and talk about motorsports, and that would bore you to tears."

Her father was taking everything she thought she

understood about the past and shaking it like a can of whipped cream.

"I know I haven't made enough of an effort with you since we moved back to the States," he said. "You went off to college, and I was so relieved to be getting out of an unhappy situation that I threw all my focus into building something new, instead of honoring the family I'd already built. I'm so sorry. Do you think you can forgive me?"

"Yeah." Emotion prickled the back of her throat. "I can."

"As for Thanksgiving, I spoke with Amy, and we've found a bigger place to rent that will fit everyone, then we'll drive to and from her sister's house."

"Dad, stop." Sloane held up her hand. "It's fine. You don't need to rearrange everything for me. I was upset, sure. But I'm not unreasonable. I understand your situation."

"If you want to come, we'd love to have you." He looked sincere.

"I appreciate that, but I'm going to stay here and…do some reflecting," she said, smiling. "You've given me a lot to think about."

"Now there's a change," he said with a chuckle. "Normally, it's you giving me something to think about."

She smiled. "I love you, Dad."

"I love you, too, Slo."

She ended the video call and closed her laptop, sinking back into the couch. It felt like the whole world looked different now.

Everything had revolved around her mother's career, and Sloane and her father were expected to pack up their lives whenever she said so. In fact, Sloane barely saw her mother for more than a few minutes at a time her whole life. A quick hello in the morning, a kiss good night in the evening. Even if she was home, she'd be working, and if Sloane entered her office, she always felt like she was on a timer, trying to snatch a minute before the next conference call or before she was asked to leave.

She blamed her mother's career for *years* for the demise of her parents' marriage. Of course, they'd never discussed it with her at the time—it was private and painful and she was still a teenager—so she'd been left to draw her own conclusions.

And she'd been wrong this whole time.

Had she made a mistake pushing Ryan away, fearful his ambitions would drive them down the same path?

You can't love a man who loves his job more than you.

If she went with Ryan to Toronto and it was the same thing, battling for his attention, being stuck at home on her own, and having to start over by making new friends *again*… The whole reason she came to Kissing Creek was to build a life.

And she had built something she loved. Her head said this was the place—a place where she could stay forever. And she'd finally started to make a real friend. How could she give that up? But her heart asked an important question—*why stay in one place if you don't have the man you love by your side?*

"Can't I have both?" she asked to no one in particular.

She still couldn't see how she and Ryan would make things work. Yet she couldn't shake the epiphany that had come to her today. A home was pointless without love, because bricks and mortar and a mailbox did not make a life. Hugs and tears and kisses and whispers made a life.

And communication was the most important thing of all.

Her father's call today had patched the fissure between them. Yes, he'd made mistakes, but Sloane always believed a person should be judged on how they acted *after* making a mistake, not whether they made it in the first place. Her dad's apology meant a lot.

And she believed Ryan cared about her.

But believing wasn't the only barrier. He might make her feel like she'd come home, but she couldn't be in a relationship with someone unless they respected her dreams, too. Unless they were willing to meet her halfway.

And that was the one thing she wasn't sure Ryan could ever budge on.

• • •

Ryan walked through the doors of an exclusive

Toronto restaurant, following the head hostess. Outside, the CN Tower glowed in bright colors, the city skyline splashed across floor-to-ceiling windows like a piece of art. Food smells and something peaty, like scotch, which normally would have had him salivating, turned his stomach.

He'd been out with his friends last night—partying, drinking, drowning his sorrows in flashing lights and thumping bass and bottle service. He'd shoved all thoughts of Sloane to the back of his mind, determined to move on and bring his focus back to life in Toronto. He was lucky to have a close-knit group of friends within the Blizzards, though they were all still in their twenties and jokingly called him "old man Bower."

He'd kept up with ease, downing shots and shoving the other guys toward pretty girls and signaling to the servers to bring yet another bottle of Dom to their table. He'd stumbled home sometime after four a.m. and collapsed into bed, sleeping until two p.m.

That was the thing about your mid-thirties: you could party hard with the rest of them, but the hangovers were a bitch.

Tonight, he had dinner with his coach. The invite had come as a bit of a surprise. Not that he didn't get along with the guy, but last-minute invites were not John Castellano's MO. It meant he wanted to talk.

As Ryan walked through the restaurant, nerves twisted in his gut. He tried to distract himself by focusing on the lights twinkling and shifting outside. His gaze broke from the window as the hostess motioned toward the table where his coach was sitting, white shirt unbuttoned at the collar and big gold rings glinting in the light.

"Welcome home, Ry." John stood and clapped an arm onto his shoulder. "It's good to have you back."

This place *had* been home for the last seven years. Ryan had arrived in Toronto at twenty-eight, entering the peak of his career, traded for a playoff run that crashed and burned. The rebuilding started and he'd stuck around, determined to help build a championship-winning team. Now, this season was over, and his boys had come close. *So* close. The underdogs sadly hadn't been able to clinch the World Series.

But they were all hungry—eager to get themselves some winner's hardware. Eager to take another swing. Eager to claim what they believed was the outcome they deserved...next year.

When Ryan thought about next year, it was like looking into a pit—black and empty. The future, which once felt like a shining star, was now murky.

"Thanks, Coach." Ryan forced a smile as he pulled his chair back and sat.

The server immediately came over to take his drink order, but Ryan decided to skip the hard stuff, opting for a beer instead. John nursed his usual, an Old Fashioned.

"How's the family?" he asked.

"Good." Ryan nodded. "The same."

"Most people say 'the same' with a sense of disdain, but you say it like it's something positive." John nodded. "I appreciate that."

"That's because you're a family man."

He expected his coach to laugh, but instead the older man scrubbed a hand over his face. Ryan had been so in his head when he first approached the table that he hadn't noticed how tired John looked. But now that he was paying attention, he could see the silver-speckled whiskers lining his jaw and the extra lines around his eyes.

"What's going on?"

"It's nothin' for you to worry about." He shook his head. "The missus and I are having some troubles, that's all."

"Oh no." Ryan liked Mrs. Castellano. She was very active in the club and did a lot of fundraising for the charities they supported locally.

"I promised her this was going to be my last year and then I'd announce my retirement. But…" He shook his head. "We came so damn close, ya know?"

Ryan nodded. One of the main reasons he stuck around through the rebuild was because he believed in his coach. John was one of the most passionate, visionary guys he'd ever worked with. This year showed that every brick he'd put in place was the right one.

They could win it next year.

"So you're staying?" he asked.

"I can't walk away. But Iris…" John shook his head and reached for his drink, taking a long gulp and draining the glass. "She wants to move down south, be close to the grandkids. Spend time with them before it's too late and they're grown up. But what am I supposed to do? Walk right up to the finish line and then quit?"

He'd never heard John talk about anything personal before. The man was Mr. Professional, but they'd worked together for the last seven years. There was a lot of trust between them.

"If she wants to leave, fine." He clenched his jaw. "But I gotta see this through."

Ryan waited for the "you're right" to materialize on his lips, but the words never formed. John and Iris had been married almost forty years. She'd supported him the whole time—when he got his first big league coaching gig, when he got fired in L.A. after only a season because the team manager expected miracles, when they came up north to Canada.

When was it her turn to call the shots?

You're supposed to side with him.

"Anyway, I didn't bring you here for a shoulder to cry on," John said roughly.

They paused as the server delivered his beer and some appetizers. He also sheepishly asked for an autograph, which Ryan obliged—signing his name on a napkin. The young man scampered away, a huge smile on his face.

At least someone didn't think he was washed up.

The sports gossip sites had been rife with rumors of a trade the past week. Then John had summoned him for dinner.

"Why *did* you bring me here?" Ryan asked.

"I know you've probably seen all the shit floating around online," John began, reaching for a croquette. He popped it in his mouth and chewed, waiting to see what response he would get.

"Was there a question in there?"

His coach chuckled. "Not wearing your heart on your sleeve, are you?"

"You know I don't want to go to another team."

"Good."

The word lingered in the air like smoke.

"Good?" Ryan asked.

"Yes, good."

John reached for another appetizer and didn't elaborate. The negotiation process was a delicate one, regardless of who you were and how good the relationship with your coach and your team. Both sides were cagey, and any official discussions would need to include Ryan's agent.

But John was telling him, without actually saying anything, that he wanted him to sign another contract. He was telling him not to worry about the rumors.

"How good?" Ryan asked.

"I can't say. But my lucky number is three."

Three years. That would take him to being thirty-eight. Three more years to keep the dream alive. He'd be in an elite group of pitchers who'd lasted in the league for more than fifteen years. Three more shots at winning the World Series.

"I've got your back, Ryan. We're in this together."

He waited for the relief to set in. For the elation to flood his veins. But the only thing he could find it in himself to ask was, "What are you going to do if Iris leaves?"

John shot him a look. "Seriously? I show you my cards and *that's* what you want to know?"

"It seems important."

"Look, you don't get to make it to this level without sacrifice. Everybody pays the price eventually."

John liked to eat early, and Ryan made it home by eight thirty. He gazed around his apartment. It was comfortable here, with the cozy yet modern furniture and a big-ass TV that was great for watching sports and playing video games. His kitchen allowed him plenty of space to experiment, and he loved sitting on the balcony and having a drink while watching the lake shimmer.

Yet, if he thought about it—which he hadn't ever before—every memory he had of this place was of him alone. Sure, his folks had come to visit a few times, and Mark and Ace came up when their schedules allowed it. And yes, he had good friends in the league that he liked to hang out with.

Most of the time, though, he was here by himself, comfortable but...stuck in a hamster wheel. For years, he'd never been bothered by that, because the only thing that mattered was getting ready for the next season. He'd always taken a break during the off-season, have a vacation somewhere remote and warm and relaxing. Then it was training, studying the previous season, counting down the days until it was time for spring training.

Yet, now, Ryan felt like there were ants under his skin. What the hell was he going to do for the months between now and next season? How the heck had he filled his time before?

In Kissing Creek, he'd gotten a glimpse of what more his life could contain. What was missing. What he *wanted* for the future. Because when he thought of the future, that image wasn't just a mound and a ball and his glove. It wasn't just a packed major league stadium and the din of cheering fans. Hell, it wasn't just the dazzle of a world championship ring.

He saw her—Sloane. The wind rustling her glossy hair and a mischievous twinkle in her eyes. He saw limbs entwined beneath a duvet and figures cuddled up on a couch. He saw a dazzling ring…but this one only had a single stone and small, dainty band designed for a woman's finger. He saw a round stomach and heard the wail of a child.

He saw a life that didn't end at forty.

Glancing at his phone, Ryan decided to call his brother. If anyone could give him an honest, bullshit-free opinion, it was Mark. He held his phone up, waiting for the video call to connect, while he settled into his couch.

"Hey, bro," he said when Mark answered.

"Whoa." His brother did a double take. "You look like… Did you ride a goose back to Canada?"

"You're such an oil painting yourself," he deadpanned, swiping a hand through his hair to tame it back into place. "And I walked back from dinner. It was windy."

"What's up?"

"Coach let slip that they're going to offer another three years."

"That's great." In the background, Ryan could see the sparse interior of the cabin.

For some reason, it made a lump stick in the back of Ryan's throat. Freaking Mark. He was so responsible and had his head screwed on properly and lived this family life that made him seem older and wiser and more…together.

"Is it great?" Ryan asked.

Mark didn't look as shocked by the question as Ryan would have thought. "You tell me."

His mind drifted to the day Mark had shared his different views about their childhood and what he wanted for his own kids. His life was about building something for the people he cared about…and Ryan had never done that. Mark had a real vision. A plan that wasn't contingent on him staying as young and fit as possible. He embraced the process of getting older and looked at the years stretching out before him as being ripe with opportunity instead of fear and scarcity.

"Mom told me you and Sloane split up." Mark

held up a hand. "Don't get mad."

He didn't have the energy to be mad right now. "It's true."

"What happened?"

"Coming here isn't the right move for her." He blew out a breath. "Which I respect, of course. She loves Kissing Creek and wants to stay there."

"Right."

"And she wasn't open to talking about the long-distance thing, either." He couldn't help the frustration that crept into his voice. He knew they had something special. And he knew she felt it, too.

Yeah, but you thought John and Iris had something special and now they're on the verge of separating.

Mark bobbed his head in a way that indicated he was going to say something Ryan wouldn't want to hear. "So, when you asked her to give up her life in Kissing Creek, she said no. That's not exactly surprising."

"I never actually asked her." The fact that Sloane had cut him off before he could say it was a minor detail. "And you make it sound like I was expecting her to do all the heavy lifting. It wasn't like that. I was willing to look at options, see what we could do to make it work. I wanted to *try*. But I didn't even get that far. She cut me off at the knees as soon as I told her how I felt."

Knowing her history, he understood why. But still, it had stung. To be prepared to tell someone he thought he might love them, and get shot down like that…

Where had it even come from? He hadn't been planning to use the L-word, but when he realized that Sloane was slipping through his fingers, it popped out. Did he mean it? *Could* he even mean it? They'd only known each other a month.

"I'm not saying you're selfish, Ry." Mark sighed. "But what concessions were you willing to make? What sacrifices would fall on your side of things?"

Ryan opened his mouth to respond, but he didn't have an answer. His career was...well, it was who he was.

Just like John.

A hard lump settled in the pit of his stomach. Seeing his coach like that...it was like staring into the future, and he wasn't sure he liked what he saw. In his sixties, the guy was still making sacrifices, still not seeing his family, still willing to walk away from relationships.

When would it end?

"None," he admitted. "Not a damn one."

"But you got what you wanted, right? Three more years. So, it's worth it?"

"I don't know if it is. My head is telling me I should be over the moon, because I know it could have gone either way. But..."

"Your heart is saying something different?"

"Yeah." He sucked in a breath. "I don't...I don't want to regret choosing the wrong path ten years from now."

Ten years from now, he wouldn't be playing

ball—not at the majors, anyway. Ten years from now, he'd be retired from that job, and what would he have to show for it? An empty apartment and a championship ring. Hopefully. But if he walked away now when they were so close…

Could he sacrifice his career for love? Would he regret it? Or would he regret giving up the woman who'd shown him there was more than one path in life?

"I can't tell you what to do, bro." Mark shook his head. "Only you can make that decision."

"John would hate me. The team…" He let out a breath. "The media…"

They would dine on this story forever. They'd speculate he was pushed out, that he couldn't hack the pressure. That he never fulfilled his potential. More importantly, would Ryan think those things about himself?

"I need to sleep," he said, unable to think through the swirling thoughts. Nothing was clear anymore.

"The answer will come if you let it," Mark said sagely. "Give it time."

Unfortunately, time was the one thing Ryan felt that he no longer had.

CHAPTER TWENTY-THREE

Three days later...

Outside, the weather was turning. They'd had snow flurries earlier, little swirls of white that drifted down and melted on contact with the ground. Nothing stuck, and now it was raining, teaming down in heavy sheets and keeping people inside. Sloane was still in her work outfit as she puttered around her kitchen, making a hot cocoa and watching the weather batter her poor backyard. She couldn't find the energy to change.

No matter what she did, she could *not* get Ryan Bower out of her head.

It was ridiculous.

He was long gone. Hell, *she* was the one who pushed him away when he'd tried to express his feelings. The chat with her father had put a lot of things into perspective—namely, that the main thing she'd blamed for the unhappiness in her childhood wasn't exactly the guilty culprit. At least, it wasn't the *only* guilty culprit.

Maybe she should've heard Ryan out. Maybe she should've communicated with him instead of shutting him down. Maybe she should stop letting fear guide her decisions. She'd even tried to call him earlier that day to wish him an early Happy Thanksgiving, but the call had gone to voicemail and he hadn't returned it.

Can you blame him? He said he loved you and your responses was six nos.

A knock at the door startled her out of her reverie. Who the heck was coming over now? She set her cocoa down on the kitchen counter and shuffled through the house, wrapping her arms around herself. The house was toasty, but there was something about looking at pouring rain that made her feel cold out of commiseration for anyone outside.

There was a figure huddled on her doorstep, head bowed, and a hood yanked up. She pulled the door open.

"Ryan? Wha—what are you doing here?" She sucked in a breath, her mind totally unprepared and starting to spiral. "Is something wrong? Is your dad okay? I saw your mom, but she didn't—"

"Dad's fine." Water ran down his face. "Can I come in?"

"Of course." She shook her head and stepped back, motioning for him to come inside.

She could see him clearer now, eyes bright and jaw set. His dark hair looked almost inky black, poking out from his hood. Rain splashed against the ground, and Sloane shivered as Ryan took his boots off before coming in. Not that it mattered much, because he was dripping water all over the place.

"What are you doing here?" she asked, her mind whirring. When had he returned to Kissing Creek? How long was he staying?

"I've come back to deal with some unfinished business," he said.

"With what?"

"Not what. *Who.*"

He couldn't be here for her. That would be… She shook her head. "What?"

"I said not what, *who.*" He chuckled as she wrinkled her nose.

"Sounds like you're doing a Dr. Seuss impersonation."

"I can't stand the way we left things, Sloane. I came back because…" The easy, joking smile slipped away, and he was Serious Ryan again. Focused Ryan. A man with a plan and the raw determination to execute it. "I needed to see you."

Water droplets clung to his hair and cheeks and eyelashes. He looked so beautiful that she had to turn away from the glare of it. She almost couldn't breathe. Her lungs felt tight and restricted as if she'd wrapped a corset around her body and laced it as tight as possible.

She busied herself with fetching him a towel and thrusting it in his direction. "Here. You're soaking."

"Thanks." He pulled his hood back and mopped the rain up with the fluffy fabric. When he was done, he caught her staring. She didn't even try to pretend she wasn't. "I miss you."

The sincerity flowed off him, deep and resonant in his voice and the way he looked at her like he was willing the rest of the world to melt away.

I miss you, too.

But she couldn't bring herself to say it. She wanted to—but it felt vulnerable and scary, and she wasn't sure whether she was making a mistake anymore. In some ways, the night of trick-or-treating had felt easier, because she'd had a strong belief about what to avoid. Now, after speaking with her father, she understood that the failure of a relationship was more complicated than one, single, easy-to-identify issue.

"Can we talk?" he asked. "I've got my car here. We can go for a drive and…well, it was really hard last time not being able to see your face."

"You've never broken up with a woman dressed as a dinosaur before?" Sloane tried to make light of it, even though her legs felt like jelly and her hopeful heart felt like a butterfly trapped in a glass jar.

"I've never broken up with *anyone* before, because that would mean I had to care about someone enough to be in a serious relationship. I never cared about anyone like that before," he said. "Not until you."

"Did you fly all the way back here to tell me that?" she asked, half joking.

"Yes."

Sloane swallowed. *Wow.* If Ryan was abundant in anything, it was intensity, and she felt the full force of it now—in his stare, in the set of his jaw, in the heat radiating from him.

"So soon," she whispered.

"Not soon enough. Every day…" He sighed.

"And why can't we talk here?"

"I feel like neutral ground might be good. Plus…" He raked a hand through his hair. "I need to keep my hands busy."

Oh.

Her cheeks warmed. "Sure, let's go for a drive."

She grabbed an umbrella from the stand by the door and handed it to him after they'd put their shoes on. It never made sense for the shorty to hold the umbrella. Outside, he slipped an arm around her shoulders and pulled her close, keeping her as dry as possible. It was so natural, their steps falling in time and her body fitting perfectly in the crook under his arm. He unlocked his car and held the umbrella over her as she got in, ever the consummate gentleman.

Sloane tried to collect herself as he jogged around to the other side and slipped into the driver's seat. All month, she'd been trying to tell herself to get over him, to understand that sometimes things didn't work out and being an adult was accepting it. But having him back here now—close enough to touch— was like taking a knife to the stitches over her heart. Stitches that hadn't even *thought* about healing yet.

Inside the car, it was quiet, and rain drummed on the roof, relentless and steady. Ryan started the engine and eased the car onto the street, the passing streetlights illuminating the perfect lines of him in yellow flashes.

"How's Toronto?" she asked, unsure what to say or how to manage this conversation. Like Ryan, she'd never really done the relationship thing. Any "breakups" barely earned the right to be called such, because Sloane had never quite found a guy who was a perfect fit for her dreams.

And yet, now, she had a man who was still a questionable fit—at best—and he made her heart sing.

"Weird," Ryan admitted. "I always come home to Kissing Creek for a bit over Christmas, and never once have I felt homesick returning to Toronto. But this time it felt like…like I was running away."

"Running away from what?"

Ryan's car—which was actually Gaye's car—navigated the quiet streets, his hands resting easy on the steering wheel as though he didn't even need to think about where he was going. As though he knew this place well enough to traverse it with his eyes closed.

"The future," he said eventually.

"Your future is in Toronto." Sloane frowned. "Isn't it?"

"They offered me three more years. Unofficially, but I trust my coach."

"Congratulations," she replied numbly.

Was he going to try to convince her to leave Kissing Creek? Her heart sank.

Is he worth the pain of starting over? The pain of always being second-most important?

Yes.

The answer hurt, because it wasn't the answer she felt like she should give. Sloane was an independent, self-sufficient woman. What would it say about her if she gave up everything for him? That she'd learned nothing.

But what you thought you learned wasn't actually the truth.

Her father's view of his marriage had rocked Sloane to her core. It made her reevaluate what she was sacrificing in having dreams that didn't flex or bend. Having goals that were so black-and-white she'd be willing to walk away from love.

Love?

Yes, love. She sucked in a shaky breath.

Before she could respond, the car rolled to a stop, and she realized where they were—outside the Bower residence. The Halloween decorations were all gone, but Sloane could still sketch her and Ryan into the spot where she'd walked away. She was ashamed to say she'd avoided his mom at the supermarket—not because she didn't adore Gaye Bower, but because it hurt a little too much to think about how she missed the nights building the float at their place.

"Why did you bring me here?" she asked, looking out the window. There was a glow inside the house, and the warmth called to some damaged part of her soul.

"I never wanted this." He gestured to the house. "The house in a small town, the big family dinners, the lawn, the festive decorations. It all felt like a ball and chain. Something to hold me back."

"And I saw it as security." How different they were in their wants and needs. The hope that had flickered in Sloane's chest started to harden. "The kind of life I'd always wanted."

"Here's what I learned. It's neither of those things."

"What do you mean?"

"Coming home last month was hard. It felt like punishment, like failure. And yet, in getting to know you and helping you with the parade and reading *Stormy Pleasures*…I saw this place with new eyes." He turned in his seat, setting his heavenly blue gaze on her once more. "I saw the beauty that you saw. I spent time with my family in a way I hadn't in a long time. I had real conversations with my brother. And suddenly I realized why I was so fearful of my career coming to an end."

"Why?"

"Because I know that without it, my life is meaningless. I've spent years sacrificing literally everything else—family, relationships, socializing, education. Everything." He sucked in a breath. "It's too much. I've given up too much."

"But you love baseball."

"I do. And it's been an incredible experience. But…" He reached out for her hand. "When I got back to Toronto and realized I might never see you again, I felt sick with it. I had to ask myself whether this—us—was something else I could sacrifice in the name of my career."

And? The word danced on the tip of her tongue, expectant and frightened and a little hopeful. But his gaze held her captive and frozen. Nobody had ever looked at her that way before him. It was intoxicating. Validating.

But she couldn't give up her life here, could she?

"I can't do it, Sloane. I can't walk away and spend my whole life wondering what we might have done together. What we might have *been* together." His thumb drifted to her jaw, tracing the line there so gently that it had no more weight than a breeze. "That's what I mean about the house and the lawn and the white picket fence. It's not a ball and chain, and it's also not a goal. Because none of that matters without the right person. None of it has meaning without the right relationship. It's the people who make or break the dream."

Wasn't that exactly what she'd learned from talking to her father? It wasn't the constant moving or her mother's career that had ruined their marriage—it was the lack of communication. It wasn't her mother's long hours and the new schools that had made Sloane's childhood lonely—it was that she'd never been taught how to be vulnerable and let people in. All that came from people, from relationships.

"I understand that now, too," she said. "And I'd be lying if I said I hadn't thought about you every night since Halloween. When you said you thought you loved me…"

She shook her head.

"I was wrong," Ryan said. "I said I *thought* I loved you. But even that was about protecting myself.

Because I knew. Even though it didn't make sense and it didn't seem to fit with my life, I knew."

"I feel the same way. You don't fit with my life, but I've never met a man more infuriating and wonderful and sexy and stubborn and focused than you."

"That's quite the description," he said with a soft chuckle.

"I don't want to love you." Her voice wavered. "Because I'm terrified that if we don't make this work, then I'm going to feel even more lost than before. I'm terrified that one of us will have to give up what we want in order to be together and that it will slowly eat away at us."

"I'm saying no," Ryan said.

"No to what?"

"To the contract. I'm going to turn them down." He squared his shoulders, like he was psyching himself up. "I'm going to retire."

Sloane gasped. "Why?"

"Because I can't keep going like this, only caring about one thing. Only *being* one thing." He shook his head. "I've played longer than most people ever have the chance to. I've achieved more than most."

"No. You can't…" She shook her head. "You can't quit."

"I am." He nodded. "I couldn't even be there for my team when I was injured because all I cared about was what *I* was missing out on. Then when I fell for you, I was expecting you to make all the sacrifices. This job has made me selfish."

"You're not selfish, Ryan." She swallowed. "You're driven."

"I live like I'm an island, and I'm sick of it. It's… lonely." The sadness in his voice made tears prick in the back of her eyes. "I have to face what I fear and realize that one thing ending isn't everything ending. I don't want to lose you, Sloane. I want us to have the life we deserve, together."

"You would give it all up to be here with me?"

"Yes."

Ryan's answer echoed in the car, smoothed over by the steady drumming of the rain. Shadows shifted inside the house—his parents must be home. Emotion clogged the back of her throat. This man. This amazing, incredible, wonderful man.

"I don't know what to say," she replied, shakily.

"Tell me what you want. I'll make it happen." He brought his hand to her cheek, his electric blue eyes glowing with sincerity. "Whatever hurdles are still in front of us, we'll make it work. Anything we face, we can overcome it."

"Just you," she whispered. "I just want you."

He tugged her closer, resting his forehead against hers. "I love you, Sloane, and that makes me more excited about the future than ever."

Warmth expanded in her chest, filling her up so that she felt like a helium balloon about to float away. Yes, this was scary. And yes, she still had old scars and old fears. But she knew one thing for certain: letting the past dictate her future would be the biggest mistake she could ever make.

What she felt for Ryan was special. And it was worth making a go of it.

"I love you, too." Saying it aloud was nowhere near as scary as she thought it might be. In fact, saying it felt right in a way nothing ever had before. Like finding a snuggly sweater that fit perfectly.

It was everyday magic.

And yet Sloane knew that her life was about to shift course—love was something she'd always known she wanted, but chasing after it had seemed daunting. She'd never felt ready. But now, staring into Ryan's handsome face, her entire life was a jigsaw puzzle with the pieces clicking into place.

Only there was still one gap.

If he was sacrificing it all, then how was this any different to him expecting her to follow him to Toronto? It was the same—one-sided.

"Can you delay one more year?" she asked.

"What do you mean?"

"Ask for one more year with the Blizzards. One more chance to win." She sucked in a trembling breath, her heart fluttering in her chest. "Retire after next season."

"But..." He shook his head. "I thought you wanted..."

"Knowing that you would give it all up for me means everything. It shows that this situation *isn't* the same as what my mother and father had. It shows that you see me and you respect my dreams and..."

She let out a breath. "You love me."

"I just said that."

"No, Ryan. You *showed* it." She brushed her lips over his, holding herself back from kissing him hard. Because she wanted to be sure they were on the same page. "I'll come with you for a year. I can take a sabbatical from my position here and cheer you on from the sidelines. Then we'll come back and make a life."

"Sloane." He closed his eyes. "I want you to know that my word means something, okay? I've seen men I know and respect make promises and break them, but I will *never* do that to you."

"I know. I trust you." She smiled. "I've been miserable without you, too. I kept telling myself it would get better, but every day was more painful than the last. And…"

"Tell me."

"I realized that in not even wanting to listen to ways we could make this work, I thought I was shielding myself from loss, when I ended up guaranteeing it." She shook her head. "I had a good talk with my dad, and we cleared a few things up. I was trying so hard not to repeat their mistakes, when really I didn't ever know the full story."

"I'm glad you're working through things with your dad."

"Me, too." Sloane nodded. "Family is important to me, even though I've never quite had the family life I wanted. A family like what you had."

"You're going to be part of my family, Sloane." His sweet smile turned slightly wicked, the lights outside enhancing his cheeky expression. "And maybe we can do our bit to expand the family. After lots of practice, of course."

"Practice, huh?" she said with a chuckle. "I like the sound of that."

Ryan leaned forward, his nose brushing hers before his lips descended in a whisper-light kiss. They hovered there for a moment, as if wanting to capture this memory forever. Sloane let her eyes flutter shut in anticipation as she made a promise to never forget how good it felt to be vulnerable and open with him.

Ryan's warm breath skated across her cheek, and then the soft yet firm pressure of his lips melted her as he kissed her again. Deeper, harder. And filled with so much love she thought she might burst. She reached out, catching the fabric of his jacket so she could tug him closer.

"Your parents are going to catch us making out in front of their house," Sloane said huskily as she pressed a kiss to his jaw. The gentle prickle of the day's stubble was a delicious friction against her lips.

"Worried you're going to get me grounded?" He grinned.

"Uh huh. We should have stayed at my place."

"We'll go back later. We've got the rest of our lives to practice, but I'm betting you're probably starving right now, so why don't we go inside and grab a bite to eat? My parents would love to see you."

Ryan shot her a look. "I heard you scampered into the other aisle at the supermarket when you saw my mom last week."

"She saw that?" Sloane cringed. "Oh no, that's so awkward."

"Come on, that's what family is all about. No grudges, no holding on to bad feelings." He pushed his door open, and Sloane followed him.

Truthfully, she wanted to go inside and spend some time with his family—even if she did want to get Ryan alone and all to herself. The Bowers had embraced her, their kindness and inclusivity a core family value.

They walked up to the quiet house. Lights glowed in the main window, but as Ryan unlocked the door, it was still inside. There was no television or music playing, no clatter of movement in the kitchen, though she could smell something absolutely delicious.

Ryan helped her shrug out of her coat, and then she followed him through to the kitchen. As soon as she set foot into the room, a group of people jumped and yelled, "*Happy Thanksgiving!*"

Sloane gasped and clamped a hand over her mouth. In the Bowers' family dining and kitchen area were all her favorite Kissing Creek residents—Gaye and Alfie Bower, Mark and Mandy and their kids, Trudy, Pat from the library and her date, Hot Grandpa. Even Douglas Shaw from the Kissing Creek Volunteer Committee was there.

That's when she noticed the kitchen table—

covered with an endless amount of food, roast vegetables, salads, mashed potato, bottles of wine, and an empty platter in the middle.

"About time!" Gaye said, opening the oven and sliding out a giant turkey. "I was worried the bird was going to get dry, you two were taking so long."

"I figured, since you were missing out on Thanksgiving with your dad, then we could give you a Thanksgiving eve right here," Ryan said, looking pretty darn happy with himself.

Everyone rushed over to Sloane, enveloping her in hugs one by one. She was almost certain she'd never received so much love in a single moment in all her life. To her mortification, a big fat tear plopped onto her cheek because she was so overwhelmed.

"Is Sloane Rickman actually speechless?" Ryan pumped a fist into the air. "Yes!"

"Hey!" She tried to punch him in the arm, but he caught her into a big hug and kissed the heck out of her while the rest of the room cheered and teased them.

"You planned all this?" She shook her head.

"Well, I floated the idea with Mom and she told me to get out of the way because I would probably mess it up." He laughed.

"Damn straight." Gaye had the turkey on the table, and Alfie was carving it up while everyone took their seats.

It was a beautiful sight—people young and old, pouring drinks for one another and passing plates around and talking animatedly.

"Sorry it's not on actual Thanksgiving Day, but I wanted to make sure we got everyone here that you'd want to see."

"It's perfect." She held him tight, knowing with every fiber of her being that no matter what the next few years held, this man was the one for her. "What if I'd said no and all these people were waiting in here? That's a risky move."

"I never throw a pitch thinking I'm going to miss," Ryan said, kissing the top of her head and giving her a gentle shove toward an empty chair. "Now, sit down. It's family time."

"Thank you," she said, her eyes watering.

"No, thank *you*." Ryan nodded. "I've been taking all this for granted for a long time. Being with you has brought me back to what's important."

"Love?"

"Yeah, love. And I'm never going to put that in second place ever again."

Sloane grabbed a seat next to Trudy, and Ryan took the one on Sloane's other side. For the next hour, they ate, and Sloane felt more at home with these people than she'd ever felt anywhere before. It was a beautiful thing—knowing it wasn't a place that made you feel stable and secure, but the love of the right people.

And now she had that in spades.

EPILOGUE

One and a half years later…

There was nothing better for Ryan than seeing his wife pregnant. Sloane was eating like a cross between a frat boy and someone conducting a science experiment, and she waddled around with her big belly sticking out front for the whole world to see.

It was cutest thing ever.

"Can you…?" She looked up at him pitifully from her position on the bench by the front door. "I hate this. I can't even untie my own shoes anymore."

"Mrs. Bower, I live to serve." Calling her by their now-shared surname always gave Ryan a thrill. He hadn't expected her to change her name when they got married, but she'd insisted. She wanted to be part of his family. Wanted to build one of their own with a name they could share with their child. "I'm here to take care of you."

"You know I hate asking for help." She watched as he untied her laces, carefully unravelling the double knot like he would do for their son in the not-so-distant future. "It makes me feel useless."

"You're not useless. You've got bigger things to worry about than tying shoes."

Her eyes softened, and her hands drifted to her

belly. "Like growing this little bean."

"I think he's more than a bean now."

Sloane narrowed her eyes. "Watch it, buddy."

"I love it." He tossed the shoes aside and pressed a kiss to her belly. Then to her mouth. She responded hungrily, and Ryan was hard as a rock in an instant. Their sex life had slowed a bit—with Sloane's body changing almost daily—but they were as hot for each other as ever. "Seeing you like that, carrying our baby…it's amazing."

"Even if it feels like you're having sex with a beached whale?" She sighed. "I want him out so we can meet him and so I can get on top of you without worrying I'm going to crush you to death."

"At least I'd die happy?"

She shook her head. "Not helpful, Ry."

"You're beautiful." He stood and tugged her to her feet, holding her as close as he could with their son between them. "Seeing you like this makes me feel incredible. We're growing our family."

"We sure are." She smiled up at him, excited and hopeful. A mirror to everything he felt in that moment. Everything that he felt daily being with her. "You don't…"

"Don't what?"

"Miss it?"

Baseball.

He'd officially retired at the end of last season. Still without the World Series hardware that he'd coveted since he was a child. They'd made it so close again. Runners-up a second time. But when he walked off the mound for the last time, he'd waited for the crushing sense of defeat to settle in. Instead, he'd felt a sense of relief. He'd made it as far as he could go.

And he was done.

Ryan was ready for the next phase of his life—being a husband, being a dad, creating something that would last forever and not just while he was young. Mark was helping him build a cottage right near his own. Mandy was pregnant with baby number three, and she and Sloane were due mere weeks apart. Even though Ryan could afford to buy the fanciest version of anything he desired, Ryan wanted the feeling of using his bare hands to build something for his family. He wanted to be close to his brother and for their kids to grow up together.

"Honestly, I don't know," he said. "Some days I miss it and other days I don't even think about it. All I know is that I made the right decision. It was time."

"Yeah?"

"Yeah."

Tears gathered in her eyes. "You don't feel like… like you might resent this life one day?"

"Never." He knew that down to the very depths of his soul.

He could have stayed in the majors. The coach would have had him another year or two, without question. But Ryan could feel his body starting to protest. He'd started suffering other minor injuries that had never existed before. At least this way, he'd gone out on his own terms rather than fading away.

More importantly, he'd seen the beauty and fulfillment in having a new goal. A different goal.

He'd always be the kind of person who strived toward something. That would never change. But his goals could and *should* change. He knew that now.

"I'll always be grateful to you, Sloane, for making me see what I was missing. What I could have kept missing if I hadn't met you." He pressed a kiss to her lips, and it turned hungry. "I'm happy to be home again."

• • •

Ryan's gaze swept over Sloane with the kind of lazy, thorough assessment that sent goose bumps rippling over her skin. Despite his eyes reminding her of a flash of blue lightning in the middle of a storm, they had none of the chill of rain or wind. Oh no. They were molten hot, like the center of a brownie straight out of the oven. Like the buttery biscuits she burned her fingers on as a child, sneaking them off the tray while her father pretended not to look.

"I'm happy you're home, too. You know, I saw a new book advertised the other day that looked pretty good. Might teach us a few things." She waggled her brows. "Maybe I'll pick it up tomorrow."

"Whatever you do, don't suggest it to the book club."

She snorted. "Trust me. After the number of

injuries caused by chapter twenty-one, I have well and truly learned my lesson."

Ryan reached down to pick up the box containing some flat-packed furniture for the nursery and carried it through the house. Sloane followed, making a mental note of everything they still needed to do. The baby was due in a month, and every day her excitement built.

The nursery was almost ready to go. Ryan and Mark had painted it, under supervisions from Grampa Alfie, of course. The walls were a soft, buttery yellow with white cornices and a white ceiling. They had a strip running around the middle of the room, which was painted using stencils featuring shapes of dinosaurs and baseballs. Something from each of them.

But just as Sloane was about to sigh peacefully, a blood-curdling noise interrupted the tranquility in the nursery.

"Not *again*," Ryan muttered. "That damn llama. I'd better call Devon."

"She's smart, really. She knows people will feed her if she hollers loud enough." Sloane chuckled. "I'm impressed."

"Doesn't take much," he quipped.

"Hey!"

"Go on, get one of the broccoli heads."

The discovery that Lily the llama loved broccoli was an accidental one. Or rather, Lily *showed* them how much she liked broccoli by getting into their backyard and eating it right out of the vegetable patch. The house they'd bought together was at the edge of town and close to the farm where Lily lived.

She visited often.

So, now, Sloane always made sure to keep some broccoli in the fridge for her. She went out to the kitchen and grabbed a nice, chunky floret. Behind her, she could hear Ryan on the phone.

"Thanks, Dev. I'll get her out of the backyard. See you in a minute." He paused. "Homemade raspberry jam? That would be great. No, no. It's fine. Frankly, I think Sloane likes it when she visits."

Sloane grinned. She *did* like it when Lily visited. Although not so much when she went chomping through their garden. But still, she found the llama amusing, and it was cool to live somewhere with farm animals close by. She wanted her son to experience all that.

She headed out to the back and whistled to get the llama's attention. The animal's head snapped up as she caught sight of the green treat in Sloane's hand. "That's right. I've got a tasty little green tree for you, girl. Don't be eating my flowers, please."

Her white-and-brown coat was decorated with some leaves and other natural debris, and she looked like she'd traipsed through some mud. The side gate was open, and it creaked in the breeze. Huh. They'd put a new lock on it recently, but Lily must've figured out how to knock the bolt out of place.

Clever girl.

"Ready?" Sloane drew her arm back like Ryan

had taught her to.

Ryan had been in talks with the local college about working with their team, the Flames. He wasn't eager to jump right back into full-time work, especially with the baby coming, but he *was* thinking about the future. Possibly moving into a coaching role, working with young players to help prepare them for the ups and downs of the big leagues. And in helping those who might not make it still find joy in the game.

For now, however, he'd practiced his coaching skills in teaching Sloane how to throw better. It came in handy during Lily's visits.

"Swing loose in the shoulder socket," she muttered under her breath. "Bend the elbow."

She pulled her hand back and launched the broccoli into the air. It sailed through the little gate and out toward the front of their house. The llama trotted happily after it, seeming to enjoy the tasty version of fetch.

"Hey, that was a *great* throw!" Ryan said from behind her.

"Thanks, Coach." She turned and grinned up at him. "Training is paying off."

"You're a good student."

"And you're a good teacher." They headed over to the gate to lock up and to keep an eye on Lily so she didn't get into any more trouble.

"I swear, that llama is a descendant of Houdini himself." Ryan rolled his eyes. "Is this what it's like living in a small town? Vegetable patches and meddlesome animals and homemade jam."

Sloane sighed. "Isn't it wonderful?"

"It really is."

Sloane's smile dissolved as Ryan's lips met hers, his kiss deep and searching. Her hands wound into his hair and she knew, in that moment, that they were well and truly home.

ACKNOWLEDGMENTS

Every book I write contains a nugget of inspiration from some rabbit hole I fell into. In this case, Ryan was inspired by the love I developed for Major League Baseball when I moved to Canada. Go Blue Jays! I must thank my husband for always being willing to help me "logic check" aspects of my story and characters, and in this case our shared love for baseball played a major part in me writing this story. I feel incredibly grateful to have a partner who is so invested in my career and my stories. Justin, I wouldn't be here without your love and support. Thank you.

Thank you to my family for fostering my love of books and story from an early age. It set me on a path that has taken me places I never thought I would go, and I'm forever grateful. To Nan and Nonno, especially, I hope I've made you proud.

Thank you to my agent, Jill Marsal, for helping me navigate the challenges of a creative career and for always believing in my voice. Thank you to the team at Entangled Publishing, especially Lydia Sharp, for helping me bring *Kissing Games* to life. Thank you to the art team for giving it such a beautiful, eye-catching cover. I truly adore it!

Thank you to all the wonderful readers who take a chance on my stories. Thirty-something books in, and it still blows my mind that people want to spend time in worlds I've created. To any reader who's ever reached out to me on social media or email, to all the people who leave lovely reviews, and to the folks in my reader group, a massive thank-you. Knowing my stories connect with you means the world.

ABOUT THE AUTHOR

Stefanie London is a multi award-winning, *USA Today* bestselling author of contemporary romances and romantic comedies.

Stefanie's books have been called *"genuinely entertaining and memorable"* by Booklist, and *"Elegant, descriptive and delectable"* by RT magazine. Her stories have won multiple industry awards, including the HOLT Medallion and OKRWA National Reader's Choice Award, and she has been nominated for the Romance Writers of America RITA award.

Originally from Australia, Stefanie now lives in Toronto with her very own hero and is currently in the process of doing her best to travel the world. She frequently indulges in her passions for good coffee, lipstick, romance novels, and anything zombie-related.